The Darker the Night

by

JP Barry

The Nearer the Dawn Saga

The Darker the Night

Contact Information: info@thewildrosepress.com

Cover Art by *The Wild Rose Press, Inc.*

The Wild Rose Press, Inc.
PO Box 708
Adams Basin, NY 14410-0708
Visit us at www.thewildrosepress.com

Publishing History
First Edition, 2024
Trade Paperback ISBN 978-1-5092-5806-2
Digital ISBN 978-1-5092-5807-9

Previously Published 2017 MuseItUp Publishing
Published in the United States of America

Dedication

For my Husband & Daughter - Everything is limitless, especially you.

Truth & Consequence—I

My Dearest Love,

Something's wrong—*horribly* wrong. After writing our last letter, my soul shuddered with realization, then fear. This will be difficult to comprehend, it still is for me, but you must believe my every word. Lying is not, and *never* will be, an option. For *only* you, total transparency exists.

I'm a prophet. The *only* prophet in existence. This means I know all. Every secret this Universe holds, I'm one hundred percent conscious of. Darkness like the world has never seen is rising. What the Mortals and Immortals have once dreaded will now become a reality. I can see, feel, experience, and am aware of things no one, living or dead, should. How else would one know the world's creation in its entire truth when those like Michael, Raphael, and your father don't? They're sword-holding Archangels—not simple Guardians, such as what I've been dubbed. The Arcs are God's messengers, His most fierce warriors. Guardians are merely protectors of those in need. I suppose a case could be made suggesting I do just that, but my love, I swear I do far more.

Allow me time to explain. When my soul passed its fate had been determined immediately in Purgatory. At the time not much stock was placed in the experience, but looking back, it's obvious. I'm afraid after reading this you'll no longer love or want me. Please, do not abandon me. I need you.

Here goes nothing…

My Mortal life was fairly typical. Of course there were hardships, but the good always outweighed the bad. Dwelling on this would be useless. Nothing exceptional or remarkable happened during this time. Death is when things became questionable. To not cause you emotional distress, I'll spare you the details surrounding my untimely demise. It could best be summed up as brutal. I'd been working for Scotland Yard as an undercover detective when my assumed cover was blown. I was beaten and tortured for days until my consciousness slipped. Honestly? Death had been what I'd been praying for from the moment of my capture.

My brief stay in Purgatory is when everything should've been realized, but hindsight is always twenty/twenty. I must end here. Michael is calling. The idea of trust is elusive these days. Michael, Raphael, and Gabriel are family. If they can't be trusted, who can?

Always,
Your Betrothed

The Darkness Continues…

In the darkest, most remote corner of The Heavens, Michael sat alone. He found himself doing this more often than usual. Faced with too many decisions and no guidance, struggling to find answers and solutions, he refused to turn to God or The Powers That Be. Doing this would be an admission of failure, a true sign of weakness. Michael was not weak. Staring into the emptiness, his restless mind wandered, finally stopping for a moment to focus on the boys—his sons.

Though biologically not his, a connection which stretched far beyond blood had always been shared. Gabriel, the oldest, his pride and joy, had become a reliable and trustworthy confidant. Michael knew children should never view parents as friends, but with Gabriel the relationship came easy. The rule was broken—a big mistake. For far too many years Michael watched Gabriel suffer. Giving Gabriel a purpose, showing him unconditional love and stability should've alleviated the pain Gabriel's mate had inflicted upon him, but the plan backfired, terribly. He, Michael, God's right-hand man, had made an epic error.

Shortly after realizing what he'd done, Orifiel arrived. Orifiel was special, "gifted" so-to-speak, and needed to be kept safe. Michael introduced the men who, much to his great relief, instantly bonded. With the unstoppable, ruthless Archangel Gabriel watching over

Orifiel, the Guardian Angel would always be protected. Initially, Michael had no idea why The Thirteen cared so much about a low-ranking Angel, but over time Michael figured it out, keeping the information and secret to himself, praying no one would ever discover it, until Raphael and Gabriel began asking questions.

Orifiel and Gabriel were polar opposites. Michael adored Orifiel's soft nature and ability to find the good in all. He hated having to train his second son to be a soldier in the Angelic Army, but what choice did he have? None. Trinity, the Angel of Prophecy, predicted a war. All of the Angels needed to be prepared and ready to fight at a moment's notice. However, Michael trained Orifiel differently than Gabriel.

Gabriel had been taught to show no mercy, to destroy, to be cruel, brutal, and soulless when fighting. Orifiel was taught war and combat were a form of art which must be respected, and to do what needed to be done in order to return to Michael's Heavenly mate, Orifiel's adopted mother, Hadreniel, unharmed. Nothing could happen to Orifiel or else Michael's head would be served on a silver platter to The Elders.

Both men had become skilled warriors, but Gabriel was undefeatable; an unrelenting force which placed him third in command in the Angelic Army under Raphael and Michael, and first in command as a Demonic Assassin. In the Demonic world Gabriel's name was feared. Gabriel reveled in this. He'd become, beyond a shadow of a doubt, the greatest weapon in Michael's arsenal, but he'd also become a liability requiring a short leash, at least until circumstances changed. Michael's hands were tied. His son's heartless soul had to be kept filled with anger and rage in order to keep The Heavens and Earth safe from the Demons.

At first he sent Gabriel into the fiery throws of Hell alone, seeking and eliminating some of the most feared monsters known to man. Michael worried every time Gabriel left, experiencing extreme relief upon his return. When Michael felt Gabriel had spent too much time by himself, Orifiel was summoned to find him. When the two were together, perfect balance and harmony existed. Good and evil melted into one, creating a powerful force. The only other person who could soften Gabriel was Hadreniel. The affection and love between adopted mother and son grew into a strong, unbreakable bond. Often, Michael had Hadreniel seek Gabriel to help him purge his sorrow and pain privately. Only she could reach Gabriel emotionally. Michael prayed one day Gabriel would embrace romantic love again, therefore restoring Gabriel's fractured soul, but secretly Michael dreaded this wouldn't happen. Additionally, a keen awareness of the destruction it might cause for all parties involved existed for Michael.

"Father," Gabriel said interrupting Michael's thoughts.

"Yes, Son?" Michael forced a smile.

"You only come to this place when you're struggling with something. What did Vincent do this time?" Gabriel asked, sitting.

"He used to be a good soul. For God's sake, Vincent was a holy man—a staunch, devout person of the cloth. What happened?" Michael spoke out of frustration through gritted teeth.

"Pompeii happened, or don't you remember what he did to that entire city and all of the helpless Mortals in it?"

"Of course I remember."

"Then why question anything pertaining to him or his actions?"

"You never question the past?"

"No. It's of no consequence. Doesn't matter. Things went down, I responded. No regrets." Gabriel's words were icy and void of all emotion.

"We need to figure out a plan of attack. One that will place Vincent in a position of severe disadvantage," Michael replied, momentarily setting aside his remorse for how he'd raised Gabriel. Stopping Vincent and the Demonic Army was far more important.

"I could pick off his inner circle one by one, but that'll take time. A lot of time. They hardly ever go separate ways, and when that occurs, the timing is too unpredictable." Gabriel paused. "Let me take *her* out. *That* would wound Vincent. I can take my time, ending her nice and slow so he feels her torture, or I can finish her with one quick blow. Dealer's choice, but I prefer the first method."

"No. You will not touch Enepsigos. That is an order."

"Why? Why doesn't he deserve a dose of Hammurabi's Code? Why are you protecting them?"

"Harming that particular Demon will start an all-out war and it won't bring Lilith back."

"Yeah, but it would make me feel a hell of a lot better," Gabriel said. As he mused over the idea of murdering Vincent's mate, a hint of delight sparkled in his eyes.

"It won't." He felt for Gabriel. Attempting to comprehend his misery was impossible, but at some point the anger had to be let go of. Moving on from the horrible moment was Gabriel's only salvation.

"What about his Hell Hound? At least allow me to strike that abomination of a *pet*." A rather commanding wicked sense of euphoria spread across Gabriel's face.

"You will also not touch Simba. Why do you actively refuse to understand that we don't want a war right now? We're not prepared for it. The Hell Hound is heavily protected. It hasn't left Hell on Vincent's orders for over a decade. You attack or touch either one of his weaknesses and we're straight up the bloody creek without a damn paddle. There are still several key players we can go after which would disable Vincent greatly. Eliminate them, then return home. Future plans will be discussed once you've completed your mission. I'm warning you, Gabriel, do not play with your prey this time. Kill them and move on. Do you understand me?"

"Fine. Will Orifiel be tagging along?"

"No. You'll be on your own. Orifiel is needed elsewhere. Same rules apply," Michael cautioned.

Gabriel laughed lightly. The sound of his mirth, no matter how small or brief, gave Michael hope.

"Nothing is going to happen, but should trouble arise you'll be the first to know, Father."

As Gabriel exited the space, Orifiel entered.

"I have a job for you, Son," Michael stated.

"What do you need, Father?" Orifiel beamed brightly.

Michael couldn't help but grin. Orifiel was always ready, willing, and able to do anything to help anyone, Mortal or Immortal, never questioning Michael's wishes.

"There's a situation on Earth. I want you to keep an eye on it for me."

"All right. What kind of situation are we talking about?" Orifiel's tone reflected deep concern.

"Do you remember the Mortal Healing Angel, Nina Luther, and the Lost Soul, Chase James?"

"Yes, of course. Is Nina okay?"

Michael found it curious Orifiel questioned the girl's well-being and not the boy's. "Nina is fine, *as* is Chase. I'm troubled though. The Lost Soul was struck by both good and evil -"

"And you want me to keep watch, reporting back with what gifts he's inherited," Orifiel finished his father's unspoken thought.

Michael chuckled. His son knew him too well, a comforting Mortal emotion. At times he'd find himself forgetting Immortality. This was one of those moments. The life he longed for while walking Earth had become his heavenly gift. A beautiful soul mate who reciprocated his love and two handsome, smart, talented boys.

"Correct. We have reason to believe Vincent may be plotting something. What? No one knows, but he's definitely up to no good. He's fueled by anger and greed. The boy escaped him even though he promised his soul to Hell, and now Vincent's on the war path. The Devil is more than likely riding his ass over this blunder, which magnifies things by a million. This is bad and only going to get worse. Chase could potentially become a very strong force, desirable in both worlds. One who encompasses both Angelic and Demonic gifts is rare. The last soul known to have this ability…"

"Lilith."

Father and son shared a look followed by a curt nod. As anguish spread across Orifiel's face for Gabriel's pain, Michael's tortured soul screamed in agony.

Clearing his throat, Michael continued. "I've spoken with Trinity. Her inner eye is too consumed with other situations allowing for nothing to reveal itself. Watch the Lost Soul and the Mortal Angel carefully. Report back directly to me daily. I'll set you up in Savannah so you can remain on Earth for an extended period of time without being noticed. The first sign of anything suspicious, call to me, immediately. Since Nina knows who you are, you may present yourself to her, but avoid Chase. By nature he's a good person, but we can't be sure of what lurks beneath the surface, yet. *Do not* alarm Nina. As far as she's concerned, you're there as an observer; to make sure Chase's transition from Lost Soul to whatever he may turn out to be goes smoothly."

"Got it."

"Give me twenty-four hours to collect the required paperwork and things you'll need to live as a Mortal again. Are you sure you can handle this?"

"I remember how to be Mortal, Father. Times may have changed, but I'm capable of blending in just fine."

Michael and Orifiel rose. Both men stared out into the deep night's sky. "What do you see, Son?" Michael questioned when a bizarre look spread across his son's face.

"The stars. Right there. It's been like that for days. Do you see it?" Orifiel asked, pointing to a cluster to the far left.

"That can't be right," Michael replied in disbelief.

"The stars are never wrong," Orifiel whispered, fired up.

"Listen to me," Michael began, grabbing Orifiel's shoulders firmly. "*That* cannot happen. The girl already has a divine plan. It's to be with the Lost Soul. The two were created for one another. It must remain that way. No one goes over, nor questions the word of God or The Powers That Be."

"But, Father."

"But, Father, nothing. You are not, under any circumstances, to mention what you saw to anyone, *especially* to Gabriel. I'll deal with him and his problems," Michael warned. "If the star's alignment is true, we're all monumentally screwed," he mumbled to himself.

****

"If at first you don't succeed, Vincent, you try, then try again. Besides, what you deem a screw-up bodes well for us. You may not have converted the Lost One Chase, but you obtained the Lost One Sean, and now Chase's soul is filled with Angelic and Demonic traits. Who knows what will develop from within his core? He'll become the best of both worlds, much like my Lilith," the Devil hissed.

"Now what?" Vincent asked.

"Watch and wait. I've taught you my ways. Figure it out, but do not fail this time. Bring me the boy."

"Yes, of course."

"Is there anything else we need to discuss?"

Vincent looked away from his ruler's gaze. The Devil wouldn't be pleased with what needed to be said next. "While pursuing the two Lost Ones, the Archangel Gabriel destroyed several of our most valuable Army members."

"How many?"

"Thirteen," Vincent replied sheepishly.

The Devil cackled loudly. "Thirteen? How poetic. There's no way you can convince him to join us?"

"I've tried."

"Lilith?"

"She refuses to go near him. She's too afraid of what he'll do to her, but she won't openly admit that. The Archangel watches her though. From afar. He still loves her and is protecting her. Michael has issued standing orders to the Angelic Army that she's not to be touched."

The Devil paused to study the starry night's sky. "Do you see what I see?"

"No. Star reading is not one of my gifts," Vincent answered, feeling like a disappointment for the second time that evening. The Devil's intentions were to create rage inside of Vincent's mind and it worked.

"Lucky for us, *I* can. The Arc won't be a problem for too much longer."

"How so?" This bit of information thrilled Vincent. Finally, he'd be able to finish off the Angel he'd tried to destroy many times, but could never.

"Oh, let's just say Gabriel's world is going to take a turn down a path he hasn't traveled for many years. One I know you'll be capable of destroying because you have in the past, and one involving an emotion he's been avoiding like the Black Plague. Until that time comes, bring me the Lost One and the Mortal Healing Angel, that is, unless you have something else planned for the girl." He broke off moving closer to where Vincent stood, stopping only a few inches away. "If you know what's good for you, you will not fail me this time, Vincent," the Devil warned.

"I already have Lahash and Vassago working together, devising a plan. We have reason to believe Michael is sending the Guardian Orifiel to Earth to watch the boy and the girl, which complicates matters. This isn't going to happen overnight. We must be patient and lay low. When the Angels turn their back, even if only for a split second, we'll attack."

"Hmmm," the Devil mumbled still staring at the stars.

An unintentional grin grew on the Devil's face causing Vincent to become insanely curious. Vincent knew better than to question anything the Devil said or did, so he remained quiet, silently hoping the Devil would share his delight. After several long moments, the Devil grabbed a pen and piece of paper, scribbling out a crude drawing. Upon completion, he handed the slip to Vincent.

"These are the Archangel Gabriel and the Guardian Orifiel's symbols. I've never seen the third or fourth one." Vincent shrugged, not fully understanding what the Devil was hinting at.

"Very good, but this one right here is also someone else's," He said, pointing to the drawing on the right. "And these two 'become' because of that."

Vincent stared at the Devil completely puzzled. Souls who shared the same Angelic or Demonic symbol were practically unheard of.

"The Thirteen made a tremendous mistake, dear Vincent, and now we must capitalize on this before the Angels figure it out. Gabriel and Orifiel are heavily protected by Michael, so by extension, the twin flame will be too."

"This can't be possible. Are you sure you're reading the alignment correctly?"

"Never doubt me," the Devil growled, locking eyes with his number one.

"The girl…she isn't…" Vincent's voice trailed.

"Yes, she is."

"Please forgive me, but what about the other two?"

"Merely pawns. This new revelation supersedes that as proclaimed by The Thirteen idiots in their treaty."

"How do you propose I handle this?" Vincent asked, not wanting to fail the Devil again.

"Like this." The Devil leaned into Vincent, pressing the palm of his hand to Vincent's forehead, and showing him the past, present, and future for the Archangel Gabriel and Guardian Orifiel.

"Will it work?" Vincent questioned, pleased over the thought of complete power and control over The Heavens.

"It better," the Devil warned.

Chapter 1

Nina

My life finally resembled a typical teenager's. I was enduring the hardships of being a pre-med freshman at South University, missing Tori who went off to Oklahoma State University to be with her beau, Tim, thrilled Jules decided to attend South University, and I was spending as much time as possible with Chase. I hated the term boyfriend. Chase James was more like my fate or destiny, but how do you say, *Hey, this is Chase and we're soul mates?* You don't. People would believe you were either crazy or a silly, young girl suffering from a severe crush. The thing is, we *are* actual soul mates. What began as shallow surface emotions evolved into powerful ones imbibed with consuming love, only growing stronger with each passing day.

A little over a year ago, my family moved from New York to Georgia. I was terribly homesick, plotting ways to get back up north when Steve, my older brother, insisted we take in the sights and sounds of our new town. He dragged me to the beach on Tybee Island and I'll always be eternally grateful for that. Sadly, an opportunity to formally introduce myself to Chase never happened that day, but watching him from the boardwalk as he emerged from the ocean and toweled off was a turning point. The seed of desire was planted in my heart. The dark cloud of restless disappointment disappeared the moment Chase came into clear focus reading a book in the school cafeteria. A few months later, after a meet cute at the mall, we started dating. Our initial romance had been shear perfection until he discovered my secret. Some of my darkest instants were experienced while we were apart. The sense of completion I'd grown accustomed to vanished. It wasn't until some months later we were told about our soul mate connection. How we were meant to be together on Earth as well as in Heaven. After that, things started making sense.

Let me slow down and explain. I am a Mortal Healing Angel. The title pretty much says it all. If someone is hurt or ill, a quick wave of my hands over the injured area will fix whatever the issue. Chase was, or rather still is, a Lost Soul. A few years back, he'd been involved in a horrible car wreck which should've killed him, but it didn't. A higher power saved him because a clear final destination of either Heaven or Hell couldn't be decided. Returned to Earth a Lost Soul, Chase was given a choice—follow the path of the righteous or the damned. Both came with rewards and consequences. Thankfully, after having to deal with a crap ton of drama, Chase chose to rise above and here we were, happy, in love, and enjoying our gift from The Heavens as soul mates.

I'm still not one hundred percent sure what Micah's, the Angel of Divine Plans and the one who caused Chase's accident, logic was, or why a Mortal Angel's mate would be a Lost Soul, but eventually we'd figure it out. There was no sense in stressing over questions you weren't supposed to know the answers to. Okay, that's a giant lie. Truth is, we were both on high alert, but were trying to conceal it, especially to the other.

Just as Chase was about to join Vincent, the Devil's favorite sidekick, a horrific battle between the Angels and the Demons broke out causing him to be struck down by both sides at once. According to Michael, the Angels' leader, Chase would gain both Angelic and Demonic powers and abilities. For the next few months we waited to see what would surface, but came up empty. I'll take nerve-wracking experiences for five hundred, please. Neither of us breathed a word of this to our parents. My family would accept it, but the James' probably wouldn't. Not wanting to press the issue, it was omitted from all conversations, but sat uncomfortably in the pit of my stomach.

"Nina?" my mother asked, knocking, not waiting for a response before entering my bedroom.

"Yeah, Mom?" I attempted to not sound annoyed over her blatant disregard for my privacy.

"Thanksgiving is around the corner. What are your plans?"

"Plans?" I'd been in college for three months. The excess of homework was crushing me and wreaking havoc on my social life, particularly when it came to spending any time with Chase. Taking a much needed break from life was the grand master plan.

"Well, will you be here or with Chase's family? The two of you seem pretty serious again these days."

"Uh, here."

Don't get me wrong. Chase's parents were nice enough and hospitable, but the atmosphere at that house always came across as cold and distant. Strong tension definitely existed between Chase, George, and Blanche. His mother and father's relationship screamed marital discord. George was rarely home, and Blanche made me feel ill at ease, often wanting to engage in disturbing mother-daughter style chats.

"Will Chase be joining us then?"

"No idea. I'll ask."

"Please do. I need to know how many of us are going to be here."

"How many of us *are* going to be here?" Large family gatherings are the worst, specifically ones involving the entire Luther clan.

"Steve and his girlfriend Scarlett, Jenny, Charlie, Bridget, Jerry, all of their children, and Jeff," she said, using her fingers to keep count.

"Why can't they celebrate the holiday alone, in their own homes?" Dealing with family in close quarters sucked, and even more so when Demonic-like children were thrown into the mix. "Going to Chase's doesn't sound that bad anymore," I added.

Recently, the entire Luther group relocated to Georgia. We always had to move first because we were seen as the stable ones. Once settled, after being completely sure the Healing Angel secret was safe, they'd follow. Mortal Healing Angels lived by one simple rule—always stay close.

"Oh, Nina. They're family. Yes, your aunts and uncles can be a bit strange and opinionated at times, but it's the holidays. We all have to make sacrifices."

"Whatever."

"Let me know about Chase, *and* soon please."

"On it."

In an hour Chase would be here and all would be right with the world again. Family drama and lunacy would cease to exist. An intense feeling of excitement and anticipation caused an epic smile to spread across my once lifeless lips. It had been too long since we were alone. After a quick shower, I dressed, and raced down the stairs.

"Where's the fire, princess?" My father laughed. "Chase is here. He's waiting for you in the living room."

"Thanks, Dad."

"Hey, you," I said out of breath from sprinting across the house to get to him as fast as possible.

Man, I'm out of shape.

He looked gorgeous. His thick, mahogany, tousled hair had grown longer, adding to the incredible sex appeal his presence already exuded. His unruly locks resembled organized chaos. Any girl in her right mind wouldn't be able to resist the urge to run her fingers through each soft tendril. His green eyes boldly stood out against the fitted, light blue muscle shirt he wore, which also showed off his stellar body tone.

Out of nowhere, an abnormally weird sense of excitement set in. My sense of smell heightened reaching a fevered pitch. It was almost as if I was experiencing the thrill and smelling capacity of several people at once. As Chase got off of the couch to greet me, the sensation increased. His scent, that thrilling aroma, overpowered everything. A fuzziness set in my head. The kind one experiences right before the flu strikes.

"Hey, baby," Chase said, pulling me into a long, deep embrace.

The closeness drove me to the edge of all reason. I felt like I'd drunk twenty energy drinks and could run a three-minute mile without breaking a sweat. When he pulled away, the feeling subsided slightly, but the sensory overload caused an awful headache to brew.

Crap. Am I coming down with something?

"I've missed you, baby. Maybe we could spend a nice quiet evening alone? You know, to catch up," Chase whispered, pulling me back against his chest and pressing his soft, full lips to mine.

"Sounds good to me." A murmur was all I could manage, mainly because punch drunk waves were crashing against my skull.

"You wouldn't object to dinner and Tybee after?"

Over the past year, the beach at Tybee Island had become our alone place. Somewhere to escape to, free of judgment, where we felt comfortable and secure enough to be ourselves. Tybee would always be special because that was where we, technically speaking, connected for the first time. Often I'd get lost imagining us getting married on the sandy beach overlooking the beautiful ocean on a perfect spring or fall day. Not anytime soon, but definitely in the future.

"Nope. No objections here."

Another dose of extreme excitement surged, but this time anticipation spiked the mix. Again, the feeling slightly subsided once Chase backed away, though it lingered heavy in the air.

You must be more excited than you thought. Guess absence really does make the heart grow fonder. That, or when you get home later, flex those healing skills because you definitely don't have time to get sick, especially with a break coming up, and this being the only time you'll get to be with Chase until the Christmas holiday.

Perhaps our strong desire to be with one another had something to do with the strengthening of our divine plan. Micah could've been messing around with our story in The Heavens which, in turn, was causing my senses to go buck wild. Who knows? Who cared? We were together. That's all that mattered. It's best when dealing with both worlds to roll with the punches.

"Mom, I'm leaving. I'll be back no later than two."

As we headed for the door, the clopping sound of shoes against hardwood floors followed us from behind. Stopping and turning, a silent curse crossed my lips.

Oh, God. What, Mom?

She reeked severely of vanilla extract. The pungent aroma caused me to throw up a little in my mouth.

"Chase, will you be joining us for Thanksgiving?"

Snapping at her over this ridiculous obsession of who would be coming for the holiday and for delaying my plans was out of the question. If my mouth opened, vomit would come pouring out.

"Thank you for the invitation, Mrs. Luther. I'll stop by after dinner. Some family is coming in from out of town and my mother wouldn't be too terribly pleased if I wasn't around."

"We'll see you for dessert then. Have a great time tonight. Drive carefully."

"Of course." Chase smiled.

As we turned to exit, I noticed her sniffing the air and her apron, mumbling something about using far too much vanilla in the cookies and praying they weren't ruined.

Okay, you're not going crazy just yet. There's no time to deal with anything out of the norm tonight. Crazy off kilter senses be damned.

Chapter 2

Chase

Damn it. Here we go again.

For months everything was fine. Truth be told, my life finally resembled "normal" even though dealing with trying to mentally merge two vastly different existences wasn't easy. Nina and I were happy. We were soul mates. Happiness, contentment, and security with one's partner isn't something an Angel or Demon can manufacture, but rather an emotion created on a strong foundation of trust. Yes, I trusted Nina Luther. Being madly in love with her helped reinforce this bond. We'd become unbreakable because of *us*, no one else.

The wrinkle in the contentment plan? Something was wrong. I knew it the second my eyes fluttered opened this morning. The objects around me appeared odd, and a horrible headache set in. Initially believing this was only a cold or the flu had been foolish. Nothing is *that* easy. Wrestling with the gut feeling the moment of truth had finally come, I panicked. This panic produced a physically painful and terrifying effect, bringing an anxiety attack chaser along with it.

My first semester at South University studying criminology had gone smoothly. Traveling down a path *I'd* chosen for myself to become a lawyer made me feel like every other person in class—typically average. Home life? Another story all together. My father had been away for two months causing my mother to constantly harp on everything due to his absence. There were no business trips. Only a girlfriend in California.

Several months ago, while using his laptop, I came across a series of emails between him and the woman. He knew I was aware, but we never spoke of it. What's the point? Attempting to rationalize how wrong this was to a man like him was an epic waste of time. Dealing with myself took every ounce of my energy leaving no stretch to endure the fallout of whatever mess dear old Dad created and how Mom would handle it. Spoiler alert—probably not well.

As the day progressed, the headache worsened and strange things occurred. At times, my eyes saw even the tiniest speck of dust. My ears tuned into conversations people were having from a considerable distance away. Food tasted oddly different, and clothing fibers drove me insane. Praying this change away didn't work. It never does. Taking a nap didn't help either. Riding this wave was the only thing left to try. Now, here we were, sitting in Gino's with me feeling as if my damn head could explode.

This too shall pass. It has to, right?

Whatever was going on had to play out on its own. Telling Nina my tail of freaked out woe seemed the right thing to do, but she appeared off herself, hardly touching her dinner, agitated, and over stimulated. This wasn't the time to dump more drama on the table.

Swallowing my food whole and guzzling water by the gallon sucked. The combination of potent aromas and the way each bite felt became overwhelming. By the time we got back to the car, my stomach had it. The smell of leather cleaner mixed with Nina's strong perfume had to be the vilest combination ever. We needed to engage in an outdoor activity where clean, fresh air existed. The beach on Tybee Island would work.

Opening the windows and focusing on driving provided some relief. Thinking about holding the most beautiful girl in the world tightly relaxed any remaining tension. However, the thought of being alone with Nina led way to an unstoppable hormonal overdrive shift. Her soft, tanned skin rubbing against mine. Her lips pressed against any part of my body. It all drove me crazy. Once parked and the engine was killed, raw animal instinct took over causing me to grab her and crush our frames together. The more intense the situation grew, the more she followed. We were in sync, experiencing the same internal surges. Nina's mouth tasted like ambrosia. This experience was the first positive one all day and damn it, it wasn't about to end.

"Chase, hold up a second," she said winded.

"What's the matter?" I tried to maneuver her waist closer so she couldn't escape.

"Let me catch my breath."

After a very brief pause, the beast within me took over and started pulling at her clothing. Our first time should've been romantic, definitely not in a car, but right now that didn't matter. Her soft moans fed my lust. The urge to melt into one grew deeper and deeper with each passing moment. Finally, unable to withstand another passing second, I made the decision for both of us—tonight would be the night. Reaching for the button on my jeans with one hand and the zipper on Nina's with the other, she immediately tensed.

"Don't you want this, baby?"

She didn't answer with words, but rather with

actions. Her lips found mine again, but this time the movements were unhurried, replacing thirst with love. Nina may have wanted to slow things down, but I had no intention of doing so. Indulging the request for more passion proved too difficult for my hands, which finally won the internal war, working even faster to remove any remaining clothing. Again, she tried to take the situation down a notch.

"I thought you wanted this?" I questioned mustering a seductive southern drawl.

"Not like this. You seem different tonight. What's gotten into you? Are you feeling okay?"

Nina's concern over my behaviors caused me to take pause. Regret, embarrassment, and frustration coursed throughout my core. I'd acted like a pig and worse, it was directed at Nina. I'd made a vow when we first started dating we wouldn't rush the physical aspect. We had forever and because of that, hurrying any part of our journey wouldn't occur. I'd pushed certain situations with my ex prematurely and I wasn't about to have history repeat itself, especially negative history.

"I'm sorry, Nina. There's no excuse. I'm ashamed of my actions. I'd never force myself on anyone, particularly you. Forgive me?" The way her lips tasted on mine lingered, which wasn't helping the situation one bit.

Good God, man. Get a hold of yourself.

"Damn, baby. Why do you have to be so frigging hot?" I felt temporarily possessed. The beast rolled back on top of Nina, aggressively attempting to take her again.

"Whoa. Stop. What did you just say?" she asked, forcefully pushing me away.

"Huh?"

Please don't let this end up as a let's-discuss-our-emotions-and-feelings conversation. I hate those. They last too long and end up going nowhere.

"How are you feeling right now?" she demanded.

Crap.

"Fine. How about you?"

"No. You said you were feeling ashamed."

"Yes, but it's all good now."

Please, Nina, pretty please, let this go.

Out of nowhere the thought of sleeping with Nina returned with a vengeance. Rapidly, my hands slid around her neck, gently tugging her forward until our lips were a hair apart. "Kiss me or better yet, let's go somewhere else where we can be alone. Maybe somewhere more romantic with a bed," I whispered, dying to further what we were doing, and hoping she'd break and give in. Part of me wanted to stop pressuring her, to keep my hands to myself, but that wasn't an option. These lewd desires were disgusting, but there was no way to end them.

"No. There will be no kissing or hopping into bed with you because you're *not* fine. You're anxious and edgy. Why?" she said agitated, shoving me far away. "You stay there on your side of the car and don't you dare cross the gearshift line. If you do, whatever part of your body that ends up on my side will become broken and I will not heal it. Currently, I don't give a rat's ass which part ends up getting hurt over your stupidity."

"What do you want from me, Nina? Tell me. I'll do or say whatever." Why couldn't we go back to quietly making out, possibly more, and not chit-chatting about our feelings?

"Now you're getting annoyed and irritated, boarder-lining on angry, but you're trying to suppress the desire to touch me."

"Excuse me?"

"Confused. You're jumbled." She paused. "You're aggravated again. Enough with the wild mood swings. They're affecting me too, and holy crap, Chase. How many bottles of leather cleaner did you use on these seats? Open a freaking window or something for crying out loud."

Oh my God...

I couldn't speak. Backing all the way up into the driver's side door, the color drained from my face while my fingers and toes tingled. More than anything I wanted to jump out of the vehicle and run, but the warm sensation of Nina's soft fingers stopped everything.

"Let's try something, okay? Try and think really happy thoughts."

"All right." The thought of Nina, and Nina alone, materialized, creating a moment of euphoria.

"I can feel your emotions, and with your mood change, you can dictate what I smell," Nina marveled.

"Do you think this is an Angelic or Demonic ability? Do you think other people, aside from you, are affected by this?"

"I don't know, but it's time. We have to tell at least my parents because neither of us knows what we're doing, and that's not good. There's safety in numbers." Her eyes lowered while speaking.

Trepidation, the kind you know will be staying for a good long time, settled in. The potent smell of leather cleaner, a vanilla air freshener, and Nina's perfume raped my nostrils making the desire to hurl bubble up yet again. Since this nightmare began, all Nina wanted to do was tell her parents, but quite frankly, it wasn't her story to discuss. It was mine and it happened to be a story I wasn't too keen on sharing, if ever. Begrudgingly, my wishes were honored, until tonight. This event was bound to come, but hoping it happened later rather than sooner had always been the plan.

"I'm not ready for this, Nina. Not right now at least."

"What you're going through sucks. I'm sorry." Sympathy hung off of each spoken word while she attempted to provide comfort by inching closer until our bodies touched.

"How do you deal with this?"

"You find a way and remind yourself that you're not alone. This world isn't new to me. There are days when it still drives me crazy, but then there's you. Without the insanity there never would've been an us, and that in itself destroys any doubts or fears known to man. We can handle anything as long as we're doing it together."

Her sweet sentiment sparked a small amount of inner strength from deep within me. We sat in silence while my fingers stroked her long hair. For the first time all damn day I felt absolutely nothing, and it was the best feeling ever. My heart craved to believe Nina's credence of us being in this together was true. Maybe the Luthers having knowledge of the situation might help in the long run. Perhaps they could make sense of everything being we were all part of the same other world, only them having dealt with it for a lot longer. To them this would seem normal. Just another typical day.

"Call your parents. See if they're up." The numbness inside of me couldn't vanish because it was the only thing keeping me sane.

She reached for her phone, hesitating before hitting

the talk button.

“Are you sure?”

“Is there any other choice?” I answered, staring out of the windshield.

She smiled warmly while squeezing my hand. “Hey, Dad. Are you and Mom still awake?” She forced her voice to remain cool and calm. “Yeah, I’m fine. Chase and I need to talk to you guys. We’ll be home in about fifteen minutes.” There was a pause. “No. Not at all. It’s a good thing. We’ll see you soon. Love you, bye.”

Yeah well, we’ll see just how good of a thing this is…

Chapter 3

Nina

For the first time tonight my nostrils weren't being assaulted by funky combinations of odors, and I was truly grateful for this. Either Chase wasn't feeling any emotion, or he somehow found a way to control himself because the entire ride back to my house nothing lingered. Telling my parents about Chase was the right thing. They'd be able to provide assistance. In the meantime, I'd be the rock in our relationship.

"Everything is going to be fine, Chase."

Our fingers found each other's, weaving together. A grin of contentment crossed his lips, but his jade green, hypnotic eyes told a totally different story, which hurt. There are millions of words in the English language and no combination of them could mend his fear and confusion. Watching your soul mate, a man who's always been strong, crumble before you destroyed me. Not being able to heal him caused a deep sensation of uselessness to settle in. Hand in hand we walked through the front door and into the foyer.

"We're in here, kids," my father called.

Slowly we made our way into the living room. Mom paced expecting the worst, while Dad sat in his favorite chair appearing balanced, almost unaffected.

"What's going on? Both of you look awful," my father stated in a serious, but smooth tone.

"Nina. Oh, Nina. Please tell me you're not pregnant," my mother said freaking out.

"Really? No, Mom. What the hell?" How could she even think something like that?

"Let me see your fingers then."

"What are you doing?"

"No ring. Oh thank Heaven. They didn't elope." Her hands stopped wildly flailing. Her shoulders returned to a more relaxed position. An overall sense of cooling down entered her core.

I glanced at Chase. He wore a shocked, jumbled expression suggesting at any moment he'd bolt from the house, never to return.

Great. Just great. Freak out the guy who's already seconds away from jumping off of the roof. Good job, Mom.

"I'm *not* pregnant and we're *not* getting married. What do you think of me? It's not like that. *We're* not like that." My voice grew progressively louder with each spoken word.

"Let's all take a breath. Chase and Nina, please, tell us what this is all about," my father requested.

"We're soul mates. He's one of us," I blurted out still taken aback by the wild accusations being thrown around. The relief of purging, being free from this burden, was bittersweet. Anything past the doling out of information hadn't been thought through. Bad move. Always have a plan before opening Pandora's Box.

"What do you mean, Nina?" My father's voice was still unnaturally level.

"Chase is a Lost Soul."

"Okay," my father replied treading cautiously.

"A few years back I was involved in a car accident,

died, went to Purgatory, then was sent back to Earth with a choice. About a year later a man started following me. That man turned out to be Vincent," Chase answered.

"Vincent? *The* Vincent? The Devil's right hand man Vincent?" My father sounded rather stunned.

"Yeah. The one and only. A friend of mine, Sean Logan, had been followed as well. Long story short, we met with Vincent to see what he wanted. Turns out he wanted our souls in exchange for power and wealth. I said no. Sean said yes. The more one resists Vincent's will, the more force is applied to bully and persuade you. The night Tori fell and got hurt, Vincent made sure light was shed on Nina's secret, then used confusion and anger as a weapon threatening Nina's life, which is why we broke up. Who would trust someone after seeing what I saw? After being told your feelings aren't real, but rather an Angel is making you love another person because you're their property?

"Unwillingly Vincent got what he wanted. The day we were supposed to transition, Nina figured everything out. She followed me to the meeting point where a fight broke out between Demons and Angels. An Angel and Demon struck my chest at the same time creating a purple flame—or something like that. I have no recollection of this due to being knocked out. I'm still considered a Lost Soul, but according to this Angel named Michael, powers and gifts will start developing over time. We should've said something sooner, but Dr. Luther, no offense, all of this is crazy. I'm still trying to wrap my head around it. I'm sorry."

My mother walked to where Chase stood and embraced him tightly. "There's no need to be sorry, honey. We're here to help." She smiled then turned, glaring harshly in my direction. "You, on the other hand, have been a part of this world since birth. I'm beyond aggravated with you for putting yourself in harm's way. You should've said something the moment you suspected Chase knew something he shouldn't have. How could you have been so reckless?"

She was right. With no plausible excuse to provide, I stood in silence, staring blankly at her forehead, avoiding eye contact at all cost.

"Don't blame Nina. Blame me," Chase offered.

"You don't have to take the fall for this," I said. If throwing myself under the bus meant he'd dodge a bullet from my parents, so be it.

"You were in a compromising position, baby. If I would've stopped and let you explain everything none of this would've happened."

"You don't know that." I moved closer taking his hands and gazing into his jade green eyes. Nothing but pure love radiated from them.

"The past is the past. We must leave it there in order to move forward to sort through this," my father interjected. "What happened to Sean?"

"He's a full Demon now. Vincent changed him that night."

"How do you know for sure that you and Nina are soul mates?"

"Vincent told me, and an Angel named Micha told Nina."

"You mentioned you could acquire new gifts or abilities. Have you developed anything?"

"How do you feel right now?" Chase questioned.

"A bit anxious, maybe a little confused." My father's tone reflected stated emotions.

"The same," my mother said slowly.

"Can you smell anything stronger than usual? See anything sharper? Hear anything crisper? Physically feel anything different?" Chase questioned, briefly shutting his eyelids.

"You're controlling the room," my father admired. "You're dictating our emotions and senses. We're feeding off of you. Chase, you have the ability to calm people down or start a riot. You could possibly make people's pain go away or make them experience intense anguish with only a thought. This is a rare and powerful gift. Only the Angel of Emotions is known to possess this."

Chase stood stone still wearing a blank expression. The hold he had over the room dropped causing an instant return to normalcy.

"Can you read others' emotions?" my father asked.

"No. I have no idea what you're thinking or feeling."

"When did this start?"

"This morning. I woke with a bad headache. As the day went on, my body felt off, like the flu was coming on."

"How is your head and body feeling now?"

"Okay. My head is still aching a bit, but not as bad."

"Chase, if the pain gets worse you have to tell me immediately."

"Am I dying?" The question caused fear to flood the space. An overwhelming desire to grab hold of and embrace him, never letting go, developed inside of my core. My pillar of strength was crumbling, scared over mortality. Admitting I too feared this wouldn't help the situation. Anything aside from assuring him this wasn't the case wouldn't alleviate the panic currently engulfing

Chase. Sadly, I couldn't provide that. Knowing your hands are tied, particularly when the situation pertains to a loved one, is one of the most unsettling feelings.

"No. Please don't be afraid of this. As new abilities develop from within, you may or may not experience growing pains so-to-speak. It's important we monitor them."

"How many more abilities do you think I'll get?"

Chase's emotions reached the point of suffocation causing me to use the wall as a brace.

"Honestly, I don't know. You're what would be considered a first-generation soul. To be struck by good and evil at the exact same instant is something more powerful than any one single Angel or Demon could ever imagine."

"Can this be controlled?" Chase asked.

"We can try. This must be a lot for you to take in, but now that we're all on the same page, we can help. You should've told us sooner, but never-the-less, you're part of our family, Chase. The first step is accepting who you are. Have you talked to your parents about any of this?" My father's manner remained easy up until the point of inquiring about the James' knowledge.

"No, and I'm not going to."

"All right, first things first. We need to figure out how to control this, then we'll figure out how to explain everything to your parents."

"I'm sorry." Chase's voice sounded tired, spent of all emotion, but mentally there was still a lot going on. How could there not be when his inner thoughts were spreading like wild fire around the room? Being controlled mentally by someone else, intentional or not, was indescribable. You couldn't fight the grip, only give into it.

“Don’t be. This is wonderful news. In time you’ll see this situation not as something evil, but rather as something good. Everything will work out fine,” my mother said, who’d been mostly quiet throughout the entire conversation, patting him on the shoulder.

“I better go. It’s getting late and well, honestly, it’s been a long night.” Chase stood, poised to leave.

“We’ll get to the bottom of this,” my father assured.

“Thanks. Goodnight,” Chase replied, heading for the door.

Desperately I wanted to say something smart, witty, intellectual, pretty much anything to make this garbage dump of a situation better, but in truth there were no words or actions to right the wrongs.

“Call me tomorrow?”

“Of course, baby,” he said softly.

Wrapping my arms around his waist, pulling him closer was all that could be done. Hopefully this simple gesture would sooth his restless soul. A mountain may not have been moved by this action, but for the moment, he appeared relaxed.

“No matter what, Chase, we’re in this together. You know that, right?”

“I know. I know.”

After a few seconds he pulled away, softly kissed me, and left. My heart instantly ached for his return. Whenever he’d leave I’d feel like this, but tonight for purely selfish reasons, the ache wasn’t as bad. My internal balance craved restoration. With Chase hanging around that wouldn’t happen. It may have been a tough night for him, but it wasn’t exactly a walk in the clouds for me.

Enjoy this while you can because you can trick yourself into thinking otherwise, but you know deep down this situation is going to get a whole lot worse before it gets even an ounce better.

Chapter 4

Chase

Run as far away from here as you can, Chase James. Do it now and don't ever look back.

As soon as the car revved, all I wanted to do was hide. My head started aching again, and my vision grew blurry. With an abundance of caution and every bit of focus mustered, I merged onto the main road squinting, trying to make out where the other cars were on the somewhat busy street.

You can't do this.

Pulling into a parking lot and cutting the engine had to happen before someone, namely me, got hurt. Never had such an overwhelming desire to let go and cry been felt. Life was insane. If I wasn't living and experiencing all of this firsthand, shit, I wouldn't believe it myself. Vincent or Michael for that matter were owed nothing. Leaving Savannah, moving somewhere else, surviving just below the radar where nothing abnormal existed was a strong option. If the new abilities were suppressed upon developing, they couldn't affect me.

This crap isn't for you mainly because you don't want it.

What do you want?

Nina.

Thinking her name made the world stop spinning and the tingling sensation in my hands and feet subside.

As if someone flipped a switch, my dicey vision snapped back into sharp focus. Getting to and being with Nina made everything seem right again. She'd make this better. She *always* made things better.

Chapter 5

Nina

After a distracted goodnight to Chase, worry hung heavy from my every bone. Though it was late, being able to sleep seemed like an indefinable concept. Drawing a bath and taking a soak usually alleviated my stress. The aloneness and silence allowed for decompressing and for the processing of difficult thoughts. For forty-five minutes, the hot water and mixture of lavender and peppermint oils fought my anxiety, finally winning the war, leaving behind a somewhat relaxed body. Comfort was found in knowing my father would be able to make heads or tails of all of this. Everything would be fine in the end.

After toweling off, the ever-elusive idea of sleep finally settled in. No sooner did I enter my bedroom, an overwhelming sense of stillness and peace washed over me. The heavenly smell of chamomile and rose imbibed the space.

“I missed you too much, baby,” Chase whispered from the window seat.

“I missed you too.”

Chase randomly popping up after hours wasn’t new. It used to scare the crap out of me, but his visits had become more regular and frequent over the past year. He walked to the bed, pulled back the pale lilac comforter, and laid down while I locked the door.

"Are you okay?" I slipped between the sheets beside him.

"Yeah," he murmured.

"Chase, it's me you're talking to. Our souls are one. Please don't hide what you're thinking or feeling when it comes to us." The tone taken was soft and gentle, the kind someone would use with an upset, frightened child. My fingers delicately grazed his cheek before reaching over and taking his hand in mine.

His breathing became shallow. "Nothing makes any sense."

"It's not going to. At least not now it won't. In time it will. You'll get used to the new you, and eventually that person will become you."

"I don't want to be someone else."

His naked admission of truth urged me to simply hug him. If never letting go was an option to ease his pain, I would've taken it, no questions asked.

"You'll still be Chase, just an improved version."

He didn't say anything in response. Instead, he stared at the ceiling, not blinking or moving an inch.

"Remember the night of the dance when Tori got hurt? If I wasn't a healer she would've been seriously messed up. When you came here that night your hand was busted up. You were experiencing physical pain. I healed you too. My gift, this ability, makes pain and suffering disappear. We don't know much about your new gift, but I'm sure we will figure it out and there will be a worthy use for it where you can use it to help others. Don't you want to help people? Make lives better?"

"Who's going to use their gift to make my life better?" he snapped.

"Me. That's who. Chase James, you're acting like a

spoiled brat. This is it. You are who you are. Don't bother wasting any amount of time thinking you can escape this because guess what? You can't. I've tried, many times. You can run and hide from the Angels and Demons, but you can't from yourself. We have each other. We have a soul connection. Love, Chase, that's the most powerful force of all."

"What card or movie did you steal that line from?" Sarcasm dripped from his every word.

"Forget it. Go ahead and fight with yourself. Let me know how that works out for you," I replied, pulling the covers up, and rolling away from his embrace.

Screw him. You want to act like an ass and ignore my advice? Dismiss my comfort? Fine. Ultimately he'll wake up realizing I was right. When that time came, he could fully expect a heaping dose of, "I told you so."

"I need some time to get use to this, baby." His attitude was much softer now. With great caution, he turned my body back around, not stopping until we were face to face again.

"You will. I'll be right there next to you the entire journey no matter how long it may or may not take."

"Promise?"

"I swear," I said, kissing his soft, warm lips. "Let's try to get some sleep, okay?" My head fell to his chest where it belonged.

"Sweet dreams, baby."

Before the dire need for sleep overtook me, I silently prayed he'd come to terms with everything and soon. Deep down a scared little boy lived inside of Chase's mind which he covered up with strong tendencies. At the heart of it, he'd been taught to be a true southern man—never show emotion. Unfortunately, this wasn't the time to repress anything. He needed to purge to keep his inner balance and mental stability intact. If not, everything, including the unbreakable bond that we shared would be jeopardized.

Chapter 6

Chase

"I can still feel your anger, Chase," Jack Luther stated evenly.

We'd been working for days on how to control the new ability, but kept coming up empty. As each hour passed, I became increasingly tired, annoyed, and doubtful. There was no sense trying to hide anything because my emotions controlled every room I walked into. I'd been spending most of my time at Nina's house, nights included, because paranoia struck when evening fell. I'd leave the Luthers' and sneak back in through Nina's unlocked bedroom window. It was safe here. If the severe headaches returned, or something went wrong, Jack could and would help me. It didn't matter if he or Ellen found out I'd snuck into their daughter's room. Yeah sure they'd be put out, but I'd be safe because he'd provide healing. After all, helping those in need was a Mortal Healing Angel's calling. Besides, technically speaking we were family now.

My parents still had no idea about anything. I intended to keep it that way for as long as possible. Tension, unspoken words, and thoughts filled the unwelcoming James household. Who in their right mind would want to be there? Not me, that's for sure. Strange life or not, no thanks. The only sense of normalcy to be had was with Nina in one of the most abnormal places on Earth.

"I'm trying," I said frustrated.

"Don't be upset, Chase. We've only been at this for a few days. We *will* figure it out," he assured, getting up, and patting my right shoulder in a rather fatherly fashion. "How are the headaches?"

"I haven't had one since the night all of this began." A lie. Truth was, the headaches had become a part of my daily existence, but what could he do about them? Nothing. Besides, they weren't severe enough to prohibit me from carrying on with my routine.

"That's a good thing. How are you feeling otherwise?"

"Dr. Luther, no offense, but you can feel and sense how I've been coping."

A slight chuckle rolled off of his tongue. "This is a difficult time. You can talk to me about whatever's on your mind. No judging. No lectures."

Okay, Jack. I'd love to chat with you about my inner most thoughts. Who wouldn't enjoy having a heart-to-heart with their girlfriend's father?

"Thanks. Honestly, I'm good."

"I'm not trying to pry into your personal life, but perhaps talking about your emotions might make controlling them easier. If we can find the root of the anger or confusion, we may be able to turn a negative into a positive."

There were two choices. The first, talk. The second, keep quiet. With little time to weigh the pros and cons, I felt trapped, but maybe he was right. At this point I'd try anything. I'd keep it simple, but perhaps expressing some fears would do the trick. However, once my mouth opened, so much came pouring out. Everything about my ex-girlfriend, Sean Logan, my mother's neediness, my father's absence from our lives and cheating ways, various encounters with Vincent and how they still haunted me at idle moments in the early hours of dawn, how I wasn't sleeping properly, and *finally* how much I loved and couldn't live without Nina, all spewed out. Jack sat, listening, never once interrupting. His eyes were filled with kindness, concern, and understanding. If my emotions were controlling the room, I had no idea and quite frankly, I didn't care. It felt good to release. The experiment proved cleansing; a truly detoxifying experience.

Maybe Nina and women in general had this "talk until the other person can't stand the sound of your damn voice" thing down to a science. All of these years of suggesting everything was fine when it wasn't had been stupid. Women of the world were definitely on to something. Would I admit this out loud? Hell no.

Every time Nina had held me prisoner wanting to drone on endlessly about feelings and all of that crap was her way of purging. Perhaps had I been a more active participant in those conversations I too would've walked away with some form of emotional relief instead of a throbbing headache and indigestion.

Jack patiently waited for my ranting to end before speaking. He started from the beginning, breaking down each issue piece by piece, not necessarily solving the problems, but rather rationalizing them, and pointing out which should be let go of and which needed to be dealt with.

"Your ex-girlfriend, how much does she know about your other life?"

"Nothing."

“Sean’s other life?”

“Nothing.”

“Then forget about it. Sean won’t go looking for her. If he should decide to, we’ll deal with it then. Generally speaking only a select few Demons and Angels are given the right to return to Earth. We can’t sit here stressing over every possible thing that could go wrong. We’ll drive ourselves crazy.”

I nodded.

“Your secret is safe, Chase. No one will ever find out unless you tell them, and I strongly advise that you don’t. I’m sure Nina has told you why we move so often. We have to protect ourselves. People wouldn’t understand or believe we mean no harm. Look at your own initial reaction to having witnessed Nina use her gift for the first time.”

A slight cynical laugh fell from my lips. “Yeah. Terrifying. Honestly unbelievable stuff,” I said, rubbing my eyes and forehead.

“When was the last time you had a good night’s sleep?”

“It’s been awhile.”

“Would you be open to taking a sleep aid?”

“Will it stop the dreams?” It seemed every time I’d drift off, visions of Sean, Vincent, my ex-girlfriend, Nina in danger, and a variety of other horrifying images whipped in and out of my consciousness, resulting in me waking and struggling to clear my head enough to go back down. It didn’t matter the location of the attempted rest, Nina’s bed or not, the same scenario repeatedly played out. Since there were no words to accurately describe the mental mind screw currently going on, waking Nina would’ve been useless.

"Sleeping pills will help you sleep better, but everyone dreams. However, it's more than likely when you take a pill, you'll feel refreshed the next morning and won't remember anything. They won't stop the imagery from occurring, but because you'll be experiencing such a deep sleep, your brain won't store them. It's your choice, Chase. Through purging your anger and stress, getting back on a healthy sleep schedule, and by finding your new version of what a normal life should look like for you, we can control your gift."

"Why can't you heal me? Can't your ability stop the headaches and mental craziness?"

"I wish it could, but it can't. Healers can't fix mental distress such as depression, stress, or anxiety. The headaches you're experiencing aren't true ailments. They're bigger than that."

"All right. Seeing how I'm out of options, give me the pills."

It's not like I have anything else to lose.

Chapter 7

Nina

Over the next few days, Chase and my father took advantage of every free minute trying to figure out how to use and control Chase's new ability. The emotions inside of the house were out of control. My mother had enlisted me to help her prep Thanksgiving dinner which turned into a schizophrenic experience. At times we were laughing and having fun, but at the drop of a hat we were at each other's throat. With each mood swing came a severe heightening or lessening of a sense. After losing our sense of sight twice, use of knives or the stove became prohibited. We knew we were being driven by Chase's thoughts and feelings, but the ragdoll effect of being tugged and pulled in every which direction had to end. The night before Thanksgiving a noticeable wave of relief had spread across Chase's exhausted face.

"How are you feeling, Nina?" Chase asked cautiously from the kitchen doorway. My father stood behind him eagerly awaiting an answer.

"Fine?"

"That's good, but *what* are you feeling right now?"

"Nothing," I said trying to concentrate on my inner thoughts and surface senses. I'd gotten used to feeling every emotion known to man these past few days. Not feeling like myself had become a common, unnoticed practice. "Yeah. Nothing."

"Excellent. See, Chase? There is a light at the end of the tunnel and we found it," my father said, patting him on the back.

"How did you do it?" I asked.

"We still have some more research and work to do, but for now, as long as Chase can keep his emotions from going to extremes, no one other than himself can experience them. We're trying to figure out the connection between emotions and senses, and we will in time. We've covered a lot of ground in a few short days. You should take a break. Try to relax." My father sounded rather proud of Chase.

"Nina," my mother called from the laundry room.

"What?" Whatever was required of me held no importance. There were other things of far greater standing, like making sure Chase was really okay, that I needed to concern myself with.

"Please finish up the remainder of the prep. There's really not that much left. Your father and I have dinner reservations with Stan and Mary tonight and I can't cancel on them again," she informed, returning to the kitchen.

"Sure. I'd *love* to."

Don't be too snarky. They're leaving and even though you have to cook and clean, you and Chase will be alone. Technically speaking it's a win.

"I'll help. It'll be fun," Chase offered with a playfully evil wink, followed by a devious smirk.

"We'll be back soon. Your father's cell phone is on should something come up. And Nina, honey, I expect the kitchen to be tidy and the house to be in one piece when we return," my mother said.

"Bye, Mom."

Just go, please.

Finally, the front door shut. Chase and I were by ourselves.

"It's a good thing you're studying to become a doctor. You're going to need the money to afford eating out every night and for a housekeeper. It couldn't be more obvious domestic chores aren't your thing." Chase laughed, grabbed a dishtowel, and wiped down the disaster area of a counter.

"Shut up," I said lightheartedly, snapping him with a wet rag.

He reached out seizing the end of the cloth mid-snap, pulling me into a deep embrace. His brilliant, green eyes resembled two perfect emeralds. A strange emotion bubbled inside of me. Attempting to put my finger on exactly what it was proved totally useless. Our lips slowly met. He tasted beyond good.

"I love you, Nina. More than you could ever imagine."

"I love you too. Always have. Always will. No matter what. Forever." Finding myself lost in all of him came easy. "How are you feeling?"

"Perfectly fine."

I pulled away slightly, shooting him a quick look of disbelief.

"Really, baby. Your father seems to know what he's doing. We're making progress. Rome wasn't built in a day. Am I okay with all of this craziness? No, not really, but there's no other choice. Sooner or later everything will get figured out. Please stop worrying. If things start going south, I'll give a shout. Deal?"

"Deal." The new calm version of Chase was a refreshing change, although some doubt lingered. He'd been a hot mess since all of this started. To have such a bold turnaround this quickly? A bit odd, but if he wanted to shift gears, start looking at the situation differently, I could too.

He winked, gently pressing his lips to mine again.

"Hey, hey, hey. Cut it out," a deep voice spoke, followed by a bear-like laugh.

"Steve," I exclaimed, pulling away from Chase's strong arms and into Steve's waiting embrace.

"What's going on, Sis? Chase? Where's Mom? Dad?"

"Out to dinner. What's up with you? Sit. Talk to me. It feels like it's been forever since we saw each other."

"First, welcome to '*the family*,' Chase. Dad told me what's been going on. I'll be careful not to piss you off now that I know you can mess with my head. Other than that, everything is going really well. The trip home sucked. I'm not looking forward to having to do it again, but I'm happy to be here," he said, joining us at the table.

"Thanks," Chase replied. For some reason he appeared tense, almost as if being nice to Steve caused him internal distress. His body went rigid, but no outward emotional hold existed.

He's probably tired. He's been working non-stop with Dad, and now that we have a quiet moment alone, Steve barges in ruining it.

"Here. Help me peel carrots and potatoes," I said, thrusting a bowl at him, hoping Chase would move past whatever and would see how great of a guy Steve was. "How's Scarlett? Where *is* Scarlett?"

"We kind of broke up two days ago. She wasn't *the one.*"

"Mom is going to be pissed. You're throwing off her

perfect Thanksgiving."

"She'll cope. Aside from Chase being one of us, what else is new?"

Chapter 8

Chase

Forced to sit for two long hours at the Luther's kitchen table pretending to give a damn about Nina's brother was difficult. The first time we met it was obvious he didn't care for me and honestly, the feeling was mutual. Steve loved himself. He thought he was God's greatest gift to women. He wasn't. Aside from being a Mortal Healing Angel, nothing extraordinary existed within him no matter what he may have believed did. Now that certain situations had changed, we had no choice but to act like we liked one another.

Nina adores him. You love Nina. For her sake, try to maintain a friendly relationship with this idiot.

Suppressing the desire to use my gift and screw with his head was hard. If I did, Nina would be affected too, and that wouldn't have been fair. Besides, focusing on fighting yet another throbbing headache was of higher importance. Gone were the days of experiencing a few migraines. Often the pain became rolling, ebbing and flowing all of the damn time. When one subsided, a few minutes later, another developed. Sometimes the discomfort would be mild and dull, other times it grew sharp and piercing. Initially, telling Jack seemed like the smart thing to do, but I wasn't a research experiment or a project. He wanted to help me and that was appreciated, but not everything could be fixed by purging stress or by popping a sleeping pill. Finally, Jack and Ellen returned, providing me with an excuse to leave.

"Chase?" my mother asked the moment my feet hit the foyer of my house.

"Yeah, Mom."

"Come to the kitchen, please."

Unwillingly I went, but all I really wanted to do was lay down. Hopefully sleep came for a visit tonight and would take the damn headache along with it.

Nice. Dad finally decided to come home. How good of him.

"What?"

"Don't speak to your mother that way," my father growled.

"I'm sorry, but who are you?"

He didn't verbally respond, but rather stood, attempting to slap my face. Grabbing his wrist mid-thrust caught him off guard. Holding the position, squeezing as tight as possible with every ounce of strength inside of me felt powerful.

"I wouldn't try that again," I hissed.

Our eyes locked in mutual disdain.

"That's all right, George. He's tired. It's late," my mother said.

As soon as I released his arm, the stare dropped. My mother came rushing over, quickly positioning her body between us. "We just wanted to see how you were doing, dear. Between your father's busy schedule and mine, we feel we haven't seen or spoken much with you lately. How is everything?" she asked, looking adoringly at me.

"Everything is fine, Mom."

"Stop babying him, Blanche. He's a grown man. Where's the Logan boy, Chase?"

"Excuse me?" The question threw me.

"Where is Sean Logan?" He repeated.

"No idea. Why?"

"Drew and Eve stopped by earlier. Sean's still missing. No one seems to know what happened to him. Eve is worried because the police stopped looking. They suspect Sean ran away and doesn't want to be found. If you know something, or if you've heard from him, you need to tell us," my mother explained.

"I told the cops everything I knew. I have no idea what's become of him." It wasn't a lie. I really didn't know what happened after that horrific night.

"His mother found this," my father said, shoving photocopies at me.

Arrogantly I snatched them from him, scanning the content. An instant eerie feeling gripped me. My brain drew a blank. Honestly? Hitting the floor from passing out over this seemed possible.

Stop. Calm down.

"So?" I questioned, tossing the papers on the table.

"So? That's all you have to say for yourself?" my father yelled.

"Yeah, that's all."

"You saw him last, honey, and your name was mentioned several times in his notebook. Take a minute to look at these photocopies again. Maybe you'll remember something," my mother said softly, reaching for the papers, and placing them back in my hands.

I knew exactly what Sean had written, so I didn't need to read whatever words he'd scribbled down. For her sake, I pretended to review the information again.

"Mom, none of this means anything. It looks like gibberish. Sean is a weird kid who got pissed off the girl he liked wasn't interested in him. The cops aren't wrong. If Sean wanted to be found he would've surfaced by now. He ran away. Plain and simple."

Thankfully, Sean didn't write complete sentences, but rather random words, which if someone tried to string together, they would come up empty. Except me.

"That's okay, Chase. Sean was always a bit different. He's probably trying to find himself. I'm sure he'll return home soon. Until then, if you *should* hear anything, please say something to one of us. Drew and Eve are sick with grief, as is poor Bristol."

Bristol. Oh please don't say that name again.

My heart jumped and ached whenever anyone mentioned Bristol.

"You should reach out to her, Chase," my mother encouraged.

"That's not a good idea."

"We all make mistakes."

"I'm tired and have a massive headache. Goodnight," I said, exiting the kitchen as fast as possible.

As much as sleep needed to happen, it wasn't going to. I stared blankly at the ceiling trying not to think about Vincent or Sean. I knew Sean well as a Mortal, but as a Demon imbibed with strength and power, who knew what he turned into. I was afraid of him. If the Angels were watching me, that meant Vincent would be too, which posed more of a threat than Sean. Until something huge happened, I'd be spending most days looking over my shoulder, living in utter fear. This wasn't a life, but rather a punishment. Things would've been easier if I'd given into Vincent's will. Nina would've found a way to cope with the loss and she'd be safe—unlike with the current situation where neither of us was.

Controlling my inner emotions so others wouldn't have to suffer my wrath was more of a burden than gift. Every ounce of self-restraint needed to be in play twenty-four hours a day, seven days a week. If not, I'd be outed. The world would know the freak I'd become. My head pounded. My body, mind, and soul were spent, and now all I could think of was Bristol. Sweet, beautiful, innocent Bristol. She'd always hold a special place in my heart. Reaching for the phone, I dialed.

"Hello?" Her soft voice spoke.

"Hey." I smiled.

Chapter 9

Nina

Catching up with Steve had been fun, but the gnawing urge to head upstairs kept biting at my nerves. Something deep within me suggested Chase would be there waiting. His needs were greater than anyone else's.

Listen to your gut.

"I'm sorry, baby," Chase's voice whispered faintly.

The only light shining in the room came from the dim moonlight. A lone silhouette revealed a hunched man. His head resting in his hands highlighted just how broken he truly was. He didn't move, nor look up when speaking.

"Are you okay?" I asked concerned, shutting the door as quickly and quietly as possible.

"Don't know."

Normally, pressing the matter until a dialogue opened had always been Plan A, but not tonight. Instead, being near him to provide comfort was a better approach. Moving to the window seat I sat, placing my arms around his broad shoulders. Slowly he turned making sure our eyes met.

"There's really nothing I can say that hasn't already been said. What you're dealing with sucks—plain and simple, but it's easier to embrace who and what you are when you stop denying who and what you are to yourself. Wasn't it you who said things always look the worst in the darkness of night, but appear better in the light of day?"

"Yeah." He smiled. "I'm afraid, and *hate* that. I can't stand being weak and vulnerable."

"Afraid? Afraid of what?"

"I've been doing a lot of thinking about everything. There's a chance this might turn out badly. Michael's not the only one waiting to find out what happens. Vincent is curious too."

"True, but if Vincent tries anything Michael and the rest of the Angels will stop him."

"You don't know that, Nina. Vincent is smart and cruel, which is a lethal combination. Between his mind games and manipulations, who knows how he might spin this. What if you become his greatest weapon again, but this time you end up hurt? I don't know what I'd do."

His rage, anger, and despair rose to the surface. My sense of touch instantly heightened. Every single thread in the cushion we were sitting on appeared almost alive against my bare skin. Obviously, he'd lost his internal control.

"You can feel my emotions, can't you?" he questioned frustrated.

"Yes, but you only figured out how to deal with this. Ease up on yourself. Practice makes perfect."

"That's the problem, Nina. There's no time for practice. We have to be ready at any given moment for Vincent. This damn gift needs to be shut off or he'll find a way to use it against me, against us." He stood and paced the length of the bedroom.

"You have to stop, Chase. You have to relax. You're not alone." I grabbed his arm pulling him into an embrace.

He was right. His anxieties were completely justified and founded, but he couldn't know that. Chase had to remain balanced and keep his focus or when Vincent did find and confront us, he'd destroy him. However, keeping Chase at ease and sane proved difficult while I was drowning in a sea of my own panic.

"Let's not do this tonight, Chase. You may think otherwise, but Vincent isn't going to surface anytime soon. Like you said, he's smart. He'll want to wait and see what else is going to transpire. We need to work on one issue at a time. Before you deal with anything else, accept—*fully* accept yourself, then work on your divine gifts," I said, trying to repress a yawn, but failing.

"Let me help you sleep, baby. You're exhausted." His tone softened, but his once vibrant, gem-like eyes revealed a tired, beaten man.

"I'm fine. Let's keep talking."

"Who's lying now?" He smirked. "We can talk tomorrow and every day after. We have an eternity of conversations ahead of us. Lie down with me. I'll help you relax. Allow me to shut off your mind so you won't toss and turn."

I didn't say anything as he led me to the bed. Within seconds, Chase's gift entered my core, drawing sleep in. Nothing aside from peace and comfort existed permitting me to get lost in a wonderful, deep, dreamless sleep.

****

"Rise and shine, baby," Chase whispered.

"You stayed all night." A smile stretched across my face.

Usually Chase left long before dawn's first light. This morning he appeared calmer which made me happy, though this contentment didn't last long once the alarm clock revealed in a few hours' time my family would be arriving and my mother would probably want me downstairs in the kitchen helping.

"Crap. You better go before we get caught."

"Calm down," he hissed, grinning devilishly. "Maybe I'm not ready to let you out of this bed yet."

Well played, Mr. James. A very tempting offer.

"Nina," my mother called. The sound of her shoes climbing the steps rang loud and clear.

"Holy crap, Chase."

Before another word was spoken, Chase was out of sight. Quickly I cracked the door, positioning myself in a way no one could see inside of the room.

"Hey, Mom." The breathlessness of my voice was too strong to hide.

"Good morning, honey. I need you to shower and get downstairs as soon as humanly possible." She paused. "You seem a bit uptight. Is everything okay?"

"Totally fine. Just realized how late it was and how you probably needed my help ages ago," I lied.

"That's all right. Just hurry up?"

"Right. Sure."

After she exited my eyes frantically scanned the room to see where in the world Chase had disappeared to. He'd vanished into thin air. I whisper-yelled his name a few times, even once out the window, but nothing. With no time to investigate his potential whereabouts, showering then calling him once I'd gotten to the kitchen would have to suffice. As I grabbed my cell phone to call him fifteen minutes later, mine rang.

"Hello?"

"Hey, baby," Chase's smooth voice spoke.

"Hey, you." Thankfully he was okay and hadn't

broken his neck falling the two stories down.

"No problems, right?"

"No, you didn't wake me. I'm actually in the kitchen with my mom."

"Oh. Can't speak openly, can we?" Chase said deviously teasing. "I guess I shouldn't tell you that you're the sexiest girl I've ever known and I can't wait until we're alone again. Waking up next to you was one of the most amazing experiences ever. I can still smell your perfume on my clothing."

"Yeah, you probably shouldn't. Not right now at least." I laughed, happy his good mood hadn't gone away. "*But*, it's nice to know. When do you think you'll be here?"

"Can't stand being away from me, huh?" He chuckled. "Probably around five. Is that all right?"

"Yeah. That's totally fine."

You should be here right now. Stupid family holiday.

"I'll be there before you know it. Go help your mom. Had to make sure everything was okay on your end and I needed you to know you're on my mind. I love you, baby."

"I love you too. See you soon," I said, grinning.

"Promise me you'll finish school before you decide to get married, *and* promise me you'll be smart and not have sex, but if you do you'll be careful," my mother begged.

"We're not talking about this, Mom."

"Come on now, Nina. I remember what it was like to be your age."

"That's great, but no one is getting married anytime soon. Additionally, we aren't doing anything we shouldn't either."

"Do you have any questions you might want to ask?"

"No, Mom. Again, we're not having this conversation."

Please stop. For the love of God, please stop.

"If you ever have any questions," she began.

"I'll find you. Can we chat about something else?"

My mother filled me in on the family gossip for the next few hours while I provided my best kitchen slave labor. A chef this chick was not. Getting burnt or cutting myself always seemed to be the end result of too much time spent in this space. It would be much easier to avoid this practice all together, opposed to having to stop every five minutes to focus on healing myself. During times like these, possessing my gift thrilled me because if I were "normal" I'd probably live on a gurney at the local emergency room. Around two the doorbell rang. The once quiet home turned into a loud, crazy madhouse.

Dinner couldn't end fast enough. Once my aunts found out I had a boyfriend, that became the center of discussion, which proved uncomfortable. I'm the type of girl who likes to be on the sidelines watching everything go by. Not in the thick of things.

"Nina, tell us about this boy," Bridget pressed.

"His name is Chase."

"How long have you been together? Where did you meet? What does he look like? Come on, Nina. Give us some details," Jenny added.

"A little over a year. We met at school. He looks like a guy."

"Chase is a wonderfully polite boy who's Nina's age. He's well-mannered, and very handsome. He's attending South University with Nina, and is studying law. He's bright, well-spoken, and talented. We recently found out he's Nina's counterpart so-to-speak," my mother added, sounding quite fond and proud of Chase.

"Really?" Bridget appeared shocked.

"That's amazing, Ellen. You usually don't find your other half until later on in life. I assume he's a healer like us?" Jenny inquired.

"Not exactly. His abilities are still developing. He's a first-generation soul. His parents do not possess the divine gift. It's a long story, but you'll meet him later," my mother said, trying to avoid giving out too much information.

"Well, what are Chase's abilities?" Bridget queried.

"Altering moods and senses is all we know of. Jack thinks more are developing though," my mother replied in an almost bragging tone—completely uncharacteristic behavior for her.

"Like the Angel of Emotions? Muriel, I believe her name is." Bridget's face etched with surprise.

"Sort of." My mother's demeanor returned to evasive. "Dinner is ready."

"How did Nina and Chase come to find out about their bond?" Bridget wouldn't let the topic rest.

"Divine intervention created circumstances like it has for all of us. Here," my mother said, shoving a casserole dish into Bridget's hands. "Bring this to the table." Grabbing the turkey, she pushed past her sister-in-law. When Ellen Luther wanted a conversation to end, it ended.

Great. Can't wait for Chase to show up now…not.

Chapter 10

Chase

Channeling my inner acrobatic skills wasn't the best idea, but it was the only way out of the Luther house without being seen. Thankfully, the tree outside of Nina's window broke most of the fall. The irony of the situation was laughable. For the first time in a while the headaches were gone, but now my back and shoulders were killing me.

Some days it doesn't pay to get out of bed, Chase.

After a long, hot shower, which I hoped would alleviate the body ache—it did not, and a quick call to Nina, I intended to get some sleep. However, my ringing cell phone thought otherwise. Reaching over and grabbing it, a smile appeared once the screen revealed the caller's name.

"Hey, you."

"Hey, yourself," she said coyly.

"What does a lowly southern boy owe the pleasure of this call to?"

She laughed lightly. "Just wanted to say hi is all."

"Hi."

"Hi."

"Seriously, beautiful. What's up?" I knew this girl well enough to know something was going on.

"You haven't called me that since." She paused. "Well, you know."

"Yeah."

"You're probably busy because it's Thanksgiving, but could we maybe see each other?" Her voice was full of hesitation over the request.

"I can make that happen. When?" I answered without thinking.

"Now? I'll grab coffee. We can meet up at Forsythe Park by the fountain?"

"I'll get the coffee, beautiful. See you in fifteen?"

"Sounds great." Her infectious grin translated through the receiver.

"Half caff, white chocolate chip, frappe blended cream?"

"You remembered."

"You never forget something like that. It used to take a team of specialists to create it every time. Rarely did anyone ever make it to your liking," I joked.

"Oh, whatever. Don't put something on the menu if you can't make it. I'll see you in a few."

After digging around for a pair of jeans and a snug-fitting, green polo, a hasty exit from the house was made. Coffees in hand, relief washed over me when her car came into focus in the parking lot. She was here, waiting for me on the same bench Sean and I sat on the day we met Vincent.

Irony at its best, yet again today.

The moment our eyes met, she threw herself into my arms, holding on tightly.

"Chase."

"It's good to see you too. What's going on?"

"I miss you." She pulled my body closer to hers.

"Miss me *how*, Bristol?" I questioned, attempting to create some space between our frames.

You'd better tread lightly and proceed with caution.

"Having you in my life."

"I'm here, aren't I? I'm still in your life." I said, finally able to free myself from her grip.

"Not like this. Like it used to be."

"You do know I'm with someone, right?" Her heart had been broken once by my careless hands. I had zero intentions of doing it again.

"No," Bristol said mellow, but not distraught. "Tell me about her. What's the lucky girl's name? How long have you guys been dating? Is it serious?" She attempted to sound perky.

"Nina. We've been together for a little over a year, and yes, it's serious, but it's also complicated." Discussing your future with your past was weird and uncomfortable.

"Complicated good, or complicated bad?"

"Complicated. How are you? What's new in your life?" I said, quickly changing the subject. Talking about Nina was too awkward, especially when I had to tap dance around the bond we shared. Making our relationship as vague as possible and answering surface questions with basic facts was best. Case closed.

Next subject please.

"Nothing much."

She dropped the Nina topic, and for the next half hour talked about random odds and ends. It felt nice to experience normal and healthy again. No headaches, no drama, no unexplained occurrences. Nothing but peace.

"I better get going," I said, reaching for our empty coffee cups.

"Oh, okay," Bristol answered softly, taking my hand in hers. "Can we hang out again?"

Before I could rationalize how seeing her on purpose in the future would be wrong, my mouth automatically agreed. “Yeah. Of course.”

“I’ll call you,” she said. Her index finger and thumb grazed the side of my face the way she used to when we were dating.

For one brief moment my sanity vanished. Leaning over and softly brushing my lips against her ear, I whispered, “And, I’ll answer.”

Chapter 11

Nina

At a painfully slow pace, dinner finally ended. Needing an escape from the white-hot interrogation spotlight, I hid in the kitchen, dragging ass while loading the dishwasher. The doorbell's chime instantly lifted my spirits. Immediately Chase's emotional presence awakened all five of my senses.

"Hey."

"I missed you, baby." Chase pulled me outside of the house and into his arms.

"I missed you too."

My hands reached behind me to close the door. Obviously he wasn't ready to come inside just yet.

"You're nervous," I said in response to the rapid change in emotions I was experiencing. "Don't be. My family's not that bad. Besides, they already know all about you."

"I have something for you."

"Oh?"

Reaching into his pocket he produced a small, black, velvet box. Slowly opening the lid, an edginess and anxiety radiated throughout the space causing my sight to sharpen. Tucked in between a slit of onyx velvet rested a ring. A three stone, sparkling, diamond ring to be exact.

"It's a promise ring. I'm eternally yours, Nina. You have to know, I'd do *anything* for you, and would *never* do anything to intentionally hurt you. I'd walk to the ends of the Earth, face my darkest fears for you. I'd follow you anywhere, and will always do what's best for you, for *us*. I love you so much," he said softly, slipping the ring on my finger.

Tears clouded my vision. Last year Chase James had been nothing more than a crush, someone I wanted to talk to but could never find the courage to, and now here we were. Things weren't perfect, but we were facing life's drama together. That's all that mattered. Nothing could break us.

"I love it, Chase, and I love you."

"You deserve so much more for putting up with me." He laughed, gently instigating a long, passionate kiss. The sensation of his laughter against my lips set my soul ablaze.

"We better get inside," I said, holding his strong body against mine, kissing him one more time, silently praying this moment could last forever.

Chapter 12

Chase

Guilt is an awesome force. A force so strong and powerful my body, mind, and soul were consumed with it after leaving the park. Between that and the heartache it brought along, my headache returned, but this time a strange surge of power and an edgy anxiety set up camp within me.

What you're feeling has nothing to do with your other world. It's disappointment and stress. You went behind your girlfriend's back to see your ex. You flirted and pretended with Bristol while your soul mate waited for you to show up. You don't deserve Nina.

Aggressively I turned the car around, got on the highway, and headed to the mall. An hour and several hundred dollars later, balance was restored. Fortunately for me, my departed grandparents had left behind a sizable inheritance some several years ago in my name. Sizable meaning I'd never have to work a day in my life or ever worry about money. Finally being of age, the funds could be freely drawn upon.

If my father could use material items such as jewelry, cars, spa visits, clothing, and purses to right his wrongs with my mother, why couldn't that tactic work for me right now? What he'd done to her was far worse and scummy than me simply sharing a cup of coffee with Bristol. Clearly this was an acceptable approach which yielded desirable results.

Hey, what dear old Dad does is a thousand times uglier, but he's definitely onto something because the guilt you were walking around with has somehow magically disappeared.

By the time I returned home, my parents and a few other family members were getting ready to eat dinner. Having to engage in small talk with any of them sucked.

"I have to go, Mom, unless you need help in here?"

"No, everything is under control. Where are you off too? Nina's house?" she asked, smiling.

"Yeah."

"You know you could've invited her here."

"She had a lot going on today. Another time."

"Maybe you'll invite her over for Christmas?"

"Sure. Maybe."

"Have fun. Please say hello for me."

"Will do." Thankfully the conversation wasn't going to drag on for an hour. As my right hand pushed the kitchen door open, it paused. "I love you, Mom," I said, not looking back at her, but rather still at the door.

"I love you too, Chase," she responded, hugging me tightly from behind.

For a brief moment, I felt childlike again, holding onto my mother's arm, silently hoping she'd be able to make the bad things disappear.

"Got to go." A strong overwhelming desire to purge everything had surfaced. It was time to leave before I said something I couldn't take back or worse, outed my secret.

Neglecting to say goodbye to anyone else felt good. It always did. I could've cared less about any of them. No connection, no emotion, nothing existed between any of us. They certainly didn't give a damn about me. Why waste an ounce of energy on them?

Giving Nina the ring erased my sin. She was happy and blissfully unaware of any wrongdoing. Everything went smoothly at the Luther house until Ellen announced dessert was ready. The moment I stood my head pounded and my vision sharpened. Not collapsing became a fulltime job. Pushing myself to act normally was an amazing feat.

Thinking or functioning on any level seemed impossible. All I could do was sit at the table propped up on an extremely hard chair hoping no one wanted to chat. They already knew I was one of their kind because everyone spoke freely about healing in front of me earlier. By the grace of God, no one asked any questions about my abilities.

What happened next is still a mystery. Nina lifted a coffee pot and was pouring the hot liquid into cups. One of her aunts shrieked something about us being engaged. Nina dropped the pot, which happened to be inches away from scolding her legs. Without thinking, I stood and reached for it. I caught it by the handle and placed it on the table.

Crisis averted. Hopefully you'll be able to go home soon and lay down in a dark room forgetting this day and this massive migraine ever happened.

Chapter 13

Nina

Momentarily, something felt strange. Like time had slowed down and the world only operated in slow motion. Everything from thoughts, movements, even words, weren't functioning properly. It wasn't only me though. Everyone in the room acted parallel, except for Chase. A few seconds later, reality caught up allowing life's natural rhythms to resume, aside for the fact Chase was placing the coffee pot, which seconds ago slipped from my hands, on the table.

"Are you all right, Nina?" Chase asked calmly.

"Yeah, but how the…what the," I started to answer, but the wild sounds coming from my family cut me off.

"Do you know what just happened, Chase?" my father questioned.

"Yes. I caught the pot Nina dropped," he replied in a matter-of-fact tone.

"You temporarily slowed down time," my father stated in amazement. "Another gift. Incredible."

"Okay." Chase looked around the room. His expression resembled a deer caught in headlights.

My mother placed her right hand on Chase's left forearm. Her warm eyes were full of concern. "Enough, Jack. Now is *not* the time. These past few days have been hard enough on him. He needs a break, and I will make damn sure he gets what he needs."

Chase and my father exchanged a quick glance. The unspoken communication led way to a sudden shift in the room. The once heavy deepness had turned into a light, carefree environment.

Chase.

He was successfully controlling the dynamic of the room. At once the conversation picked up. All parties involved were rather cheerful, not even mentioning the incident at all. It was as if it never happened. Masterfully Chase maintained the atmosphere for the rest of the evening. Once the house emptied, his body flopped lifelessly on the couch.

"How are you feeling, Chase?" Concern dripped from my father's every word.

"Completely and totally tired. Like I ran one hundred miles without stopping," he said, closing his eyelids, and leaning back against the cushions.

"Does your head hurt?" my father questioned, reaching for Chase's wrist to check his pulse.

"Yes," Chase whispered almost inaudibly. "You have to make it go away. Do whatever necessary. Just make it stop."

"Steve," my father called.

"Yeah, Dad?" Steve appeared, stopping dead in his tracks the moment he saw Chase. "You okay, man?"

"Help me," Chase slurred, attempting to stand, but failing.

"How bad is the pain? Are you feeling anything else, aside from a severe headache?"

"Can't focus. Everything is blurry. Hard to speak. It's bad," he panted while struggling to communicate, clumsily grabbing at his hair.

My father instructed Steve to grab a few things from

around the house and to meet him in the guest bedroom, before helping Chase up the stairs. He'd never been this weak or helpless before. I started to follow, but my mother stopped me.

"Let your father handle this," she urged.

"Something's wrong and -"

"Let your father handle this, Nina," she repeated.

"You seriously want me to sit here and do nothing?"

"Yes," she snapped. "And while you wait, there's a ton of things you can help me with to occupy your time."

A few warm tears rolled down my cheeks. Apart from powerlessness, there was nothing else left to feel.

"He's going to be fine, honey. Your father knows what he's doing. He'd never let anything happen to Chase, or you, or any one of us for that matter. Chase is a part of our family. We love him. Let your father do what needs to be done and fulfill his calling as God intended. There's a reason why this happened and is happening. We *will* get to the bottom of it," she said, wrapping her slender arms around my waist, gently pushing my head onto her shoulder.

I hope you're right, Mom. Please be right.

Truth & Consequences—II

My Dearest Love,

Keeping powerful knowledge to oneself is bloody infuriating. You have no idea how many times I've wanted to call Michael, Raphael, and Gabriel out, but I haven't. Why bother? They'd lie, cheapening the false relationship we're all already pretending to share. Stories could be told for days about the dynamic of those three. How they state bold falsehoods, then swear for the other, but I digress because Gabriel and I have done the same for each other. It's inner anger that's causing this black rain to fall upon my soul, and I apologize for my sour tone.

Shall we continue?

Purgatory is an odd place. It's a holding cell of sorts for those who have passed and are waiting to be placed for their final rest. To the Mortal eye, Purgatory appears to resemble a hospital, but it's the farthest thing from. Once there, your name is placed on a list which is reviewed by The Elder's Chief Counsel. The Chief Counsel are beings much like The Thirteen who hold no allegiance to Heaven or Hell—just the facts. Most individuals wake, then are told their fate is being determined. Once a decision is made, they're sent to Heaven, Hell, or back to Earth as a Lost Soul, but not me. Michael was the first thing I saw.

He sat on the edge of the bed, first apologizing for the brutality of my death, then welcoming me home. A lot of people would've panicked, but there was no reason to. The pain and suffering had ended. Without knowledge of how Purgatory worked, I assumed this behavior was typical, I followed Michael through a door, to a garden—Heaven's Garden to be exact. We talked and when the conversation ended, I'd been given a position in the Angelic Army, a gift, a space to exist in with Michael and Hadreniel, and I met your father. An instant bond existed between your father and me. We were inseparable. Michael often referred to him and me as "the ultimate yin and yang," but personally, having a powerful older brother meant more to me than anything The Heavens could've bestowed upon me.

Time is funny in The Heavens, mainly because it doesn't exist, but after a while something strange occurred. Star patterns suddenly told stories—stories only I could read. What's odder is they came true, like prophecies. Michael brushed off the ability suggesting several Angels possessed the gift and the Army didn't rely on the star's credibility. One night while sitting in the garden star gazing, God's Scribe, Metatron, introduced himself.

We must stop here for now. The mission I'm currently on is of great importance. If not handled properly you won't be born, and that can't happen. Until our next letter, I'll be dreaming of only you and all of your beautiful perfections.

Always,
Your Betrothed

Chapter 14

Chase

I could barely move by the time we reached the top of the stairs. All of my weight leaned heavily on Jack's shoulders.

"*Chase…Chase…Chase*," an unfamiliar voice whispered.

Immediately my senses weakened and powered down, leaving my sight and hearing severely diminished. An icy rag was placed over my eyes, which in a weird way soothed the headache. The faint smell of random herbs and menthol hovered in the air.

"How's your head now?" Jack asked, checking my heart rate.

"Calming," I mumbled to conserve strength.

"Your pulse is almost normal again and your color is returning. Your vitals are strong. The headaches are a constant in your life, but for some reason you felt the need to hide this. Chase, if you want my help I need to know *exactly* what's going on. None of this should embarrass you or make you believe you're weak. You're a part of this family. What we discuss stays between us."

"I'm sorry."

"I may not understand what you're going through, but I'm here for you. Tell me, what's *really* been going on?"

"The headaches are always present, but never as bad

as this. I thought they'd go away in time. I'm tired of feeling like an experiment and want to know what the hell is going on inside of my head. Nothing has been right since the damn accident. I'm sick and tired of this life. Nina is being dragged down too. We can't even have a normal relationship. This mind mood controlling thing sucks. Do you know what it's like to keep everything to yourself so others don't feel screwy around you? And now, evidently, the freakshow side of me can control time. But hey, let's run back to the lab where more tests can be run. We can poke and prod some more all while getting nowhere. I get it. The headaches are my brains way of coping with the new Universe I'm a part of. It's probably trying to rewire itself to accommodate the abilities, but if this is going to be a lifelong problem, I'm out."

"This will pass. You will feel normal again. Never the way you felt before the accident, but calmer and more mentally stable. We need to get each ability under control. Holding your emotions back during a stressful time like this is difficult, but everyone must endure hardships in order to find our way back to higher ground. All we've done is put a bandage on the problem. By testing different theories we will find a more permanent solution, and in turn, fix them. *You* are *not* an experiment, Chase, but we *need* to experiment to figure this out. As for you and Nina, she understands and is your mate. She's not going anywhere."

"Why is this happening all at once?"

"Truth? No idea. Working theory? When all of your abilities fully develop they'll somehow play off of each other or connect, but we won't know for sure until the change is complete. How's the head?"

"Better," I said realizing the pain had subsided and my body was in a somewhat relaxed state again.

"I'll mix more of this solution up. When a headache starts, wet a cloth, pour some on, and lay down. The discomfort should diminish quickly. Don't let the aching get out of control again, like tonight. The moment you feel anything, start treatment."

"What's in it?"

"Various herbs, oils, and a few other ingredients that when combined combat migraines. Very holistic Eastern medicine. It's not a pharmaceutical if that's what you're worrying about. How have you been sleeping? Have you taken the pills?"

"Honestly, no."

"Why not?"

"I'm afraid to. What if they mess with the emerging abilities or make them worse? What if they cause a bigger problem than what I'm already dealing with?" I attempted to stand, but Jack gently pushed my frame back onto the mattress.

"Those are all valid concerns, but if you don't sleep, you'll be in worse shape. Take the pills, Chase. There's nothing to be scared of. They'll help. I wouldn't prescribe something to you that I wouldn't take myself or wouldn't allow my family to ingest."

"How many more abilities do you think will evolve?" I asked with a sigh, while cradling my face in my hands.

"I don't know, but there's more brewing inside," he answered, checking my pulse again.

"Great," I moaned.

"Heart rate is normal. Vitals are steady. How do you feel overall?"

"Tired. Drained. Done. Frustrated."

"Do you think you could sleep naturally right now?"

"I'm not sure. Sometimes I'm beyond tired, but can't seem to fall asleep. If by some twist of fate I can, it's never for long."

"All right. What if we called your parents and asked them if you could sleep over tonight? You can take one of the pills. I'll be here to monitor you, *just in case*, but nothing is going to happen aside from you finally getting a good night's rest."

Shifting, I reached inside of my back pocket for my cell phone, and dialed home. Jack openly invited me to stay the night. I'd be a fool to leave. If things went south, this was the safest place.

"Hey, Mom."

"Hi, darling. Is everything okay? You sound ill."

"Everything is fine. Listen, I'm going to spend the night at Nina's," I stated, rather than asking for permission.

"Are Nina's parents' home?"

"Yes. Of course."

"I don't know if I like the idea of you sleeping at your girlfriend's house, Chase."

"I'm nineteen years old—not a child. I'll see you in the morning."

"Chase."

"What?"

"What's been going on with you lately?"

"Nothing."

"I'm your mother and know you well. You seem off, rather distant, and well, I can't put my finger on it, but something is going on. If you're in trouble or need help, talk to me." Her tone softened.

"Nothing's wrong. I want to spend some time with Nina."

"Chase, you're hiding something. Hopefully in time you'll share whatever it is with me."

"Goodnight, Mom," I said, and hung up.

"Is everything okay?" Jack inquired.

"My mother is picking up on all of the oddities." The statement may have appeared calm, but my frantically pounding heart told a vastly different story.

"We'll have to meet and explain the situation soon."

"Dr. Luther, there is no way, and I stress the word *no*, either of them will believe or understand this."

"You'd be surprised."

"Yeah well, I'd be surprised if they didn't have me committed. Sean's parents stopped by a few weeks ago asking if we knew anything. I told my mother I knew nothing, but I'm doubtful she believed me." My inner fears had reached the surface.

"Whatever happens, it will be fine," Jack said calmly.

"No, it won't. They can never know. Not now, not ever," I insisted.

"Chase, let's tackle one day, one issue, at a time. At some point you're going to have to tell them. It doesn't have to be today or tomorrow, but your parents will have to be told. You're their son. They love you and will love you no matter what, but for now you need rest," he urged, handing over a bottle of water and a small, white pill.

Balance and peace were required and that pill was the only answer.

"I'll check on you in a few minutes. If you need me for anything, holler." Jack smiled warmly before exiting the room.

Holy shit. This situation is beyond out of control. First and foremost, my freak status needs to remain a private matter, one that George and Blanche never know about. Whatever it takes they must remain oblivious.

A soft knock snapped me back to reality.

“Chase?” Nina’s sweet voice spoke. She was the only consistency I cherished. She walked in with a worrisome smile etched on her face.

“Hey, baby.”

“Are you okay?” Her distress bothered me tremendously.

“I’m fine, just a little tired.” I forced a grin to ease her troubled mind. This beautiful creature should never have to experience pain and suffering on any level. In a little over a year I’d inflicted too much of both on her. “Come here, baby,” I encouraged, sitting up, and extending my arms for her to fall into.

Nina, my beautiful, angelic Nina, would always be the end and be all of everything right in this world. Perfection in its purest form.

Chapter 15

Nina

In silence I fell into Chase's strong, waiting arms. There were no right words. There would never be any right words, and sadly this happened way too often lately. Feeling useless and helpless had become a constant. Instead of settling on saying something lame, wrapping myself in his embrace, burying my face in his neck, and inhaling the intoxicating scent only he provided seemed a more powerful option. Sometimes situations required more than words.

Chase always reminded me of my favorite cologne, coupled with fresh laundry, and the way the fall smelled in New York. When we began dating, I shared this sentiment with Jules who looked at me like she'd just heard the most insane thing ever, swearing he only smelled faintly of aftershave. During a mother-daughter moment, I told my mother, who explained when women like us find our mates, the attraction from both people is strong, so strong their senses become heightened which is what draws the couple together. I became curious by this and asked Chase what attracted him to me. Apparently it'd been my voice. The volume, pitch, and tone pleased him, evoking cherished memories and daydreams.

"I'm sorry, Chase."

"Sorry for what? None of this is your fault."

"We should be happy. *You* should be happy. We shouldn't be defeated this early in the game."

"We're not defeated, baby. We'll get through this and live to endure others storms by each other's side forever."

"Promise?"

"Swear."

"Can I lay here with you for a little while?" His answer didn't matter because detaching from our closeness wasn't about to happen anytime soon.

He laughed lightly, tugging me closer. Not allowing myself to think actually came easy for once. Staring at the blue walls, feeling his touch, hearing him breathe, and imagining our life together was what my soul needed. Things were rough, but life would eventually slow down and we'd be able to find solace.

Only the strong sense of contentment could be experienced while lying there as my fingers weaved in and out of a sea of tousled mahogany hair. Unfortunately, the momentary joy vanished as soon as the door squeaked open.

"Nina?" Steve said.

"Yeah," I whispered, carefully sitting up, hoping the sudden movements wouldn't wake Chase.

"He's down. Dad gave him a sleeping pill that could knock out a Clydesdale. Why don't you go to your room and get some rest yourself?"

"I'm going to stay with Chase a little longer."

"Nina, he's fine. You need sleep too. Come on. It's bedtime," he stated, taking hold of my arm, and yanking me into the hall.

"Steve," I hissed, trying to pull free.

"Steve, what? You'll see him tomorrow. Good

night," he rebutted, guiding me gently into my bedroom, and closing the door, leaving me confused and aggravated.

Whatever, Steve.

Flopping on my bed, deep annoyance and anger set in. There'd be no rest tonight or any other night for that matter until Chase was back to good.

If I could only use my gift to heal Chase we could have our happily ever after fairytale ending. Too bad I can't, but maybe...

****

No real danger presented itself, my instincts confirmed this, but my body and mind flooded with fear and great despair. Something had to be found, but what? Wildly I surveyed the room. My surroundings came into focus, sharpening the longer I stared at objects. The room was dimly lit and icy cold. A chill should've been felt, but wasn't. Instead, a fiery hot sensation from deep within me presented. A wooden table with leather restraints was placed off to the side. There were no windows, making the only source of light come from a hanging light bulb which was swaying slowly in the center of the room. Panic raged.

A door appeared to my left. Automatically I ran to it pulling the handle open. A long, dark corridor greeted me on the other side. Intuition carried my legs to the right and down a hallway. I moved like a bat out of Hell with no direction, running blindly through the darkness, not caring about tripping or hurting myself. Finding whatever was lost mattered most. Nothing else. A small dot of canary yellow came into view. This had to be my final destination.

The point evolved into larger rays and faint voices

off in the distance were now beginning to become audible. Once the source of sound and light was reached, my body stopped abruptly, nearly causing me to fall over. Cautiously peering into the brightly lit space, several hooded and cloaked figures stood in a loose circle. They appeared to be surrounding something as they chanted in monotone style voices. Trying to hold my breath and stand perfectly still to remain unnoticed proved easier than expected. In extreme slow motion, I crept closer to the figures. My hands and legs shook. Gone was the ability to not breathe. After a few carefully placed steps, the object in question became crystal clear.

It was me. My lifeless body was lying on the hard, dirty floor. A gold chain draped around my neck radiantly sparkled in the pale glow. Attempting to scream or run to where I was to help myself couldn't happen. Something tight had wrapped itself around my knees making any movement, big or small, virtually impossible.

"No. Chase. Help me." A drowsy slur of words managed to stumble out of my mouth instead of a core shaking shout.

My body sprang up, furiously trying to free myself. Beads of cold sweat rolled without pride down my forehead and into my eyes, stinging and burning. Finally able to break free, I jumped off of the bed.

Ground yourself.

My entire being felt wrong, off, almost like a stranger had invaded my soul. The world around me spun out of control. Seconds away from losing it, a strong calming sensation overtook the bad, beating it back into the bowels of consciousness.

Chapter 16

Chase

"Baby. Calm down. You were dreaming. You're all right. I'm here and I won't let anything happen to you *ever*. Okay?" If there were ever a time these freakish abilities came in handy, now would be it. We've all suffered nightmares, but Nina's current experience won the prize for the world's worst.

"Chase. Oh my God, Chase." Nina's voice appeared calm, but traces of panic lingered while she tried to fight the mental hold I had placed over her.

"Nina, look at me. Are you awake?" The balance between giving too much or doling out too little when it came to using mind control remained a mystery.

"Yeah. I'm pretty sure."

The gift may have been weakened from earlier, but apparently it still worked. "You're safe, awake, standing in your room, and nothing, I repeat *nothing*, is going to harm you."

Carefully moving to where she stood, positioning our bodies face to face would allow for eye contact. After a few intense moments, Nina threw herself at me damn near crushing my ribs with her grip, while mumbling inaudible sounds.

"I'm going to remove my hold over you, okay?"

"It's happening again, Chase. The dreams are back." Her hands shook violently.

It was obvious she still required mental guidance to simmer down, but I didn't know how much juice remained inside of me. The damn pill Jack had given me had dulled everything, including my own senses, so by default, my gift. The sleep aide worked, but not for long. After a few hours of a fairly peaceful, dreamless slumber, I woke feeling somewhat rested and grateful the headache hadn't returned, but ill at ease. Something from within me urged me to sneak down the hall and into Nina's room, which turned out to be a good thing. Pushing myself to increase her sense of smell might work being it was my scent which initially drew her in.

Maybe soul mates shared an ESP thing? Who knows? Wouldn't surprise me if they did. Hell, nothing really surprises me anymore.

"What are you talking about, baby?"

"Last year, even before we started dating there were these dreams. I was searching for something in a forest. Every night the dreams progressed until everything became clear. When we were apart the nightmares were worse, more intense, and filled with intricate details. Initially, it was a reoccurring event, but then it came to life almost moment for moment. This is going to sound crazy, but I thought for a hot second when it was all over, the dreams were a prophecy, a warning, you know? It sounded ridiculous to even think. Then the nightmares stopped, until tonight. Vincent had me, Chase. He was going to kill me while the rest of his Demon minions watched. What if this turns out to be a prophecy too?"

"Sometimes a dream, or in this case a nightmare, is just that. Nothing more. You're jumping to conclusions. You've been under a lot of stress so you're anticipating the worst out of fear. I'm not dismissing your take on the situation, but it's doubtful last year's nightmares have anything to do with the one you had tonight, nor was it a prophecy." Thankfully, my words came across smooth, masking my own internal panic.

Stay calm. Happy thoughts, Chase. Don't let her feel your emotions.

"What if it is?"

"It's not. Let it go."

Nina gave off the impression she wanted to debate the issue further, but stopped.

"Why aren't you asleep? Is something wrong? Do you not feel well?" she asked. Her voice was consumed with concern, but its quality fell flat. The little mojo left within me had dwindled down to almost nothing. The hold had to be released before another migraine set in or worse.

"I'm fine. The headache is gone. I got up to use the bathroom and heard you moving around in here."

"I'm glad you checked on me," she whispered, curling up against my waist. "Can you stay until I fall back asleep? Please?"

"Baby, you're safe. Everything is going to be fine. Do you honestly think I'd ever allow anything bad happen to you?"

"No, you wouldn't. Stay for a few more minutes? I need you," she pleaded softly.

"I'm here and not going anywhere, ever. I promise," I assured, stroking the side of her face. "Close your eyes."

It took a good thirty minutes and a ton of focus before my ability kicked back in at full strength forcing sleep upon Nina. Beating back every thought so she wouldn't feel my own worry and trepidation proved exhausting in itself.

Damn it. Now what? As if dealing with my screwy situation wasn't enough, now she's seeing the future via dreams? What the hell?

Somehow a keen awareness grew the instant she shared the information, Nina possessed seer abilities. This inner eye of sorts reared its ugly head the moment I entered her life.

Maybe we're wrong for each other?

Yeah, but there's the whole soul mate thing.

Perhaps it was a mistake and all of these warnings are a sign that nothing good could ever come from us?

No. We share an unbreakable bond. This is all one big shit test. Yes. It's a trial of devotion and strength. Couples are supposed to be a team. We have to stick together to weather this storm. We'll emerge stronger for enduring it.

Several hours later as the sun rose, Nina remained in a deep, peaceful rest. She wouldn't be waking anytime soon. The last thing I needed was for Jack or Ellen to see me in bed with their daughter. To make sure that didn't happen, I enhanced my ability to hear sharper and didn't conk out. Slowly, as quietly as possible, my feet lightly traced the floor until the door was safely closed behind me.

"Is something the matter with Nina?" Steve questioned.

I didn't expect anyone to be standing in the hall, and I wasn't about to reveal that this jackass's presence startled me.

"She had a nightmare." Our eyes locked in equally hard glares.

Oh, Steve. You really don't know who you're

messing with. Please don't make me have to show you. For both of our sakes, drop it.

"About?"

"Ask her."

"I will."

"You should."

As if the world was mine for the taking, I pushed past him, walked down the stairs, and out of the front door.

Chapter 17

Nina

Prematurely I was taken from a deep, dreamless, wonderful sleep by the sound of Steve knocking, then entering. A quick scan for Chase showed he'd left and no danger existed within the safety of the four walls. No Vincent. No Demons. Nothing. Not even the slightest trace that a nightmare had occurred several hours earlier.

"What?" I grunted.

"Rise and shine, Sis," Steve roared in his deep voice.

"What time is it?" Perhaps pulling the covers over my head would subtly cue him to go away.

"Almost eight, but I'm only here for a few more days and I wanted to spend some time with my favorite sister." He sat on my cluttered desk.

"I'm your *only* sister. What do you want to do?" I yawned, poking my head out from under the comforter.

"It's Black Friday. Let's hit the mall. Catch all of the good sales. Elbow people fighting for the last five-dollar laptop. Besides, I need some new clothes. Scarlett wasn't too happy when we broke up. She may have taken a scissor to most of my shirts. Get your lazy butt up and get showered," he said, standing.

"Fine, but we have to be back before four."

"Why?"

"I've got plans with Chase."

"I get the whole soul mate thing, but you two seem

a little too fused at the hip," Steve said displeased.

"What's that supposed to mean?" His tone suggested a fight loomed, and my gut's radar was never wrong when it came to my brother.

"Nothing. Get ready, all right?"

"Now wait one damn second, Steve." While attempting to stop him from leaving, my foot tangled on a carelessly discarded flip-flop.

Steve rushed to where I'd fallen, effortlessly lifting me onto the bed.

"You're bleeding. Hold still."

Several droplets of blood had bubbled to the surface on my right palm. As if nothing out of the ordinary, his skilled hands healed the cut, the few minor scrapes, and potential bruises. The warm sensation washing over my soul felt like home. It was the purest form of comfort. It always had been, but now having accepted what I truly was, the feeling was far more powerful.

"Good as new. Watch where you're going, Sis."

"Thanks, but I could've done that myself. What's your problem with Chase?"

"Nothing, Nina. We're burning daylight." Steve replied, brushing the Chase question off.

After his hasty exit, I showered, dressed, grabbed a bagel, and a jug of coffee. Plopping onto a kitchen chair, my full attention turned to my cell phone, which I'd accidently had left downstairs the night before. Slightly disappointed Chase hadn't texted me, I decided to shoot him one.

"Good morning, honey. What's with the frown?" my mother asked, entering the kitchen.

"Morning. Tired."

"Uh huh." Her right eyebrow arched suggesting she

hadn't believed a word of what I'd said.

"I'm fine, Mom."

"Did you and Chase have a falling out?"

"No." Her line of questioning was totally annoying.

"Okay. Where are you heading off to?" she asked.

"The mall with Steve, then later out with Chase, Mark, and Jules."

"Chase looked much better this morning. Poor thing. I can't begin to imagine what he must be feeling and going through." Her voice oozed with sympathy and empathy.

"Where is he?" On my way downstairs I noticed the guest bedroom door was open. The bed appeared made, and since Chase wasn't with me, I assumed he'd left.

"He's with your father. I believe he left around five thirty and came back maybe twenty minutes ago."

"Oh, okay," I said, casually getting up, and leaving the kitchen.

My father's office door was shut, which meant they were more than likely discussing a private matter. The inner eavesdropper within me knew that lending an ear wasn't right, but necessary. It was the only way I'd ever hear an ounce of truth.

"You seem considerably better today. I assume you haven't experienced any headaches since the last one?" My father said.

"No," Chase replied.

"Good. Whenever you feel one coming on or feel off, use the mixture. It seemed to do the trick. When you run out, let me know. I'll make more. Today we should explore your new ability. Do you feel up to it?"

"Yeah, sure." Chase sounded distracted.

"What's the matter?"

"Nina had a nightmare last night."

"I'm not following. Nightmares are a common, unfortunate part of life. Is she all right?"

"She can see the future through them, Dr. Luther." After a pregnant pause, Chase spoke again. "Nina suggested that last year she had vivid dreams about the forest and what happened, but she didn't think anything of it because, quite frankly, it seemed insane and impossible, until it *did* actually happen. Now, as of last night, they're back. A new vision is forming, but not fully developed, *yet*. Nina said that only snapshots of what's going to happen revealed themselves. Vincent was there. He had her and wanted to kill her. She's got another gift buried inside of her."

"She, like the rest of our family, is a Mortal Healing Angel. That's all. No one in our lineage has had any other gift. It's highly doubtful Nina does."

"Explain the dreams then," Chase challenged.

"Dreams are a series of thoughts, sensations, and images which happen to occur while we sleep. There's nothing more or less to them. The fact that she dreamt about the forest and last summer's events could be somewhat true. Maybe Nina did experience a nightmare about a wooded area or you being in danger, but, Chase, her mind could've been envisioning a park where you two shared a date. You being in harm's way might've been a biproduct of the breakup. When a relationship ends, the mind attempts to justify why. As humans we seek answers and closure. The brain is a powerful organ. It can make you think, act, and believe all sorts of things you typically wouldn't."

"You're wrong. Nina is part seer. I know it. We're soul mates. Our bond is strong. I'm sure she's something more than only a healer."

"Let's focus on you and your gifts right now. If Nina has another divine ability, we can deal with that issue later. There's no sense in worrying over a suspicion. For now, this stays between us."

"Hey," Steve whispered from behind me, poking at my sides.

Completely lost in snooping, Steve's voice and jab to my ribs startled me, causing me to pivot sharply and lose balance for the second time today. This go around Steve caught me before the floor met my butt. Grabbing his wrist, I dragged him outside. I was completely caught off guard by what Chase had said.

A seer? Me? Why would this information be kept secret?

"What the hell, Nina? You look like you've seen a ghost," Steve said.

I was so oblivious to anything other than what I'd heard, it hadn't registered I was now on the highway in my mother's SUV, sitting in the passenger seat.

"I'm a seer," I whispered in disbelief, feeling as if the wind had knocked me off of my feet.

"A seer? Someone who can see the future? Can you?" he asked, not appearing shocked by this news at all.

"No idea. Last year I had these crazy nightmares."

"What does that have to do with being a seer?"

"They came true."

"Okay. Why is this coming to light now? Did something happen?"

"A new *vision* started forming last night. Chase heard me thrashing around my room. After he calmed me down I told him, and this morning, he told Dad."

"How clear was the last round of nightmares?"

"Crystal."

"What does Dad say about it?"

"Nothing. Dad doesn't think I possess another divine gift because no one in our family does. Apparently, I'm not supposed to know he knows. He told Chase not to mention anything about it to me."

"Are you going to say anything?"

"Should I?"

"Well, on the one hand, you have the right to be made aware of what's going on in your life, but on the other, you overheard a conversation not meant for your ears. Sucks to be you, Sis." Steve shrugged.

"Thanks for the useless advice," I snapped.

"Look, if you say you're a seer, I believe you. Why couldn't you be given a second gift? It's not like we know much about our ancestors, other than they were all healers, which means absolutely nothing when you think about it. Besides, over time stories about the past become diluted and change for purposes of exaggeration. The more a mundane happening is embellished, the more sensationalized our powers and abilities become."

"True."

"What's been going on with you and *Chase*?"

"Nothing." There was a strong chance this simple question would turn a friendly conversation into a brawl simply from the tone he used to address my boyfriend.

"He left your room this morning."

"So? I had a nightmare. Chase was making sure everything was all right, but quick, let's hate him because he cares about his girlfriend's wellbeing."

"Last summer I watched him on several occasions scale the tree outside of your room and climb in. I'll ask again. What's going on?"

"Seriously? None of this is your business. Do I interrogate you over things you've done with your girlfriends? No. Back off, Steve."

"I'm sorry, Nina, but let's be honest. I'm not stupid, and I don't like that you're entering a world you're much too young to deal with. You're headed for more pain and suffering than you've ever experienced." His demeanor went from light to hard.

"You've got to be kidding me."

"I'm all about who and what we are. Carrying out our mission as healers is a top priority for me, but something isn't right with Chase. Don't get me wrong. What he's going through sucks, but he's off. Chase isn't like us. Call it brotherly intuition if you'd like. I don't trust him. He says he'd do anything to protect you, to keep you safe, but I'm not buying it."

"Really, Steve? You're honestly going to sit there and go against divine plans and intervention when seconds ago you said you believed in your heritage?"

"I do stand by who we are and where we came from. I'm damn proud to be a part of a world where helping mankind is our calling. I've embraced this life. I'm doing my part to fulfill our Mortal mission."

"It really doesn't matter what you think. He's my destiny. You're pissed off you haven't found yours yet. If the shoe was on the other foot and you were the one with the mate, you wouldn't care what I thought. Chase would never do anything to hurt me. He'd do everything to make sure I'm safe. I'm sorry, but you're wrong. *And*, if you breathe a word of this to Mom or Dad, you will feel the full wrath of my anger. That's a threat *and* a promise."

"Take it easy, Nina. You're right. I'm probably wrong, but you're my little sister. I don't want to see anything bad happen, because trust me, if he, or anyone for that matter, harms you or puts you in danger, they're going to feel *my wrath.*"

"I can handle myself just fine." My arms tightened around my waist, while my hips grounded me farther into the soft, leather seat. Major irritation flickered from within me.

"I hope you know what you're getting yourself into," he replied, pulling the SUV into a parking spot.

It was obvious Steve regretted ever mentioning his true feelings for Chase as he desperately tried to change the subject of conversation over and over again as we walked through the mall. I allowed the topic to be dropped, but a part of me was hurt over the harsh words he'd spoken. It didn't matter what Steve had to say anyway because I really had no desire to talk about college, friends, our parents, or whatever other things came up. Mulling over the whole seer thing was my top priority. Chase would be easier to pump the information from, but my father possessed more knowledge. Researching seers seemed the best option, but how far could one really get on an internet search weeding out fact from fiction? Absentmindedly clothes were taken from various racks and handed to Steve.

Being trapped in the damn mall for hours was pure torture. Normally shopping was an enjoyable experience. Something I could spend days, no, *weeks*, doing without complaining once, but not today. Answers and closure were sought, not fun shoes and cute tops. Since Steve couldn't provide this information, he was useless. When he realized my preoccupied state, he suggested we head home. A wave of relief washed over me when Chase's car, still parked in the same spot from this morning, came into full view.

My father and Chase were sitting at the table talking in quick, hushed voices. The moment I entered the room, both stopped whispering and turned.

"How was the mall?" my father asked.

"Fine," I said, grabbing a drink from the refrigerator. "Does anyone want anything while I'm up?"

Both men shook their heads.

"No bags?"

"No, Dad. No bags."

"What's the matter, Nina?" Chase chimed in.

Holding my tongue when something bothered me had never been a strong suit. Trepidation loomed in Chase's eyes, but his emotions seemed contained.

"When were you going to tell me?" I demanded, placing both hands firmly on my hips.

"Tell you what?" Chase questioned cautiously.

"Don't use your gift on me, Chase." Unnatural relaxation with a heightened sense of touch causing the soft cotton material of my sweater to feel heavenly washed over me. Laying down and enjoying the calming sensations sounded like the best idea in the history of ever.

"All right."

Almost instantly, my muscles tensed. My clothing felt like cotton and denim again. "What exactly is going on? And don't lie to me or look to him for answers." This whole unspoken communication thing between Chase and my father was annoying as hell.

"I think you have the ability to see the future through your dreams."

"Okay."

"We don't know for sure which is why we weren't going to say anything. There's a *slight* possibility you *may* have some seer-like traits. In the past you've never shown signs of having this power, and there are no known relatives who possess this gift either, *but* that's not to say you couldn't be the first. Your dreams *might*, and I stress the word *might*, be a window of sorts into the future," my father clarified.

"How can I know for sure about the dreams?" Fear and curiosity collided within my core.

"You don't, Nina. We have to wait and see. For now, out of an abundance of caution, you're not to be alone. Someone, anyone of us, needs to be around you at all times. Should you experience another odd nightmare, you're to let me know immediately if not sooner." My father's tone was soft, but firm.

"That's ridiculous," I protested.

"Baby, please don't fight this. Do it for me, for us. I hardly ask you for anything, but I'm begging you to listen to me," Chase rationalized.

Up until that moment, caring for myself had been something I'd been quite capable of handling. For crying out loud I lived in New York City, meaning being tough and alert while aware of my surroundings became second nature. However, the mixed signals radiating off of my father's faux balanced attitude caused me to take pause. If he was dead sure the nightmares meant nothing, he'd never suggest a personal escort. Deep down he believed Chase's theory to be true, even if the words never left his mouth. Lifelessly my body flopped on one of the hard, wooden kitchen chairs. There was no sense in arguing the matter further. Chase stood, cautiously approaching me. He dropped to his knees making sure we had full eye contact before speaking.

"Nina, nothing is going to happen to you, your family, or me for that matter. You have to trust me. Okay?"

"I do, but you can't keep secrets like this from me. We're supposed to be in this together."

"I promise, but for the foreseeable future, I'll pick you up and take you to your classes, or wherever you need to go. At night your parents will take over."

"What about you and your classes?"

"I'm dropping this semester. There's too much to deal with and no time for school. My parents are going to flip out, but this is far more important." Chase didn't seem fazed by this at all.

"The hell you will," I snapped.

"It's already done. Case closed. I'll reenroll in the fall."

"I can't believe this craziness. It's insane." My head involuntarily shook back and forth.

"It seems like light will never shine through this darkness, but it will, baby," he said, standing and kissing me softly on the forehead.

"I have to get ready for tonight. You should too."

The hour alone spent getting ready to head out proved a pleasant distraction. Instead of focusing on being a seer or seeking answers to questions which probably had no answers, something different was done. For sixty wonderful minutes—technically forty-five because getting myself to shed the stink of stressful thoughts had been an epic bitch—I got lost in being me, concerning myself with only finding the perfect outfit and accessories, flawlessly applying makeup, and feeling excited about seeing Jules.

"Are you almost ready, Nina?" Chase asked, knocking on my bedroom door.

"I'm actually ready right now," I answered.

Glancing at me, then at his watch, a rather surprised expression spread across his face. "Wow. Only an hour. That's a record, baby."

A laugh rolled off of my tongue. It was the first genuine laugh I'd experienced in a while and boy, being at ease with myself had been terribly missed.

Chapter 18

Chase

The second Nina mentioned getting ready, annoyance struck me. Mark and Jules were okay to be around, but today wasn't the best day for socialization. However, this crap was important to her, for who knew why, but she did deserve normalcy—hence the only reason I'd endure the evening. Feeling like Hell frozen over while pretending to be fine had become common practice lately. Tonight would be just another award-winning performance. Running home to shower and change was a nice break. Getting away from all of the supernatural insanity and back to my own personal corner of the world proved refreshing, even though the Nina being a seer issue kept playing on a loop. Nina, now aware of this theory even if Jack wasn't fully on board with it yet, was a good thing. It was out in the open and because of that, out of my hands. In time Jack would come around. Hopefully sooner rather than later, but for now, he was at least taking it seriously by having Nina's movements carefully watched. One less thing to worry about.

My sense altering ability had become considerably easier to control and handle. Turning it on and off at the drop of a hat was effortless. Maybe Jack's influence had something to do with it or my body and mind were finally accepting the transition. Whatever the case, the problem was solved. The time trance gift was another story. I had no idea how to provoke it or which part of my brain housed it, but how it worked needed to be figured out as soon as possible. The mixture Jack had made seemed to be warding off the headaches. None had been experienced in twenty-four hours. A true, epic win. At some point I'd have to tell my parents I'd be dropping out of school, but how does one bring that up? Better yet, what does one even say when it would appear they're throwing their life away and couldn't be truthful as to why?

You could always tell them you're enlisting in the military. That would make the old man happy. He wouldn't be able to look down upon you and your existence whenever you're hanging around house anymore.

Various excuses formed while getting ready to head out. Nina required round the clock protection and that was far more important than an education which could still be obtained at a later date once everything had calmed down. Initially, Jack didn't think Nina required additional defenses. I hated having to secretly use my gift to persuade him, but what else could be done to express the importance of this matter? Gradually, throughout the conversation, he was fed emotions and bad vibes so he'd become consumed with worry and doubt. It worked because an hour later he agreed. Taking time off from school was my idea. Honestly, school and studying, shit, even my future, didn't matter. There were really only two choices. Drop out for a semester and see what happened, or flunk out, in which case the school wouldn't let me return. Withdrawing made the most sense. Eventually things would settle. They had to, right?

Carelessly I grabbed a t-shirt and pair of jeans from the closet. After a quick run of my hands through my chaotic hair, I darted from the house by means to avoid any and all potential conversation with either parent.

"How's your head feeling?" Jack asked, after he ushered me into his home.

"Fine, actually." A masking smile flashed across my lips.

Anxious to leave as soon as possible, Nina's forgetfulness hindered that plan. She and I made it as far as the damn front door before she realized she didn't have earrings on causing her to run back upstairs leaving me waiting in the foyer.

"We need to discuss your parents at some point in the near future," Jack urged.

Before I could respond, Nina returned.

"Just when I thought you couldn't look any prettier, you proved me wrong," I said, ignoring her father's comment.

Perfect timing.

"Awe, thanks. Ready?" Nina beamed.

I've known a lot of girls, and most of them had no idea how to take a compliment. They'd either blush and become embarrassed or think you were lying to them, but not Nina. She knew how and it was quite an attractive trait. Nina had self-assurance, a confidence about herself that was beyond sexy. No one needed to validate her presence or appearance. Tonight she appeared particularly attractive wearing a pair of tight jeans, her signature heels, and a tailored white button-down dress shirt.

"Yeah. Let's get going. Where are we supposed to meet Jules and Mark?"

"Gino's in about fifteen minutes," Nina replied, grabbing a sweater coat from the hall closet. "We'll see you later, Dad."

"Have fun and be careful. Try not to go too far. Call if something should come up," her father answered.

We drove in silence to Gino's. It's not that I didn't want to talk, there was simply nothing to say. My body, mind, and soul were spent. Instead of words, I reached for her soft hand, lacing our fingers together. The gesture felt nice and rather comforting. We were at a stage in our relationship where we didn't have to fill voids of time with mindless banter.

Something you never had with Bristol. She always had to talk, or rather fight, with you. Every damn thing you ever did or said was placed under a microscope. Yes, Bristol is a good girl who deserves nothing but happiness, but not with you or from you.

We entered the small restaurant, which had become a date night staple, and found Mark and Jules waiting.

Keep calm and focused. You'll have a good night. Forget about the supernatural freak you've become for a few hours. Consider it a well-earned break.

Ha. Yeah, right. It's nice to have a dream.

The thought made my lips curl slightly, but yet sent an icy chill up my spine.

Chapter 19

Nina

Chase's arm wrapped around my waist as we entered the restaurant felt amazing. At that moment in Gino's—this little hole-in-the-wall Italian place where we shared our first date, everything seemed balanced again. His touch possessed a powerful, commanding control.

Mark and Jules were already waiting. Mark was a good-looking guy with short, spiky, dark brown hair, cool, ocean blue eyes, and a tall, toned body. A true jock, but in no way, shape, or form could he ever hold a candle to Chase James. Mark and Jules had been dating for over a year now. They hooked up around the same time Chase and I did. It'd been awhile since Jules and I had a free second to hangout making tonight special. Though plain on the outside, a strong, sweet, sincere, beautiful inner goddess lived on the inside. No matter what, Jules always shined.

"Hey, guys," Jules squealed, running up to me, throwing her arms around my neck.

"I've missed you," I responded, embracing her tightly.

"You look great."

"Awe. Thanks. You're looking pretty great yourself, *especially* in that dress." After many trips to the mall senior year, she'd finally caught onto the concept of highlighting her assets, of which there were many. The knee length, fitted, blue dress showed them off perfectly.

Jules's face flushed crimson. Her head lowered. "Uh, thanks. How are your classes going?"

"Hey, Nina," Mark said, interrupting us by leaning over and giving me a side hug.

"What's going on, Mark?"

"I'm starving."

"You just ate a double bacon cheeseburger and fries an hour ago," Jules said.

"Which is why I'm hungry now. It's been sixty minutes since my last feeding," Mark quipped, tugging Jules's slight frame against his hip.

Usually on a Friday you couldn't find a free table, but tonight the eatery was fairly quiet and empty. Once seated, Chase and Mark immediately started chatting. They'd actually become somewhat friendly over the summer which made me happy seeing how Chase's old best friend was now working for Vincent as one of the Devil's servants. Truth be told, Sean Logan had never been a personal favorite of mine. He was one of those guys you either loved or hated. A part of me wondered if Chase missed their friendship. The two had been close for many years, how could he not? We never really discussed Sean, and I often internally questioned how Chase would react if we were to ever run into him again.

"Y'all ready?" our waitress asked.

"I think so," Mark answered, scanning the table to make sure we all nodded in agreement.

We ordered and picked up where we left off in our conversations. Chase and Mark continued to engage in a rather animated discussion, while Jules and I caught up on life. The dinner conversation had been light, and the food tasted unreal, leaving me to wonder if Chase had altered the dynamic of the table, or if we were simply having a good time.

Glancing at him all that could be seen was complete perfection. Strands of his chaotic hair fell into his face. Every so often he'd push it back revealing his bright green eyes which sparkled with intensity. I loved how he showed off his body by wearing fitted muscle shirts. Hey, if you got it flaunt it, right? A large part of me craved his touch and wanted more from our relationship, but Chase wanted to keep things the way they were for the moment. Mark and Jules had already consummated their relationship, as did Tori and Tim a long time ago. When they'd discuss matters of intimacy, I'd feel left out, and at times, rather jealous. Jules comforted me by saying it was sweet and romantic Chase wanted to wait, but that just made the situation worse.

A couple of hours later, Chase and Mark paid the bill while we tried to figure out where to go next. Mark suggested the batting cages, to which Chase quickly agreed. Jules and I shrugged in response. We honestly could've cared less.

Once there Jules and I found the bleachers and sat. We continued our conversation from the restaurant as we watched Mark and Chase try to out swing each other in the ninety mile per hour cages. Chase proved to be a fairly good batter, making smooth, solid contact with the ball each time. It actually looked like he knew what he was doing. Not that I was an authority on this. I hated sports.

See, Nina? Life can be normal if you let it.

I smiled at nothing in particular while inhaling the cool, crisp night air. Leaning my forearms against the bench behind me, I allowed myself to laugh and live freely—even if it would be for only a moment.

Chapter 20

Chase

Enduring dinner wasn't as bad as I'd feared. No headaches presented and I felt in full control of my every action. However, toward the end of the meal, a cagy sensation set in. Intense energy charged my veins. Doing something physical to burn off the sensation needed to occur. When Mark suggested the batting cages, I couldn't agree fast enough. Nina wouldn't be a huge supporter of this activity, but I'd done plenty of things like marathon shopping and watching endless chick flicks with her that sucked the life out of me. It was my turn. Besides, she could talk with Jules, an activity she'd enjoy, occupying time for a long stretch.

"Heading for that twenty mile an hour cage, bro?" Mark razed.

"Ha, ha. You're funny, but in case you forgot, I played shortstop, one of the hardest positions in baseball, *and* was captain of the varsity team for a year. If memory serves correct, it was the *only* season we went undefeated—winning the state title. *Additionally*, I did all of that while you were catching butterflies out in left field."

"Well then, *Mr. Captain*, let's just see how many balls you can crush," he challenged.

"It's on. Ninety mile an hour cages, *Princess*."

Prior to my life changing accident, we'd been

somewhat decent friends. We were never close like Sean and I, but we had a good relationship. It felt nice to have even a small part of the past back. A chunk of me worried about Mark, him and Jules to be exact. Sean had been madly in love with Jules, and after seeing the contents of his locker, now post change, I feared what he'd do to them. The stalker pictures and notes were safely buried in the back of my closet in an old shoebox. It was highly doubtful Sean would surface anytime soon, but deep within me, certainty remained he would attempt to kiss and claim Jules. How or when, who knew. What Sean grew capable of would remain a mystery until said time arrived. The friendship we'd once shared was long gone. If it ever came to blows, I'd destroy him without a second thought. We were enemies. The past no longer mattered.

Now isn't the time for this, Chase.

Pent up anger and frustration found an immediate release from the hurling balls. The need for self-control wasn't required here. We were at a place where it would be safe to channel emotions and no one could get hurt. As long as focus on the matter at hand was maintained, what could go wrong?

"Whoa, bro. You broke the damn bat. Holy crap," Mark howled.

After a few seconds, I realized Mark had directed his statement at me. Slowly looking down at the bat, comprehension that my hands were holding only a piece of it struck. I drew a blank.

Quick. You have to say something fast.

"The bat was crap," I said making sure I sounded as casual as possible. Thankfully Nina and Jules were still chatting and hadn't seen, nor heard, what happened.

"Try not to kill this one." Mark chuckled, tossing

another bat over.

“No promises will be made.”

The more the desire to keep it together and stop thinking about Sean, Jules, Nina, Mark, Angels, and Demons, and so on, the more the rage inside of me cultivated. Channeling the intense vibes proved difficult at first, but as time passed the task became easier. Cracking the balls as hard as possible provided a cathartic experience and forced me to maintain my typical composure.

“What the hell, man?” Mark asked in a state of utter disbelief.

“Cheap bats,” I answered, shrugging, and stepping away from the cage while holding the remnants of a second metal bat.

Change the subject.

“Hey, baby?” I called to Nina.

When Nina turned and looked up she appeared surreal. Her beauty overtook my every thought. Panic and discomfort made a speedy exit as desire and love took its place. Casually Nina rose, steadily making her way over.

“What’s up?” she questioned.

That voice—it drove me wild. Between that and the way she’d glance through those long, perfectly curled eyelashes was absolutely addicting. A compulsion that couldn’t and wouldn’t be kicked. I wanted to grab hold of her right then and there, but I didn’t. Public displays of affection, aside from a quick peck on the lips or hand holding wasn’t my style.

“Your turn,” I said, brushing away the hair that was obscuring the most beautiful face in the world. Covering or shadowing this excellence would be a crime.

"Oh no, no, no. You must have me confused with one of your other girlfriends because this chick doesn't do sports. You already know this," Nina quipped.

"Jules, look at this ball," Mark marveled.

"That was a ball?" Jules questioned, taking the destroyed leather and examining it.

Oh, man. Use your gift, Chase. You have no other choice.

Carefully infusing the air with confusion, smell and touch of those around me heightened. There were patterns between emotions and senses. Though I still wasn't one hundred percent sure of every detail, I knew what adding misperception to a space would accomplish. Anger caused a lack of vision, but a heightened sense of touch and above average hearing. Happiness seemed to heighten all senses. More experimenting needed to be conducted, but at least a foundation to build on had been established. An extreme curiosity to see if emotion could be separated from senses drove me to continue on with the research. If feelings I desired were granted while giving or taking away senses, the power I'd possess would be unstoppable. Any situation could be manipulated in my favor. In time, I'd master this skill.

At least you're finding little things to look forward to.

"You'll be fine. I'll help," I replied, turning my gift up another notch, hoping Jules and Mark were feeling the effects. However, a proper read on Nina couldn't be obtained.

Jules dismissed the ball tossing it to the ground and stared aimlessly into space. Mark did the same. Neither were speaking or touching one another, just gazing blankly into space. Nina seemed unaffected, checking her cell phone.

Strange. Jules and Mark can feel me, but Nina doesn't. Maybe she's used to experiencing my gift, or maybe she isn't influenced by it anymore? I'll have to test this later.

"Guys?" I questioned.

"Huh? Oh, hey. Isn't the sky simply amazing tonight?" Jules asked dreamily.

Too much juice, Chase. Take it down a notch.

"Sure," I answered, pulling my hold back gradually. Truth be told, having control over them was rather enjoyable. I dictated their every move, every thought. I could make or break them. Never in my life had anything ever felt this commanding, and it was awesome.

Chapter 21

Nina

Against my better judgment, Chase led me to one of the batting cages. For a few minutes, he stood behind me, showing me how to stand and swing. After a few solo practices, Chase exited. Seconds later, balls started catapulting toward me. With every ounce of might I'd swing, coming up empty each time, feeling like an absolute idiot while spinning in circles. What made matters worse was each time this happened, Chase snickered loudly. Jules seemed to be doing well. Unlike me, she'd at least been somewhat capable of making contact with the ball.

Seriously, Nina. If Jules can do this, so can you.

If my head wasn't somewhere else, I might've heard the pitching machine release another ball. A crack and a crunch cut through the air before the most intense pain ever throbbed. Every bone shook while bright flashes of stars appeared before me.

"Holy crap," I screamed, dropping to the ground, clutching my right hand against my chest.

"Nina. Are you okay?" Jules shrieked, rushing over, trying to push me out of the line of fire.

Practically on her heels were Chase and Mark. The moment Chase touched the injury the pain subsided and deep comfort soothed me. He was actually making the pain go away by dulling my senses. I knew what needed to be done, but that required getting far away from Mark and Jules. As long as Chase continued to absorb the pain, everything would be fine.

"Just breathe, baby. You're going to be fine," Chase said calmly.

He knew panicking was moot. The instant we were alone, I'd be able to heal myself. Scaring Jules, a natural born worrier, would've been silly. Between the instant swelling, horrific pain, and barely moveable hand, I didn't need to be a master surgeon to figure out that the bones were broken.

"We should go to the hospital and get an x-ray," Chase said as he helped me off of the ground.

"I am sorry, Nina." Jules was practically in tears.

"It's not your fault. I'm athletically challenged. It's fine. Stop stressing."

"Here, use this until you get to the ER. Coach used to make us carry these in our equipment bags. Because I'm epically lazy, I never cleaned anything out after last season. It should still work," Mark said, handing me a snap and shake ice pack.

"Thanks."

"We better go," Chase instructed.

After assuring Jules that I'd call her once I got home, Chase practically dragged me back to the car. Luckily the windows were heavily tinted, making healing myself without being seen possible. The second he shut the door and started the car, my good hand went to work healing the other. It was comforting and freeing to be able to do this openly in front of Chase—no gawking or questioning. If anything, his face wore a blank expression as if this action didn't faze him one bit.

We've come a long way in a little over a year.

My healing ability was strong, stronger than anyone else's. My parents and brother spent countless hours mastering their God given gift, whereas I hadn't. Some might consider that unfair, but a deeper reason for this existed. This gift and the power it owned would be needed for something one day, something major. What? Who knew, but at some point the reason would present itself. Honestly? This thought made me feel authoritative. It erased my distain of having to be a freak.

In a matter of a few mere seconds the faint glow radiated, growing into a great bright light. Warmth crept into the injured hand. Once the glow and warmth subsided, I examined my work, flexing my fingers, and balling them into a tight fist.

"Good as new."

"What am I going to do with you?" Chase laughed.

"Don't know. You tell me."

He put the car in drive, and took off out of the parking lot. Placing his right palm on my left thigh, he squeezed it tightly.

"I'm sorry about tonight, but you knew going in this girl was not an athlete."

"Don't be sorry, baby. You didn't mess up anything. Besides, now we can be alone for a while before your curfew, *and* that's a win."

"Thanks for helping before."

"Helping with what?"

"You used your gift to make the pain stop. Didn't you?"

A brief smile flickered across his face, but he didn't respond. Pride. Chase was secretly proud of what he'd done. The emotion, no matter how quick, was enough to satisfy me. This was a good thing, a very good thing, actually. For me, once I realized and lived through a situation where my cursed gift helped another human, acceptance eventually followed. At the heart of everyone, an individual who wants to help resides. How awesome was it that we, Chase and I, could assist mankind on a deeper, more meaningful level than most? Not many could say they were part of a special select group who were granted an ability, by God no less, to better the world.

As soon as the car merged onto the highway it became obvious we were heading to Tybee. An unexpected alone moment with a content Chase. Could life get any better?

Chapter 22

Chase

The thought of not knowing if my damn gift still worked on Nina played on a loop to the point of obsession. I'd tested it when she broke her hand, but I couldn't get an accurate read. Attempting to force her pain away proved damn near impossible with the prying eyes of Jules and Mark, leaving an unsettled, unsure vibe inside of me until Nina finally expressed her gratitude. I probably should've accepted the thankfulness, but instead, I didn't say a word. A large part of me was elated Nina could still fall victim to my will. I, and I alone, could dictate what she felt, how situations were perceived, and her reactions.

Not replying to her question regarding if I was the reason her pain subsided shielded the internal joy I was experiencing. Drunk off of the power of being aware I controlled unpredictable variables drove me to seek more. How far this ability stretched required further testing, and what a better time than right now? Nina wasn't expected home for another few hours and here we were, alone for once.

After pulling into our usual spot at Tybee, it was time to turn up the charm. This irrepressible primal part of my brain kicked in causing my lips to crush hers; showering every inch of her soul with hard urgent passion. Nina's mouth tasted divine. It always did.

Carelessly fumbling for the handle to recline her seat fueled the beast within me. Raw, wild movements took over. If Nina Luther could've been devoured right then and there, I would've gladly accepted the Karma.

To suggest the rational, logical, and loving parts of my being were in control would've been a lie. Something far more potent took control dictating my each and every move. Inner forces demanded sating. Nina tugged at my shirt feverously trying to rip it off.

Your gift is most definitely affecting her. Too bad something stronger than you is controlling the situation.

Who cares? Shut up and stop thinking.

Relieved I still maintained control over her, the notion was quickly dismissed because thoughts were now jumbled and fuzzy. This inner guiding energy yanked Nina nearer. Once my shirt had been removed, her lust grew stronger and more forceful. She dug her long nails into my skin, racking them across my bare shoulders. Our bodies were flush. Our hearts pounded in sync. Being any closer would be impossible. To the average person my actions may have appeared soulless, void of all emotion, but that wasn't the case. Though adulation for this beautiful girl was felt, there was a fine line between love and desire and I'd crossed it.

"Chase…Chase…Chase."

I pulled away slightly.

"Chase." Again.

The exact same voice from before had returned. The sound was oddly familiar. Placing it was impossible.

"Did you hear that?" I whispered, moving completely back into the driver's seat. My left forearm wiped the fog which had formed on the windows. Once the glass was clear, my eyes wildly darted from side to side trying to see something, anything.

"Hear what?" Nina asked, sitting up, sounding rather annoyed.

"Shhh."

Without thinking I pumped up the volume on my hearing and vision to such a sharpness, things a normal human ear or eye could never experience were clearly seen and heard. It didn't matter if any of this messed with Nina's head. Protecting us was far more important. She lay back down, remaining quiet, not moving a muscle.

"Chase…you know what has to be done. You know what you want to do. You know what you should've done." The voice shrieked angrily causing my head to turn suddenly and twitch uncontrollably. Grabbing my temples and pulling my hair tightly to stop the involuntary movement was fruitless.

"What do you want? Who are you?" I shouted over the ear-piercing voice which had now taken control.

"Oh, I think you already know who I am. You're too afraid to admit it. You have two choices, Chase. You can either procreate, presenting me with the child as a fitting, appropriate apology, or you can kill her."

"Get out."

Forcing the voice away caused my head to jerk a few more times before stopping. Seconds later, the makings of a crushing headache erupted. Nina had to be taken home before the full effect of the pain settled in.

"Chase, what's going on? What are you hearing? Are you okay?" Nina fired off tragically concerned.

"You can't escape me forever, Chase James." The voice hissed its final farewell before my head felt like it was about to explode.

Did you hear that?" I barely whispered.

"Hear what? Chase, are you all right?"

"No. You need to drive home. Now." Somehow the words managed to stumble out. Every sound, every letter was like a bomb discharging. My abilities had been stretched to the limit. Ousting the voice and its owner's thoughts away caused my entire being to dangle in a state of hung-up limbo.

"Uh, okay," she answered, getting out of the car, and helping me into the passenger seat.

Nina and stick shift driving did not go well together, but it honestly didn't matter as long as she got me somewhere to lie down and fast. About thirty minutes later when we pulled into the driveway of the Luther house, the pain had reached its worst. Slowly, like a drunken man, my legs staggered out of the car. The world spun. My ears throbbed, ringing without relent. A blurry version of Nina raced in front of me, opening the door. A distorted version of her normally beautiful voice called for Jack. Finally making my way up the stairs with the aid of an unstable banister, I stood in the foyer trying to find a wall that wasn't moving to lean against for support.

"Chase?" Jack questioned. His voice was odd as well.

I tried to reach for his hands and speak, but I couldn't. A pop in my head caused me to fall, rather hard, to the floor, then nothing. No pain, no spinning, no heightened sound, nothing. Just peace and quiet for once.

"Enjoy it while you can, Chase James, because it won't last forever. I will be back to collect what's mine," the phantom voice threatened.

Chapter 23

Nina

"Chase," my father yelled, trying to catch him before the ground did. "Ellen, call nine-one-one now."

"What's wrong with him?" I panicked.

"Chase? Can you hear me?" he asked. "Unresponsive." Grabbing a pen light from the table by the door, he opened Chase's eyelids examining his pupils before taking his pulse.

"Dad."

"Did you two drink or do any sort of drugs tonight?"

"No." If I wasn't panicking his question would've pissed me off.

"What did Chase eat? Did he complain about any pain?"

"He had some kind of chicken dish at Gino's and no. We went to the batting cages where he broke two bats and destroyed a ball. A little later, Chase said he heard something and kept asking if I'd heard it too, which I didn't. After that, he got all weird and asked me to drive home. What's wrong with him?"

Every time I tried to move closer to where Chase lay, my father used his body to create space between us.

"What did Chase hear? Where were you? What were you doing?"

"I don't know. We were at Tybee Beach."

"What were you doing at Tybee?"

"Being alone." Now wasn't the time to discuss my and Chase's personal life. "What's going on, damn it?"

"I have no idea, but he needs to go to the hospital."

"Why? Can't you help him?"

"No, because without the proper tests there's no way to be sure if this is his body and soul adjusting to being one of us, or if he's seriously ill."

"What kind of *seriously ill*?" Tears rolled down my cheeks. The thought of losing Chase consumed me.

"If he's sick I'll be able to help, but we won't know anything until tests are run."

"Why can't you try to heal him now?"

What are you waiting for, Dad? What if Chase dies before these stupid tests are conducted?

"You're not a doctor, nor are you well versed with our other world. If you were you'd know what our limitations are and what boundaries we can and cannot cross, Nina," he snapped.

Before another word was spoken, my mother opened the front door. Three paramedics rapidly lifted Chase's limp body onto a stretcher. Nothing made any sense, but yet everything was crumbling before my eyes.

"Ellen, follow the ambulance to the hospital. I'm going to stay with Chase. Call his parents, please. Be as vague as possible. I'll deal with them when they show up at the ER."

"Mom?" I asked in a dream like trance.

"Not now, Nina. You have to hold it together. Let's go."

My mind went blank, void of all thought and emotion while I listened to my mother speak with Blanche James. The buildings, homes, and scenery flashed in and out of focus as we sped down the highway.

Fifteen minutes later, we were sitting in the waiting area of the Emergency Room.

"Mom," I whispered choking back tears.

"He's going to be fine, honey. Your father is with him. Dad is a talented, gifted doctor and healer. Have faith," she said, placing her arms around my shoulders. This simple gesture provided more comfort than I'd ever known.

Chase's parents eventually arrived, but it didn't matter. No one aside from them was allowed to see him. Stuck in the waiting room, my thoughts raced with all sorts of crazy scenarios. Every time the door opened, hope swelled someone would appear to state everything was fine—that Chase would be released soon. No such luck. A numb, cold feeling settled in. Trying not to think the worst, but not being able to stop at times was infuriating. My entire being felt caged. At any given moment I'd snap. Reassuring myself Chase suffered a mild stress related episode of sorts didn't help. What if this wasn't stress induced? What if I lost him? The thought of losing Chase forever scared the life out of me.

"Nina, honey, come sit down. You're going to wear a track in the floor from all of that pacing," my mother urged.

"We've been sitting for hours, Mom. When is someone going to tell us something?"

"We're not immediate family, and since Mr. and Mrs. James are here, we have to wait for your father."

"Not immediate family? Seriously? I'm his damn soul mate. I'm the closest thing to family he's got," I snarled, walking to the triage station. I wanted answers and damn it, someone was going to provide them.

A loud buzz filled the rather quiet space causing me

to turn.

Oh thank God.

"Dad." Relief and trepidation wrestled in the pit of my stomach making a wave of nausea bubble up.

"His doctors are still waiting on some test results before they'll know for sure what's wrong, but he's awake, alert, and has suffered no memory loss. His vitals are strong."

"What kind of tests? Can I see him?" I had to see Chase with my own two eyes to fully believe everything was all right.

"You can't go back there yet, and because of doctor patient confidentiality laws, we cannot discuss what tests have been done. His parents are with him, so we should not interfere. He did ask for you and wanted me to tell you to stop worrying."

"You can't tell me what's going on and I can't see him. You've got to be kidding."

"I'm sorry, princess. I'm unsure if you'll be able to visit Chase tonight or when he'll be discharged. There's a strong chance he'll be spending the night here." My father's tone reflected a compassionate, understanding man. His eyes softened the moment several tears streamed down my cheeks causing him to pull me into a tight, warm embrace.

"Make it better."

"Everything will be okay. I promise. Why don't you and your mother go home? I'm going to stick around for a little while longer. I'll keep you posted."

"Do I have a choice?"

"Not really."

"Can I visit Chase tomorrow?"

"As long as he's in a room and everything checks

out, then yes. For the moment, Chase needs rest. He'd want the same for you. Even if you were able to speak with him he'd tell you to go home."

Not completely sold that Chase wouldn't want to see me, I begrudgingly allowed my mother to guide me to the car without a fight. The conversation had been light, filled with a lot of, "I told you Chase would be fine," and, "you'll be able to be with him tomorrow." Nodding in agreement, because engaging would only end up irritating the hell out of me, was easiest. My thoughts and emotions lingered elsewhere, not on empty words of comfort. Plotting a way to sneak out of the house and back to the hospital became an obsession. He'd tell me what the doctors were saying, I'd heal him, and by tomorrow morning this messed up, horrible night could be behind us for good.

"After Dad gets home you could easily climb down the tree, but starting the car will more than likely wake them," I mumbled to myself, while surveying the drop from the lowest limb of the oak tree outside of my room to the ground. If Chase could do it, why couldn't I?

"It's far too high. You're also frightfully uncoordinated. And please, for me, before you land square on your Auntie Annie, just don't do it, love," a sweet, soft man's voiced laced with a rich English accent warned. Though spooked, I recognized the voice instantly and spun to face its owner.

"You scared the crap out of me, Orifiel," I hissed, smacking his chest hard.

"I'm sorry," he replied with a laugh.

"It's not funny. I'm having a terrifying night as it is."

"Aye, I'm aware, but Chase is going to be okay. I

swear. I'd never lie to you," Orifiel said, squeezing my shoulders.

Peace and comfort were immediately found deep within his golden eyes. Without asking permission—who knew if he'd accept my embrace or if there were rules against Mortal to Immortal contact, I threw myself into his arms, holding on tightly. In turn, he reciprocated the gesture with equal enthusiasm.

"Don't cry, love. Your mate will return to your side shortly," Orifiel said, still holding me firmly as he stroked my hair.

"What's wrong with him? Why can't Chase be healed?" It was of no consequence to weep like a child while being surrounded by his touch. Orifiel felt safe. He'd provide honest answers to all of the unanswered questions.

"Too much is happening inside of Chase's core too soon. Don't forget, both good and evil reside within him. Right now the two forces are at war with one another. We've been watching Chase and are aware of his new gifts. To date, his ability of sense and mood persuasion and time manipulation have been deemed Angelic powers, but the strength, a gift Vincent bestowed upon him before the battle, has increased. That's a firsthand, first-generation Demonic gift. The presence of tremendous evil deep within is dangerous and consuming. Your healing touch isn't strong enough to help because this situation is beyond the scope of a healer, which is why your father hasn't tried and has resorted to conventional Mortal means to aid him." The combination of his smooth accent mixed with his deep rooted compassion could sooth even the most restless of souls.

Many notions raced through my mind. There were copious views to formulate, many questions to ask, and being exhausted wasn't helping. Because of all this, I cried out of defeat. I sobbed uncontrollably in the arms of a true Angel whose presence filled my heart with solace.

"Hey," Orifiel whispered, pulling away slightly. Softly he touched my chin, gently tilting it up to establish firm eye contact. "Nina, once Chase finds proper balance inside, and he *will*, he'll be all right. All Mortals have two sides to their existence, good and bad, but it's which side you allow to be stronger that dictates who you are and what you'll be. Love defeats evil. It's more powerful than anything Demonic you'll ever face. Do you trust me?"

"Yes, I do," I admitted. It didn't matter why or how long we'd known one another, placing faith in this man came easy and was free of doubt.

"I'll always be wherever you need me. Just call for me."

"Can I tell you something? Sort of a secret," I asked, turning away from him while wiping my tears with the back of my hand.

"You can tell me anything. I'll never judge or betray your trust *unless* it's something dangerous to you or us," he offered, placing his warm palms against my cold shoulders. "You're freezing. Go inside to your room. I'll meet you up there."

The thin button-down shirt and light weight sweater were better suited for fashion than warmth. The smell of freshly brewed coffee suggested my mother would be floating around the house somewhere. Deciding it best to not open another dialogue with her, a speedy trip up the stairs occurred. Upon opening my bedroom door, Orifiel presented himself. He was standing by the foot of the bed with his arms folded tightly across his chest.

"Hey," he said in muted tones.

Closing and locking the door as swiftly as possible, my breath caught in my throat. This wasn't the time to lose my nerve and not purge my secrets.

"Shut the lights so your parents will think you're sleeping," he instructed.

"Then how will I be able to see you?"

"I'm an Angelic flashlight, in case you forgot," Orifiel said sarcastically.

Well played.

Once the lamp clicked off his body glowed dimly.

"Can you see me and my entire perfection okay?"

"You're a jerk, and yes," I said, smacking his arm, then sitting on the bed.

Orifiel continued to stand and peer out of the window.

"What's up?" Orifiel asked. His tone and facial expressions were both serious now.

"Is there such a thing as a Mortal Angel with seer abilities?"

"Sure. Anything is possible. Usually a gift like that is uncommon for Mortals of any type, but there are a few out there. Many believe they possess a third eye, but they really don't. In The Heavens we have one true seer and dozens of partials."

"Could a Mortal Angel have two divine gifts?"

"Of course. It's rare, but not unheard of. I have no idea how it happens, but every now and again it does. The first gift is present and clear for years before the second surfaces. There are several true Angels who encompassed two gifts upon death. I, myself, was one."

"I can see the future." Instant relief occurred once the words were spoken.

"You're going to have to do a little bit better for me and explain further, please," Orifiel said, joining me on the bed, and reaching for my hands.

As quickly and quietly as humanly possible, the story was told. Nightmares, past and present, were discussed in detail while he listened with a silent, thoughtful expression.

"What happens next?" I asked, scared of his answer.

"I don't know but, Nina, Michael needs to be told."

Michael being cognizant of this could turn out to be a good thing because he'd know what to do, or at least be able to make sense of it. Granted, his existence was still a mystery, but as the leader of our kind, a position he surely earned, Michael had to have an awareness of how to handle this. Suddenly, Orifiel rose from the bed and headed back to the window. The tips of his fingers found their way to his temples. His golden eyes closed. His frame stood stone still.

"Are you okay?"

"Aye. Sorry."

"Do you not feel well?" Based solely off of his body language it appeared a sudden illness struck.

Great. Another one who's got health issues tonight.

"Nothing is wrong. My brother called to me. I was answering."

"Excuse me?"

"Inner voice is how we Angels speak with one another. Instead of using dog and bone, we reach out from within."

"Excuse me? Dog and bone?"

“Telephone. Cockney slang. Even as an Angel I’m still tethered to some of my old Mortal habits.”

“You can hear other Angels call your name, and you can have conversations with them in your head?”

“It’s a little more detailed than that, but yes.”

“Is your brother okay? Do you have to go?” It dawned on me that other than knowing his Angelic job and name, I knew nothing about this man. Part of me wanted to because an unexplainable closeness existed between us.

“He’s fine and no, I don’t have to leave, unless you want me to.”

“No. Please stay. Talk to me. You’re making me feel better.” Taking his hand in mine, I lead him back to the bed.

“I’ll talk to Michael tonight. Don’t worry about this gift.”

“You believe me?”

“Of course, but it’s highly doubtful it’s a new gift, per se. I’d be willing to bet you’ve had this ability since birth, but haven’t paid attention to it until it started including Chase. Bonded soul mates are powerful and can evoke all sorts of strange occurrences.”

“Does the connection become stronger in Heaven?”

“No idea. Don’t have a mate, therefore I’ve never experienced it first hand, but I imagine it would. Makes sense, aye?”

“You don’t have a mate? Why not?”

“She hasn’t been created *yet*.”

A sadness fell inside of me. Though things with Chase hadn’t always been good and the ups and downs were plentiful, the joy and happiness he provided was amazing. Something everyone should experience.

"I'm sorry."

"Don't be. She'll present herself."

"Didn't you have a wife or girlfriend while alive?"

"No wife. No steady girlfriend."

"Tell me about your Mortal life." Placing my head on his shoulder would hopefully keep him from taking off.

"Well, let's see. I passed away around forty while living in London. I was working as a Scotland Yard Detective. Dad went out for cigs when me and my younger sister, Beth, were kids and he never came back. Mum had to work multiple jobs to support us. Because she was gone a lot, I more or less raised Beth. I was murdered in the line of duty. Mum's long since passed, but Beth is still alive. She lives in Manchester with her husband, my six beautiful nieces, and a mess of grandbabies. Haven't the foggiest as to what happened to Dad. Now, I'm a Guardian Angel, part of the Angelic Army, and a seeker of all things lost. Pretty boring stuff."

"Were you a Lost Soul as a Mortal?"

"Nope. Just a plain old Mortal. Missions and abilities were given to me once I died. Not all Angels start as Lost Souls. Some were Mortal Angels or regular run of the mill humans, like me. Upon death I went to Purgatory and from there to The Heavens."

"Do you see your mother in Heaven?"

"Aye."

"Wait, hold on a second. You just said you only had a sister. How could your brother be calling for you?"

"Gabriel has become my brother even though we share no blood ties. Things in The Heavens are different than on Earth. You'll see for yourself one day," he spoke softly while his long fingers stroked my hair. "Close your eyes, love. Get some rest. We can gab and carry on more later. Just remember, tomorrow is a new dawn, which brings a new day, and fresh hope."

"Promise?"

"I promise, love."

I still had no idea why Orifiel felt safe or why I blindly trusted him, but in the hour we spoke, it was as if we'd been friends for years. Like we shared an insanely close bond or something crazy like that. His affirmation of hope was freeing. Clutching his arm as tightly as possible, my soul soaked in relief, finally finding sleep.

Chapter 24

Chase

Slowly my eyes opened, struggling to focus on the objects around the space. A steady beep continuously blared forcing me awake.

Must be your alarm clock.

Rolling over to smack my phone, a realization struck me. This wasn't home, but rather a hospital.

What the hell? Why am I here? The last time I ended up in a hospital I left considerably different. What now? Damn it. Think, Chase. Think. Did you dream about anything bizarre?

After a brief pause, not one single event came to mind. The moment my back arched into the upright position, a chair slid across the floor.

"Chase. Chase, darling. You're awake. George," my mother cried, rushing to the bed, and gently pushing me down on the hard, uncomfortable mattress—if one could even consider the thin board that.

"What's going on? Did something happen? Did I have another accident?"

Physically nothing felt off. There were no real aches or pains other than the pinching of the IV needle. My senses and body mobility were all intact. Quickly I whispered my full name, address, and phone number satisfying the need to make sure my brain function hadn't been affected.

"You collapsed at Nina's house. The doctors ran a bunch of tests. We're waiting to find out the results. It's possible you suffered a stroke," she said, smoothing my hair back as tears fell freely from her eyes.

"Mom, please stop crying. No one had a stroke and I'd like to go home now." Women crying always made me feel ill at ease, mainly because it was awful to experience.

"I'll go find your doctor," my father offered blandly, exiting the room.

While pushing myself into a more comfortable position, Jack entered.

"I heard you were awake. How are you feeling?" Jack asked, smiling while flipping through papers attached to a silver clipboard.

"Where's Nina? Is she okay?" Jack's question held no importance.

"I sent her home. Until we get a handle on what's going on with you, there's nothing she can do here, but yes, Nina is fine. You'll be able to see her tomorrow," he answered casually. After setting the clipboard down on the foot of my bed, his attention turned to the IV. He fiddled around with some switch, examined the needle, then proceeded to check my vitals. "We're still waiting on lab results, which we should have back shortly. However, since you're awake and alert, we can all relax a bit. Mrs. James, could you please step outside for a few minutes while I examine Chase?"

"Of course," my mother said weakly, and left.

"I have to talk to Nina."

"You will once we know what's going on with your health. Deep breath," he said, pressing an icy stethoscope to my back.

"There's nothing wrong with me. We both know that. Run all the tests you want, but you're not going to find anything because I'm not sick."

"What *did* happen, Chase?"

"There were these strange internal power surges racing through me all night. I destroyed two aluminum bats at the batting cages by just swinging them at a run of the mill baseball. Nina took a few swings and got hurt, big surprise there. After we left, she healed herself in the car. Then we went to Tybee Beach to be alone. The surge returned, but stronger this time. I heard voices. My head started hurting, so Nina drove us back to your house. When we got there this pop went off in my brain, and then nothing. Can you get Nina please?"

"The power surges are a new gift," Jack mused deep in thought.

"No, they're not. Vincent gifted me superhuman strength long before the Angelic and Demonic strike."

"Why are you telling me this now? This is something we should've discussed from the beginning."

"I forgot, you know, because nothing else is going on in this fucked up life and all," I hissed.

"All right. To date you've acquired great strength, mind and sense altering skills, the ability to slow down time, and now you're hearing voices?"

"Yes."

"Can you identify the voice? What is it saying?"

"I'm pretty sure of who the owner is, and he wants me to hurt Nina."

"Care to elaborate?"

"It's Vincent, but I'm not completely positive, and before you ask, tonight was the second time it's happened. The headache and surge at Thanksgiving had me out of it. I wasn't sure if I'd actually heard anything or not. After tonight I'm fairly certain I did."

"What were you and Nina doing when the voice presented? Also, did you by chance use any of your gifts willingly tonight?"

"Yes. Jules and Mark were asking way too many questions and focusing far too much on the broken bats and ball. My only option was to alter their perceptions. Initially, I upped the force too high which confused and dazed them, but while Jules and Mark were taking a trip to La La Land, Nina didn't seem affected by the mood change. In fact, she had no idea anything was happening because she continued to act off free will. However, when Nina's hand broke, the gift worked on her by dulling the pain."

"Nina was standing where in comparison to you?"

"Why does that matter?"

"I've noticed, at times, your gift holds no control over me, but only when I'm standing next to or behind you."

"Okay."

Where are we going with this, Jack?

"In order for your gift to work effectively you have to project it onto others. You have to focus on your targets. Jules and Mark were more than likely standing in front of you while Nina wasn't. You were only looking at the primary targets, not the secondary ones. We have to work on peripheral vision this way you can lock all of your intended targets. You're using only tunnel sight right now. If that can be accomplished, you could control an entire stadium with the greatest of ease. Thanksgiving night you controlled the room by spending a few minutes time on each individual at the table over and over again. You didn't have to do that. If you would've seen all of us from a central point, you could've handled everyone at once."

"All right. That makes enough sense. I'm willing to try anything that could potentially make my life easier."

Jack was spot on about Thanksgiving and tonight. This theory needed to be tested immediately and would be the second I was out of this hospital bed.

"What were you and Nina doing when you heard Vincent's voice?"

Making out in a deserted beach parking lot.

"Uh," I started, desperately searching for the most non-offensive way to phrase this.

"I was your age once, and I realize this is an uncomfortable conversation to have with me, but have you and Nina expressed yourselves further than…"

"No. We've kissed. Fooled around a bit—*nothing* else. I swear I've treated her with the utmost respect and have been nothing less than a true southern gentleman. Furthermore, I have absolutely no intention of doing anything else with Nina until we're at least engaged." This unsettling discussion had to end.

"I'm not trying to pry, Chase, because as a father, I don't want to know. One day when you have a daughter you'll understand. This is just as awkward for me, but under no circumstances can you be physically intimate with Nina, at least not until we figure this out. You have Demonic traits inside of you which might be evoked. Seemingly, they were tonight by a shared closeness with an Angelic enemy. To top it off, if you were to procreate, who knows what kind of child you'd create. The offspring could be all Demonic. When good and evil join forces, nothing holy ever comes from it. This isn't to suggest you'll never be able to have children with Nina. Eventually the Angelic side of you will defeat the Demonic parts which will hopefully flush out any malevolent traits."

I needed to get out of here and to be with Nina. "I'd never hurt Nina," I exploded, getting up.

"I didn't say you would, but you have a piece of the Devil inside of you. Don't be foolish or blind to that fact. Angels and Demons are enemies. Until we're sure of exactly what's going on within your body, we need to proceed with caution. You're a good kid who loves my daughter, but what you're going through is a greater force than anything in this Universe." Momentarily our eyes locked. "I never said I didn't trust you to be alone with or to look after Nina. You need to realize and acknowledge your limitations. You have to know when to get help, like you did tonight. Until your official doctor releases you, get back in bed." Even though Jack's words appeared harsh, his face was filled with empathy.

"Have any results come in yet?" I asked, sitting on the edge of the mattress. My body was exhausted. Engaging in a battle of wills with Jack Luther hadn't helped the cause.

"A few. All of your blood work is within the normal range. The brain scan was negative. We're still waiting on an MRI and a handful of other tests, but your vitals are strong and you're coherent, capable of moving all of your limbs. These are all promising signs of good health. Dr. Kennedy will probably write this off to stress. A mild breakdown, with exhaustion and dehydration. She's going to want to keep you here overnight for observation. This might be a good opportunity to tell your parents you wish to take a semester off from school. Perhaps even discuss what else has been going on."

"I'm not ready to do that."

"You're going to have to tell them."

"Yeah? And say what? Hey, Mom, Dad. Guess what? Your only child is a freak of nature. Better yet, let's tell Dr. Kennedy or a shrink about this. Which floor is the psych ward? Thirteen? Because that's where Nina will have to come to visit me."

"Chase, we can discuss it with your parents together. You don't have to go it alone."

Oddly enough, his offer to be there with and for me was comforting. "Thanks. I appreciate that, but it's not going to happen today or anytime soon."

A few seconds later my parents, followed by the doctor entered. As Jack had predicted, she said the culprit for tonight's events were exhaustion, dehydration, and abnormally high levels of stress. Once I'd been moved to a room for a twenty-four-hour observation hold and everyone had left, I reached for the phone quickly dialing Nina's number. The line rang a few times before it went to voicemail. Part of me was insulted and annoyed that she didn't answer. How could Nina feel content enough to sleep knowing that her soul mate was in turmoil? An irrational wounded mindset led to my next call.

"Hey, beautiful."

"Oh. Hey, Chase. What's up? What time is it?" Her voice was full of sleep.

"Damn. I'm sorry. I didn't realize how late it was."

"No, no. It's okay. What's going on? Is something wrong?"

"I didn't mean to wake you. Go back to bed. I'll call

later," I said, hoping she'd decline the offer and stay on the phone because talking to someone who didn't know about the other part of me and was oblivious to the presence of Angels and Demons *might* make the situation better.

"I'm awake and know you well, Chase James. Something's doing. You better start talking, mister."

"I'm in the hospital."

Come on, sweetheart. Say something to make me remember what the word "normal" means.

"Oh my God. What happened? Do you need anything?"

"You."

"Text me the address and your room number. I'll be there as soon as possible."

****

An almost inaudible knock jarred me. A slight turn of the head revealed the girl I'd tossed away and had treated like crap. She was currently sleeping on the small couch beside my bed. A few seconds later, a doctor entered, checked my vitals, and informed me discharge papers were being drawn up.

"Bristol," I whispered, nudging her thigh. "Wake up, beautiful."

"Huh?" She stirred. "How are you feeling?"

"Good. We can go. Let's get out of here."

"That's great news. Give me a few minutes and I'll take you home."

By the time she finished in the bathroom my release papers were signed, and I was dressed, ready to take off before Jack came to check in and saw me with another girl. As fast as possible I hauled ass out of the hospital to her vehicle.

"You know you never told me what happened, Chase," Bristol said, maneuvering her car onto the highway.

"Stress, exhaustion, and dehydration." In the light of day, it was evident my hasty actions were wrong. I never should've called her. Guilt and a sense of betrayal seeped inside of me, sitting like bad indigestion in the pit of my stomach.

"What's going on that's causing you so much stress?"

The fact that she still cared and came running was dangerous, mainly because it was a lead-on. In the end, I'd hurt this wonderful, sweet girl again.

"School, life, parents—the usual." I wanted to tell her the truth. Purge where Sean went so Bristol and the rest of her family could stop worrying, but I knew better. This secret could never be divulged to anyone other than freaks like me.

"Can I do anything to help?"

"No, but thanks for coming last night—for being there." I smiled and touched her knee softly.

"Where's your girlfriend?" she asked trying to sound breezy, but failing. Jealousy and hatred danced freely around her tone. It was easily detectable by even the most untrained of ears. The same way this girl knew me well, I knew her, *especially* her moods.

"Home. I didn't want to worry her. She's going through a lot at the moment as well," I lied, because in reality who the hell knew where Nina was or what she was doing other than not answering the phone. Though still ticked off over this, Bristol couldn't be made aware of that. It would only add more fuel to the fire.

"You'll worry me, but not her. That's rich."

"Awe. Come on, beautiful. Don't be like that." My response was automatic.

Holy flashback.

With that one jab, I remembered why I'd called it quits—neediness, immaturity, and possessiveness, qualities Nina didn't possess. Even when Nina had a lot going on, she always maintained a high level of outward composure. Bristol may have reminded me of simpler times, but they weren't happy, and happiness, at the moment, outweighed normal any day of the week. All ties with this girl had to be severed once she dropped me off at home.

"I hope that says something to you," she snapped.

"It does. More than you think."

A frosty silence consumed the energy of the car. After a half-hearted promise to reach out to her later and an awkward hug, I bolted into my house.

"Darling, what are you doing home? We were getting ready to come see you," my mother said, practically strangling me with a squeeze.

"Early discharge. A friend picked me up," I explained.

"We should probably talk about some things." Her face knotted with anguish.

"Chase," my father's voice boomed.

I didn't respond. There'd never be any bowing in the honor he believed he deserved.

"Sit," he ordered, attempting to mask the fact this conversation was the last thing anyone had time for.

To avoid an argument, I did as instructed. This chat needed to be over and done with as soon as possible.

Hey. You and the old man finally agree on something. Neither of you wish to speak to the other.

"Stress is for the weak, Chase. That's not how we raised you. Man up, deal with your problems, and move along. If you have to drop some dead weight, so be it. If someone or something is dragging you down, you don't need it in your life. Whatever or whoever isn't worth it. Problem solved. Case closed."

Great advice, Dad.

"I'm not weak and I always fight for what I believe in. Sometimes you can't just drop things and walk away. If you haven't realized in your fifty plus years on this Earth, life sucks. It's complicated and messy," I challenged.

"You *are* weak because if you were strong you wouldn't have ended up in a hospital bed because you couldn't cope with whatever nonsense is going on in your life."

"And you're so damn strong, Dad?" I hissed, abruptly standing so we were eye to eye.

"This is *my* house. While under *my* roof you live by *my* rules. This is how your life is going to play out going forward. You're to get rid of that girl you hang around with because she's nothing but trouble. She's dragging you down. She's not good enough for you. Your last name is James. In this town and state that name commands authority. How the hell do you expect to graduate from college with good grades if you're never home studying, but rather out chasing some low-class tramp? You don't, moron. From now on your ass is to be in this house or at school. Nowhere else. When you finish your undergraduate work you'll take the LSAT examination, obtain a stellar score, and go to law school. After that, you'll get a job, and then I don't care what you do. Marry whatever piece of trailer trash you want, but don't expect me to finance the wedding or your life. Do you understand me?" he yelled in my face.

"Your house, your rules. Got it." I smirked, turning, and exiting the room.

The moment I stepped foot in my bedroom, three duffle bags from the closet floor were stuffed with clothing, as well as other various important belongings. After a quick last check to make sure everything was packed, I took my laptop and the shoebox containing Sean's photos, journal, and papers and left without a word. I had no idea where to go or what to do, but leaving felt right. George James would never understand my other world. Never. The time had come to part ways for good—drop the dead weight like he advised.

Okay, Chase. You're on your own. You can do this, and you will come out on top. Its game time. Don't accept anything less than victory.

Truth & Consequences—III

My Dearest Love,

Your parents are going to be the death of me. They share the same psychotic, irrational, erotic, co-dependent relationship with their mates, and they simply refuse to acknowledge how unhealthy it is. It'd be much easier if they'd open their damn eyes, but in time it shall happen. The stars predict it, therefore it will be. For your information, your stubbornness comes from Gabriel. Perhaps because of this inherited trait you'll be the death of me as well, but that would be a death I'd gladly accept, almost welcome. Shall we pick up where we left off?

Metatron didn't offer up much information, but he said much at the same time—if that makes any sense. Cutting to the chase, he informed me that star reading wasn't to be looked down upon. If anything it's one of the most valuable gifts The Heavens or Hell could bestow upon a chosen few. Micha, Michael, and I are the only Heavenly entities who I believe can do this, but there may be more. Though their ability isn't nearly as accurate as mine, the Devil's is. When asked to elaborate, Metatron suggested I project beyond the surface to seek the truth, and to confirm the newfound information within the stars. The answer would present itself clear as day when this happened. Confused by what I thought to be a foolish, old secretary of God, his words were dismissed as rubbish and "life" continued. It wasn't until I'd overheard Michael and Raphael having it out with Gabriel over me being left defenseless on a mission that my attention to what Metatron had shared occurred.

I may not be as glorious as those three, but I'm certainly not weak or incapable of protecting myself, or you. Everything since day one in The Heavens was placed under a microscope to be reviewed and analyzed. First item of scrutiny? Why Gabriel never left my side and when he did, why Michael or Raphael took his place. Yet frequently told I'd be handling a mission alone, truthfully, one of the three was never far behind. Why were they always standing on guard? Whenever I'd question this, Michael would suggest he required my assistance with calming Gabriel's mind. The response made sense being Gabriel was often an extremist when it came to matters of assassination. He'd use assignments to take out personal aggression on Demons, and most times when he started utilizing violent tendencies he couldn't stop himself. That's where I'd come in; to pull him back to reality.

Other things such as simply knowing information I'd never studied or been privy to became concerning. Random pieces of facts, like creationism, which no one seemed to agree upon, melded together into the true story shared in our last series of letters. How do I know the tale is all true? Metatron.

Several other realizations struck causing me to seek him out. Once this happened, Metatron flat out admitted everything in what seemed like one long breath. The short version—God selected me as His sole prophet the moment I entered Purgatory. I'd been gifted the ability to know all of the secrets the Universe holds. Why me?

God never said. What I am sure of is only a single Prophet can exist at a time. To date, there are no known Prophets in Hell. One could surmise my predecessor's soul ended right before I came to be in The Heavens. Michael, Raphael, and Gabriel were told and instructed to never share the information with anyone, especially with me, because God feared one day I'd use this extraordinary power against Him. The three Archangels created a prison of protection around me with them as my wardens. Metatron left me with a solitary warning. I could never tell anyone aside from my soul mate about being a Prophet. He never provided an answer as to why, but his cautioning was taken seriously, and my lips are eternally sealed to everyone except you.

Sometimes they'd ask me questions. Raphael or Gabriel not so much, but Michael would, a lot actually. He'd attempt to poke into my psyche to extract what I knew without raising a red flag. After Metatron purged this information, Michael's little missions into my head made sense. The entire situation could be summed up as living a lie, surrounded by untrustworthy individuals. I suppose that's why I often feel alone. One could go further and suggest when I connect with a being who's pain and suffering resembles mine, an instant love forms.

There's more, but right now my attention must return to this current mission. Nothing can go wrong. Even though the stars suggest all will fare well, I'm consumed with worry it won't. Without you, there'll never be happiness.

Until we speak again.

Always,
Your Betrothed

Chapter 25

Nina

For the first time in a while, balance had occurred. Sitting alone at the kitchen table, enjoying a fabulous cup of coffee, reading a fashion magazine, and smiling, healthy vibes radiated out of me on every level. Chatting with Orifiel helped. Sharing my inner conflict and doubts to someone who understood both worlds proved freeing. A weight had lifted. Normal breathing resumed, replacing the suffocating sensation of emotional drowning I'd been enduring for far too long. At ten, I'd head to the hospital to see Chase. He had called late last night, but I'd already fallen asleep. I didn't think he'd reach out or even had the option to. Had I known, staying awake to talk with him would've definitely overpowered my desire to sleep. Hell, we could've spoken all night if that's what he wanted.

Everything was going to be fine. My father said Chase would be discharged at some point today, and Orifiel assured this event was part of Chase's adjustment process. I trusted him. I trusted Orifiel more than anyone right now. There were no lies or games with him, only truth and honesty. The doorbell chimed tearing me from my musings, but not enough to make me get up. Someone else would answer it.

"Who was at the door?" I asked my mother a few minutes later when she walked into the kitchen.

"Chase."

"Chase? *My* Chase?"

"How many other Chases do you know?"

I got up at once to go to the foyer, but a hand grabbing hold of my wrist stopped the action.

"Wait. Sit and wait."

"For what, Mom?" I snapped.

Her answer wasn't necessary because my father and Chase appeared in the doorway.

"Chase." Something was noticeably off in his eyes. What? No idea, but even his brief embrace came across as distant and shallow.

"In light of certain circumstances, Chase will be living with us," my father said, placing a hand on Chase's back in a very fatherly manner.

"What's going on?" There were a million other questions to be asked, but that happened to be the first one that popped out of my mouth.

"Nina, show Chase to the guestroom, which going forward is his room. Chase, please make yourself at home because this *is* your home and will be for as long as you'd like. Forever if need be."

"Thank you, Dr. Luther," Chase replied, managing to fake a slight smile.

"Oh, honey. Everything is going to be okay. Time heals all wounds," my mother spoke, hugging him tightly. "You're not some boy who happens to be dating our daughter. You're a part of our family. We're here for you and love you very much. Whatever you need or want, just ask and it's yours. I realize we're not your parents, but we will do everything we can to make you feel welcomed, happy, safe, comfortable, secure, and loved."

"That means a lot," Chase said softly.

Without saying a word, I led the way upstairs. Mechanically he placed a few bags on the floor and shut the door.

"Where the hell were you last night?" he spat nastily.

"Home."

"I called. I was worried, and then I find you sitting at your kitchen table, sipping coffee, and reading a magazine without a care in the world."

"First, my father insisted *you* wanted me to go home and get some sleep. Second, had I been allowed to see you I'd have stayed all damn night. Since a girlfriend isn't considered family, she needs to wait until God comes off the mountain to allow non-family members by your side. Do you know how frustrating that felt? To be freaking out about your boyfriend and told you mean nothing because you're not biologically related? Do you know how scared I was? What was going through my mind? You're not the only one who's under stress you know," I clapped back hard.

Our eyes locked. Neither of us spoke a word or made a sound. We held the position for a few seconds until he grabbed my shoulders, crushing his lips to mine. The kiss was strong and passionate, but filled with tension. I pulled him closer, weaving my fingers around his thick, mahogany hair.

"I'm sorry, Nina. I'm so damn sorry," Chase whispered. "Please forgive me."

"There's no reason to apologize for anything. You're dealing with a lot. I love you. We will get through this *together*."

"No matter what I say or do, promise me that you'll

always find a way to forgive me and never leave me. You can't leave. Please, don't leave me."

"We're soul mates. We'll always be together. There will always be a you and me combined as one."

"Swear to it, baby," he begged.

"Okay. I swear."

He sighed deeply, closing his eyelids, and pressing our foreheads together while gripping the sides of my face.

"What happened, Chase? What's going on?" His behavior was truly uncharacteristic. Sure he suffered temporary moments of fragility, but never like this.

"Honestly? I don't know. Maybe the good part of me is at war with the evil and the power struggle became too much. Physically, there's nothing wrong. All of the tests came back clean."

That's *exactly* what happened. Orifiel said it and Chase's suspicions confirmed it. I wanted to ask why he was moving in, but I didn't know how to pose the question. One false word and he'd think I didn't want him around or that I wasn't happy about it. Chase being in closer proximity made me happy.

"I had to leave," Chase spoke, almost as if he'd read my mind.

"Did something happen?"

"A lot of things went down, but they still don't know who the real me is. Being here with your family, people who get it, is better, healthier. The move isn't permanent. Just until this craziness settles and everything gets figured out. I'll be looking for apartments in the meantime."

"This is none of my business, but where are you getting the money for that when you don't work?"

"I'm far from poor."

"What's that supposed to mean?"

"I have money, quite a bit of it, and it's mine, not my parents. Paying for an apartment, college, and living expenses won't be a problem." Chase paused, studying all of me for a brief moment. "An inheritance from my grandparents. You can stop wondering if I'm an escort, or a pimp, or sell drugs to the neighborhood kids, or something stupid like that."

"Oh."

You think you know your soul mate and bam—you don't. What else haven't you told me?

"There's more," he added.

And there it is. The other shoe dropping. Play it cool, Nina.

"Oh yeah? What's that?"

"First of all, having money isn't important. I'm not hiding anything else except the fact Vincent's voice is what I've been hearing. I *temporarily* kept one major thing from you. Let's skip the, 'I feel like I don't even know who you are,' shit. I'm really not in the mood, Nina."

"Excuse me? How do you know what I'm thinking?" I barked, ignoring the fact that Vincent's voice now lived inside of his head, which honestly was far more important than anything else.

"No special gift is required to read your emotions. We're soul mates, therefore bonded emotionally because of that. Maybe this connection affects me more because it seems I'm the only one of us who has this direct line into the other's brain."

"Pardon me for not knowing what you're thinking or feeling all of the time."

"If you stopped worrying about yourself for one frigging minute perhaps you'd experience it too. Damn it, Nina. I just told you I'm hearing Vincent's voice. Last night he wanted me to kill you and all you're worried about is me not telling you about my financial status. How self-centered can you possibly be?"

"How dare you," I yelled, storming past him and out of the door.

Fuming with anger, pacing the length of my room, my fists balled tightly. Internal rage brewed within me, but not because of Chase, because of me. His words, though rude and overly harsh, were fact. My priorities were messed up. Instead of focusing on Chase, his hospital stay, and now living with us, I'd been too busy thinking about myself and how all of this crap affected my life. This wasn't about me. It was about him. Chase deserved an apology. The door to the guestroom was still open from earlier, but I knocked anyway. He sat on the foot of the bed, staring at his phone.

"Hey."

"Hey," Chase grunted.

"You're going to be okay."

"Yeah? How do you know that?"

"Remember the Angel Orifiel? The one who led us out of the woods last summer?"

"Vaguely."

"He came here last night. We talked. The Angels know what's going on and have been keeping a close eye out. He said what you're dealing with and experiencing is normal. Once you find balance with your new gifts, your life will start to get back on track. Maybe that's why I'm coming across as not appearing overly concerned. The Angels wouldn't lie, especially to us."

"I'm sorry about before."

"Me too."

"Listen, I have a few errands to run, but do you want to get dinner or go out tonight? Just you and me?"

"That would be nice."

"I'll pick you up at six?" He joked.

"I'll be here. Room down the hall."

I reached over and kissed his perfect lips before leaving.

Okay, joking is good. It's a tense time. Feeding off of Chase's anxiety is not the best course of action. Instead, help him beat it back. He would for you.

My cell phone buzzed on my desk. Glancing at the number, I had no idea who was calling.

"Hello?"

"Nina?"

"Orifiel?"

"Aye. It's crucial we speak straight away. Meet me at the schoolyard by your home in fifteen minutes."

"Okay. Is everything all right?" His sense of urgency suggested something was seriously wrong.

"We'll catch up in a few."

"You're freaking me out. And since when did Angels start using cell phones?"

"Don't *freak out*. As for utilizing Mortal communication, who do you think gave them the idea to create such things? Now get going," he said, hanging up.

After a brief pause to look out of the window, I saw Chase's car was gone. Reaching for a sweater, I headed for the door, praying for an easy escape. Five minutes later, my body swayed nervously on one of the swings at the school's playground.

What now? It's barely noon and this day already

blows.

“Would you like for me to push you, love?” Orifiel’s sweet English accent spoke.

“What’s up? What’s going on?” Definite traces of panic were echoed in my voice.

“There’s never a need to ever worry when I’m around. I’d sacrifice my soul so you’d never feel a second of mental or physical anguish.”

“You’re not always here.”

“Oi,” he said, walking in front of the moving swing, stopping it, and kneeling down. His fingers gently caressed my cheek. “I am *always* around, love.”

“*Sure.*” My eyes rolled involuntarily.

“Really? You woke this morning, showered, had a cup of coffee, read a magazine at the kitchen table, Chase arrived with several duffels, and you two engaged in a rather heated spat. Again, I’m *always* around.”

“You’re following me?” Orifiel’s presence went from sweet to creepy in a matter of seconds.

“For the time being. Michael needs to know what’s going on with Chase. I’m not listening to your calls or watching you utilize the loo. This isn’t an attempt to strip you of your privacy. I respect you and your boundaries.”

Great annoyance should’ve been felt, but it wasn’t. It didn’t matter that his actions were that of a stalker’s. Knowing he was near proved comforting, providing a certain amount of safety no one else could—maybe ever.

“I wanted to tell you something,” Orifiel added.

“What’s that?”

“You are, in fact, fifty percent seer. You could be more, but you’d have to strengthen it. Currently, Michael is against that idea. He wants your ability to grow stronger from within before you explore it further. No one in The Heavens has the foggiest idea where you obtained the gift from or why, but never-the-less it doesn't matter because you possess it. I thought you'd want to know so you could stop thinking about it. Free up some space inside of that otherwise overworked brain of yours. You have to do me a favor though. Michael doesn't want you to mention this to anyone else. If someone who already knows questions you about it, tell them the dreams and visions stopped."

"Why?"

"We don't question Michael's orders, Nina. We listen. We do what we're told."

"You mean to tell me no one has ever defied the great Michael's rules?"

"*No one*. Well, perhaps Gabriel has at some point, but that's another story for another time. Can you do this for me, love? I normally wouldn't request someone act deceitfully, but please try and understand that my hands are tied this time."

"Yes, I can and will, but what if the dreams come back revealing more of the vision?"

"Call for me and *only* me. Scream my name as loud as you can inside of your head or out loud."

A horrifying image struck me the moment two and two were put together. I was a seer. The vivid dreams which predicted the future, my future, ones which included Vincent trying to kill me, were still ever present.

"Oh my God." Panic caused me to jump off of the swing. My hands shook uncontrollably. My eyes darted from side to side. Getting out of the wide-open space and back to my room was an absolute must. Being in a confined, safe area, locked away from the world and all of its evil had to happen this instant.

"Talk to me, love," Orifiel said cautiously, slowly approaching me.

"I have to go. I have to get out of here."

Taking me by the hand, he casually and calmly guided us away from the playground, where several children carelessly ran around as their parents looked on. Drawing attention to our presence had to be avoided. Letting the people around us think we were a couple was normal and socially acceptable, whereas Mortal Angel and True Angel appearances and conversations weren't, especially when the Mortal Angel wore a freaked-out expression. We stopped in a remote spot behind the school. Before speaking he gently placed my back against the brick wall.

"What's scaring you?" he asked, caressing the side of my face.

"In the visions Vincent has me imprisoned. He intends to kill me. I don't want to die, Orifiel." A raw panic attack had erupted.

"He's not going to harm you on my watch, Nina. Vincent is aware I've been hawking you. He won't risk it."

"You don't know for sure. What if you turn around for a hot second and he strikes?"

Please, Orifiel. Prove me wrong. Say something so I'll be able to sleep in peace again.

"I've been trained to never close my eyes, Nina—as a Mortal and an Immortal."

"There's always human error."

"Then let's be thankful I'm no longer human." He leaned closer. "Usually when I'm on Earth my brother is with me. Vincent is cognizant of that. Because of this, he'll assume Gabriel is here in a stealth capacity and won't strike. Gabriel is considered Hell's number one threat. He's is largely feared down there. This isn't our first day on the job. We know what we're doing."

"Okay." Nothing he'd said provided any ease. Not even an ounce. Confusion, yes. Comfort, no.

"A long time ago, Vincent royally screwed with Gabriel. Since then Gabriel is out for vengeance and won't stop until Vincent is gone forever. The big, strong, powerful, almighty Vincent is terrified of the Archangel Gabriel and wouldn't dare take a gamble touching you because he believes Gabriel is lurking somewhere, waiting to pounce and kill. With a one hundred percent track record for murder, it's a guarantee Gabriel will destroy Vincent. The situation Michael created resembles a perfectly crafted trap for Vincent alone."

The thought of this Gabriel person was quite relieving. If Vincent feared him, as long as Gabriel stayed close, no harm could come to me or Chase. "Is Gabriel here?"

"No. He's off on a mission somewhere, but Nina, you have me. I swear I'm just as good as him. Do you honestly think I can't protect you or wouldn't properly have your back?"

"But Vincent doesn't see you as a threat. He sees your brother as one. Why didn't Michael send him to Earth?"

An expression I'd never witnessed on Orifiel spread across his face—anger. True, wild anger. His fists balled so tightly his knuckles turned white.

You better apologize before this guy blows up.

"Let me tell you something, Nina Luther. Just because I wasn't trained like Gabriel, or hold a high-ranking position in the Angelic Army, doesn't mean I'm not capable of doing any job as well as him. *And* let me tell you something else. If Vincent doesn't fear me, he should. What he did to Gabriel was an act of pure evil. I didn't have the pleasure of knowing him prior to the incident, but I'm painfully aware that Gabriel used to be a good man. Today he's filled with such rage and hurt it's sickening. Vincent will pay for that, and dearly. My father may view me as the good son, but make no mistake. When it comes to Vincent, I'm out for blood, and I will make damn sure Gabriel gets the revenge he desperately seeks.

"You have two choices, Nina. You can trust I'll protect you and Chase, or you can doubt me. Either way, this is still a mission which must be carried out and it will be, with or without your blessing and support," Orifiel said, pivoting and walking away.

"Chase said he's hearing Vincent's voice inside of his head. That's what happened last night. Vincent told him to kill me. The visions are now corresponding with the evil inside of Chase."

Orifiel stopped dead in his tracks and turned sharply. "You need to tell me the second this happens again. You're to call to me immediately. Should you find yourself in direct danger, scream my name internally or externally. I will hear you. Voices inside of one's head are never a good thing, but can be a deadly when you're hearing Vincent's. I have to tell Michael about this and it has to be done now." Orifiel paused to scrutinize me. The angry expression he wore moments earlier had passed. A softer, more concerned look replaced it.

"There's a logical explanation as to why this is happening. I'll figure it out and share said findings. All we know for certain is both good and evil reside inside of Chase's soul. He has to do whatever possible to fight the evil. Once he can beat that part down he'll be okay, eventually becoming one of us. You have to help him. If you love him the way true mates should, show Chase our way, *your* way."

"How exactly does one do that? Chase already knows how I feel."

"Does he?" Orifiel questioned, raising one eyebrow. "I have to go. Call to me should you require anything," he added before taking off.

Chapter 26

Chase

Damn it, Bristol. Stop calling me.

I'd spent the past three hours clicking the ignore button on my phone. Inviting her back into my life had been an epic mistake. However, the idea of normality had become a lost object which had to be found again, and the last place I'd experienced it was with her. Returning to the scene of the crime became inevitable. Unfortunately, Bristol had always been a stage four jealous, needy clinger which would make dumping her for the second time complicated and it could potentially result in Nina finding out. A few unresolved emotions still lingered for Bristol, but nothing strong enough to provoke me to leave my soul mate.

Nina, the girl I'd spent the greater part of these past few days pushing away, all while nit picking her every action. I'd been stupid. In reality Nina's emotions and reactions were the status quo of *normal*. Like me, she had to find balance between both worlds, but she wasn't behaving as poorly. Instead of enduring the journey together, I'd foolishly been attempting to do it alone. Yes, part of me held anger directed towards her, but my rational side finally broke free. She wasn't the reason for all of this. Fate was to blame. Fate, something neither of us controlled, nor planned for. In essence we were both victims. Tonight, we'd start fresh, leaving the past behind us.

There were no errands to run. Being alone to process and re-evaluate my life had been desired. The solitude allowed me to call my mother, a natural born worrier who didn't deserve to be treated neglectfully by her only child, to inform her where I'd be staying. She begged me to return home and to talk, but I declined, suggesting things were complicated and this move was for the best. After reassuring her we'd still see each other and speak regularly, she hesitantly agreed, making sure to add that the door to return home would always remain open.

Fat chance of that ever happening.

Pulling up to Nina's house, which I supposed was now my house as well, I inhaled deeply.

Time to start a new chapter.

Chapter 27

Nina

The days rolled into weeks and just like that, the semester came to a close. Trying to focus on studying proved challenging, but somehow above average grades were scraped together. While in class, Chase and his actions controlled my every thought. While home, studies and finishing strong dominated my focus. There would be no complaining to anyone about anything. I had no right to bitch and moan about life and its hardships. Chase was the one who was drowning in stress, pain, and fear. He had every reason to be walking around sulking and moody.

I still wasn't allowed out of the house alone, and since Chase and my father were locked away inside of the house working and training, I became my mother's responsibility. But, with winter break finally here, devoting all of my free time to Chase was the plan. No further abilities had developed, while his existing ones strengthened daily. He could finally successfully control mood and sense altering—a huge relief not only for him, but for everyone else. Slowing down time remained a work in progress. No matter what they did, neither could evoke the gift.

Chase's strength had become his worst ability. The house transformed into a disaster zone with broken plates, glasses, doors, etcetera. It appeared working out, lifting weights, and running helped alleviate the excess of power, but the more Chase forced his emotions back, the stronger he grew. His moods flipped from happy to depressed at the drop of a hat. You never knew what you were going to get at any given moment. Mostly I left him alone, not pressuring conversations, allowing him to be the initiating party for all communication and interactions. He hadn't mentioned any more headaches or hearing Vincent again—a very good sign. At times, temptation to ask him about everything was present, but I wasn't about to poke the bear. If Chase wanted to talk about it, he'd mention it. Sometimes loving someone meant taking a step back and allowing them space. He knew I was there for him and he would often acknowledge this with words or gestures, but often he'd thanked me for laying off. From time to time, we'd experience and celebrate a "normal" moment with each other. Those brief happenings were amazing, proving rather enjoyable. I'd hold on tight, savoring every second, stretching the feeling paper thin during difficult days, praying a glimpse of happiness would find me soon to renew my faith in time being the ultimate healer of all wounds.

My mother and I spent the first few days of vacation Christmas shopping and decorating the house. The night before Christmas Eve, I decided to stay home with Chase while my parents went to the airport to pick up Steve, my brother, the man who never said goodbye when he went back to school after Thanksgiving break. The one who never replied to any emails or text messages. The one who'd been ignoring me out of envy over me having a soul mate and annoyance that I no longer hung on his every word like I had in the past.

Whatever with him.

"What do you want to do?" Chase asked. He appeared in a fairly decent frame of mind which made me feel slightly freer.

"No idea," I purred, slowly creeping up next to him on the couch.

"Oh."

Pushing him down, our lips met and our arms tangled. As we drew closer the wanton tension in the air drove me crazy. Our relationship needed to take this turn, and I'd be damned if tonight wasn't going to be that night. Desperately, my hands tugged at his clothing. I marveled at Chase's perfect body. As his physical strength increased through training, remarkable muscle mass had developed. My fingers aggressively yanked on the button fly of his jeans, only stopping when he gently pushed me back a few inches.

"Let's slow down," Chase whispered.

"Why? Why do you pull away every single time we get close?"

"I'm not ready."

"How can you *not* be ready? We're *supposed* to be together. Don't you want this to happen? Is it *ever* going to happen?" Complete aggravation, confusion, and hurt over his actions fueled the already burning fire within me. What was wrong with me, with us, that was causing him to shy away from sharing this particular intimacy?

"Baby, we have an eternity together. There's no rush. I love you, and at some point we will do other stuff, but it's not going to happen today. I can't give you what you want right now. I'm sorry. Please, be patient. Try to understand that it's a complicated situation," he pleaded softly.

"You're right. I apologize." A lie. Chase *wasn't* right and I *wasn't* sorry, but continuing to press would only toss him over the edge. Who really wanted to deal with that? Not me, that's for sure.

"Hey, I have something for you." Chase got up and produced a small box from a bag sitting on the stairs by the front door.

"What is it?" Curiosity replaced my pissed off emotions.

"Open it and find out."

"All right. You've convinced me."

Inside, a beautiful gold cross with a stunning square, red gem in the center lay on a black velvet liner. I'd never seen a stone so radiant before.

"It's gorgeous, Chase. Help me put it on," I said, leaning over and kissing him.

"The stone is beryl—bixbyite, actually. It's very rare and only used in special pieces of jewelry. Looking though the stone can reveal what was once invisible or lost to the seeker." He smiled while securing the clasp.

"It's perfect." The charm hung well off of the thick gold chain, resting flawlessly between my cleavage—a remarkable size and fit.

"Promise you won't take it off," Chase said.

Strange request.

"I promise. Any reason in particular why?"

"I just want you to wear it always."

"Um, okay."

Agreeing was the smart move—the only move. Further questioning would only start an argument or worse, make him fall into one of his bipolar mood swings. Earlier in the week, I'd run into Tori at the mall. She wanted Jules, Mark, Tim, Chase, and me to hook up over the break being it'd been some time since we all were together. Chase wasn't a huge fan of Tori, but nodded in agreement when I asked if we could go. Not wanting to open a can of worms and question if he'd be spending time with his family for the holidays became another avoided topic. Though I was dying to know exactly what was going on, my lips remained sealed. Blanche had stopped by the house twice since Chase had moved in. Both times I overheard her begging Chase to come home, and both times he refused, insisting the current arrangement would continue whether she understood or not. After spending the next hour engaging in a very exhausting one-sided dialog, relief finally arrived when the garage door opened.

"I'll see you in the morning, Nina," Chase said, getting off of the couch.

"Hang out a second to say hi to Steve."

"Yeah, I'll pass," he responded, leaning down, and kissing the top of my head.

"Why?"

"Because your brother and I have, let's call it, *issues* with each other. Goodnight, baby."

No sooner did Chase leave, a strong set of arms lifted me off of the ground.

"I have absolutely nothing to say to you, Steven Mitchel Luther."

"Aw. Come on, Sis. I'm sorry. Leaving without saying goodbye wasn't nice, and not reaching out wasn't either. School's been tough this semester."

I didn't respond. Inflicting the wrath of my hard, no-nonsense stare would be far more powerful than any combination of words.

"You're still my favorite sister."

"I'm your *only* sister." An involuntary laugh came out of my mouth as my arms coiled around his massive neck.

Steve had always been a weakness. Who else our age could identify with what we were? What we had to deal with? Growing up, we leaned on each other when we'd feel like social freaks because of having to live a double life. We had our private jokes, inside secrets, and an unbreakable bond.

"I am sorry, Nina," Steve whispered, holding me tightly. "I do miss you and worry about you when I'm not here, but soon enough I'll have you fulltime when you join me back home in New York. It'll be great. We can hang out every day doing all of the things we used to. You're going to love my apartment."

"It's time to move again? For crying out loud, we just got here."

What the hell? No one mentioned relocating to me, but apparently they did to Steve. Whatever. At least Chase will be with you this time. Silver lining.

"Can I be completely honest *without* you flipping out?"

"Try me, but no promises will be made." Worry and paranoia set in.

Mom and Dad wouldn't make you leave Savannah midyear. Never in the past have you been made to up and take off anywhere until the summer holiday. Besides, if they did try to pull something like that, you're old enough to stay behind, like Steve did.

"I didn't want to come home for Christmas, but Dad insisted. I don't like any of this, Nina. Dad told me what's been going on and quite frankly, it's concerning. Don't you realize Chase is putting you and the rest of us in danger? He's a pressure cooker that could blow at any time. Sure he's your destiny, but Nina, you don't have to follow what is thought to be. Nothing is written in stone. You're coming back to New York with me. You'll be safe there and away from him. When Dad figures all of this out, we can re-evaluate the situation."

"Excuse me, but who died and made you my father? Last time I checked you were only my brother. The brother who left me here in a strange town with new people to rot while you ran back to New York. I hated it here until Chase came into the picture. You have no say this time. If any danger presented itself at any point, Dad would tell me, and he never would've allowed Chase to stay with us."

"He has all of you brainwashed. It's truly amazing. The only reason he's here is because Dad knows if he's not, you'll run away to be with him." Steve's tone reflected frustration.

"That's *not* true. This isn't Chase's fault. None of us asked for this life. Dad wants Chase here because he wants to help someone in need. He wants to help them understand this craziness." Angry heat rose from my neck. "You know something, big brother? Go to Hell," I shouted, storming out of the living room.

Hot tears streamed down my flustered, enraged cheeks. Still seething after slamming the bedroom door, I paced the space trying to shove the anger away with rational thoughts. At the heart of the matter, Steve meant no harm and wanted to protect me, but he would never fully understand the magnitude of the situation because he never experienced the bond associated with soul mates. Trying to prove how powerful that was would be useless. I'd never leave Chase's side, not even to return to New York. We were in this together, and if that meant having to follow him into the fires of Hell or to the ends of the Earth, so be it. Nothing else mattered. Steve was going to have to accept that.

Lying on the bed I stared at the ceiling wondering what Chase was doing or thinking about. Since he moved in our late-night rendezvous had stopped. It'd been far too long since time was spent in each other's arms, talking, laughing, seeking comfort and solace from the intimacy. We needed to share that now. Once my parents and Steve went to bed, I'd make a move and sneak down the hall. Unfortunately, after an hour of waiting in the dark, sleep overcame me, peacefully allowing an unconsciousness to set in.

****

My eyes shot open. Intense fear set in as my brain evaluated my surroundings. Instinctively, I already knew the room would be dark with a door to the left which lead to a corridor. Without wasting any time, my legs rapidly headed to the hall, though the area remained foggy. The dim narrow space outside felt damp. A musty odor hung heavy in the thick air. The temperature appeared ice cold, but my skin burned. There were no hesitations this time while approaching the tiny source of light off in the distance. Stopping abruptly in the doorway, what lay in the center of the room hidden behind several cloaked figures wasn't a surprise. The sounds of the figures' monotone chanting became progressively louder with each passing second. The terror from deep within rendered me motionless, not allowing any further closeness. Like a stone statue, I watched in horror. The covered individuals carefully formed two lines flanking the sides of the room allowing for a complete view of my lifeless body.

"My children, the time has come again," a low, serpent-like voice spoke.

The owner of the sound glided from a blackened corner and into the light using swift, fluid motions, standing tall, with long, stringy, black hair. Thick, black eyebrows made his blood red eyes pop. The man studied my form, stroking his goatee with lengthy, yellowing fingernails.

Vincent.

"Foolish girl, or should I rather say, stupid boy?" Vincent laughed. "He led her right to me. Now he will pay for the shame and embarrassment he caused by his reckless actions. Bring him to me."

Two henchmen disappeared momentarily. They reappeared supporting a limp body which was thrown at Vincent's feet. The person hit the ground with a loud thud.

"Show some respect. Bow before me," Vincent yelled, raising his pointer finger, painfully forcing the man into a hunched position.

The man cried out in agony as his frame contorted to obey Vincent's wishes. The second Vincent's hold was released, the man panted in relief. Knowing the identity of this tortured soul became the object of extreme desperation. My eyes strained to see farther, but the man was now facing down and not moving.

"See what you've made me do? See what this had to come to because you couldn't do what you were told? Destroy the girl, but leave him. He's mine," Vincent hissed.

"You will not harm her." The man struggled to say, slowly rising.

The man turned, glancing at the doorway. His face was bloody and beaten. His clothing was torn and dirty. His green eyes were filled with hatred.

Chase.

"No," I screamed from the top of my lungs.

Furiously, my legs kicked themselves free from whatever had been holding them down. Drenched in sweat, but freezing cold, my hands grabbed at everything. My gaze darted wildly to gain some sort of sense of awareness. Though temporarily blinded, everything could finally be seen in crystal clear perfection.

"Nina, wake up," a calm voice urged, gently shaking my shoulders.

"Dad," I whispered loudly.

"Relax. Deep breaths. It was only a nightmare," he soothed.

"Chase. Where is Chase?"

"I'm right here," Chase said.

He appeared leaning against the bathroom door frame. The sight of him in navy blue lounge pants with a snug, white tank top was like being able to breathe again after being submerged under water for far too long. Greedily, my lungs stole oxygen, allowing balance from within to be restored. Chase looked exhausted and drained. Under the low lighting, bags beneath his eyes appeared dark and deep. There were no words because mixed emotions which were definitely mine and not Chase's, clouded all sense of reality. On one hand, we were safe and the vision had only been a nightmare, but on the other, fright still controlled every solid, rational thought. I'd caught a glimpse of the future and it was morbidly grim. However, the vision presented slightly different this time.

Yes, it did.

The revelation was sharp, rather life-like, but a haze existed around each frame. That glitch in the dream, that obscurity, provided safety for some unknown reason.

"Nina, what did you see?" Chase requested, moving closer. His tone caught me off guard. Lately, mellow, sweet, or polite weren't adjectives I'd use to describe Chase, especially with me.

"I don't remember." My voice still shook with panic. Every moment of the nightmare haunted me, but Orifiel didn't want anyone knowing about the prophecies and quite frankly, his protection was far superior to those currently surrounding me.

"Nothing at all?" Chase pressed.

"Not a thing."

He sat on the edge of the bed, placing his hands over mine. Our eyes locked on one another while my father sat on the desk chair. Both men's faces were filled with curiosity, but spiked with fear.

"What's going on?" Steve's voice boomed as he pushed the bedroom door open.

"Nina had a bad dream," my father explained.

"Yeah, I got that from the screaming. Is there something more to it?"

"No. Everything's fine," I piped up, forcing a slight smile.

If there were ever a doubt about the level of tension that existed between Steve and Chase, it shined boldly now. The moment Steve walked into the room, Chase seemed unable to control his mood. Disdain and aversion filled the space almost instantly. Steve's face visually expressed the shared animosity. Sight, sound, and smell heightened to the point of wild animal hunting status.

"Come on, Steve. Let your father and sister talk," my mother said, gently guiding him out.

Once Steve left, a calmer dynamic returned.

"Are you sure you don't remember anything?" my father queried.

"Yes."

And you both will continue to receive the same answer until Orifiel is informed of this matter, or until I feel Chase can be fully trusted and won't explode or fall off the deep end. It's time for a little self-preservation before everything sinks into the dark abyss surrounding us.

Chapter 28

Chase

Lie.

I knew when Nina wasn't telling me the truth. She was hiding something huge, but one way or another, whatever the secret, it had to be revealed. Part, if not all of Nina, possessed a seer ability. She had to open up, but unfortunately doing so would prove tricky. My behavior since moving into the Luther home had been less than stellar. A polite, megawatt smile was constantly worn around Jack and Ellen, but with Nina, no such fabrication existed. If we couldn't be ourselves around the other, what kind of relationship did we have? For crying out loud, we were soul mates. Didn't that mean total transparency? Nina received much credit for always keeping her cool, never pushing issues, or asking too many questions, but sometimes I wished she would've. My heart craved someone to scale the walls I'd put up and break in; longing to find comfort in someone's ready, willing, and able arms so I could temporarily forget everything. Nina could provide this, but she often seemed distant and distracted. Besides, it felt like every time we were physically close, all she wanted was sex. I just wanted to feel her near to experience the heat, nothing less, nothing more. Mostly Nina didn't initiate anything anymore. She waited for the first move to be made. Was this her way of backing off to give me space, or was it a by-product of her being too wrapped up in her own life to notice whatever else, such as the downward spiral I'd been swept up in? Whichever the case, the vast distance between us felt like we were slowly drifting apart. Those days frightened me. I'd force myself to act happy to close the ever-growing gap between us.

Jack had me working nonstop on developing the damn *gifts* and thankfully, progress had been made. Controlling my emotions had become easier and the migraines had stopped, but the lack of an emotional or physical outlet drained me, becoming more torturous with each passing day. When not working with Jack, I lived at the gym, hoping the exertion of energy would help, even if only in the smallest of ways. Frequently, a cagy, trapped sense of self hovered, hence the perpetual bad moods. Sleep remained the enemy. I often had to resort to popping a sleeping pill to find a few hours of peace.

Nina's parents welcomed me into their lives and home, but Steve wouldn't. We'd never be friends, and after overhearing Jack on the phone with him a few weeks back solidified this point. Steve refused to come home for the holidays because of me living in the house. Jack took my side and told him he had to learn to cope because the situation wasn't changing anytime soon. After many threats and warnings, Steve finally broke and agreed to spend Christmas in Savannah. I felt bad. Had I found an apartment this wouldn't have been an issue, and Jack wouldn't have had to deal with his unruly, spoiled, megalomaniac son. Jack had been good to me and he didn't deserve anymore grief.

Behind their backs I searched for a decent place to live, but kept coming up short. There wasn't anything out there that felt like it could eventually become home. Everything appeared cold and empty, like my soul. I'd contemplated asking Nina to move into an apartment with me, but that felt wrong. At nineteen living with a girl, soul mate or not, wasn't a plunge this guy was about to take. Truth be told, returning home appeared like a fairly decent, solid idea. All of the changes were overwhelming and having to force myself to be okay with things that weren't, like Steve and our mutual hatred, was too much. But, going home meant playing by George James's rules and that wasn't going to happen. On top of everything else, I didn't need to be dealing with a frustrating housing crisis.

Luckily, Bristol finally stopped calling and texting me. Hurting her again sucked, but allowing the reintroduction, no matter how necessary it *may* have felt, had been a mistake. All ties had to be cut before an intense situation ignited, then exploded, leaving behind damage of mass destruction.

"Baby, you're lying," I said, squeezing her hands while looking into her two weary, hazel eyes.

"I'm not," Nina started.

"Don't lie to cover a lie, please. It cheapens us and what we share. If you want to protect us, you'll tell me what you saw. If we both know, we can be prepared and possibly avoid a dangerous situation."

"Why should I trust you?" she whispered in my ear.

"Why shouldn't you?" Her bold, outrageous statement threw me for a loop. I'd never betrayed Nina, well, not that she'd been aware of. Did Nina know about Bristol, or had I treated this girl that badly I'd finally pushed her away?

"Because you'll end up yelling or moody and

honestly, my heart can't take it anymore," she replied, backing away.

"You have my word neither will happen. It's been rough, but I love you. Always will. It's you and me, alone, in both worlds, baby. If we can't trust one another to have the other's back, we have nothing," I said softly, inching closer, gently brushing a few strands of her hair from her face, finally pressing our foreheads together. Respite and shame collided inside of me. My recent indiscretions remained private, a definite relief, but Nina had been experiencing heartache and pain by my hands. The girl I'd do anything for was worth more than that. I'd been too wrapped up in me. Nina's feelings had been neglected, and she too had been enduring quite a bit. Regaining her confidence in a few brief moments causing her to purge the nightmare without the use of any divine gift would be tough, but not impossible. Repairing the fractured trust in the long run would take time. Right now, Nina needed to come forward freely without the use of force.

Perhaps if you stopped treating her like an old toy you're bored with she might realize you still want a future with her. You better turn up the charm and turn down the uncaring jerk act and fast or else she'll never tell you anything or worse, you'll lose her forever. How much emotional abandonment can one person take, soul mate or not, before they upped and left for a better life?

She looked down and sighed heavily. My heartfelt

pleading had appealed to her kind nature. "Fine. I saw Vincent, a few Demons, you, and me. The vision wasn't clear."

"Where were we?"

"Don't know. I wasn't in the situation, but rather

looking at it, and the view appeared hazy, different than visions from the past. It wasn't an actual prediction. More like a bad dream."

"Why did you scream if the vision wasn't clear?"

"Vincent being present in nightmares or reality isn't reason enough to scream? You do remember what he looks like and who he is, right?"

"What do you think this means?" I questioned Jack. My hands ran nervously through my chaotic hair.

"I'm not sure. If Nina is a seer, then we just got a blurry glimpse into the future. If she's not, then it was nothing more than a nightmare."

"You know as well as I that she's a seer."

"Chase, we don't know for sure," Jack pressed.

"Seriously? Nina saw the future last time and the same crap is happening again," I shot back, defending my stance on the issue.

"Yes, she did but, Son, a true seer can see the future for everyone. Nina can't. She's only seen your fate, once. There's no evidence to prove what she's experiencing now is anything worth fretting over." Jack playing Devil's advocate was infuriating.

"Has it maybe occurred to you that Nina's ability might not be fully developed yet? That is a possibility. Maybe her gift is not meant for others, but rather only for us. Maybe this is someone's way of giving us a heads up, letting us know what's creeping up around the corner so we can make it out of this garbage dump of a situation alive." Giving up wasn't an option. Jack had to hear and acknowledge me.

"We'll have to look into this further, Chase."

Either he's in denial or he's blind to the fact his daughter possesses another ability.

"She's a seer, damn it. I'd bet my life on it. We have a connection. Something inside of me tells me these visions are warnings."

"Again, we can't be certain of this."

"I've trusted you. It's your turn to put blind faith me."

"I need more proof, Chase. More research." Jack's tone remained cool.

"You're wrong and because of that we're wasting valuable time."

"It's late. We all could use a little more sleep," Jack said, getting up from Nina's desk chair.

"Like I'm really going to be able to fall back asleep now," Nina mumbled to herself.

"Let me help," I offered, gently pushing Nina's shoulders back on the mattress, brushing the hair from her face, and softly running my fingers over her worried eyelids. A deep sleep could only be willed upon once relaxation set in. Slowly, her sight and hearing were diminished, while touch and smell were heightened. I'd figured out how to separate senses and emotions using my brain to influence others by the power of persuasive thinking. It wasn't a mastered technique, but it was pretty damn close. Nina would've been out cold in a matter of seconds if she wasn't trying to fight the hold. The more she resisted, the harder my brain worked to control her mind. It was exhausting, but well worth the results. I could make anyone do anything or make them feel however I deemed fit. Lord knew there were many times when abusing this power would've been personally gainful, but that wouldn't happen. There were good guys and bad guys in this world. I was one of the good guys—*not* a Demon.

“Don’t go, Chase,” Nina begged in an extremely groggy manner.

“You can stay,” Jack said, shutting the lights and exiting the room, but making sure to close the door only halfway.

Yeah, like I’d really try anything with your daughter in your house.

“Close your eyes, baby. Drift away.” Kicking the gift up a notch, the desired results were had. Nina’s breathing grew rhythmic and shallow. She finally nodded off with a slight peaceful moan.

“I love you, baby. Nothing will stop me from keeping you safe. I’d give my life for yours,” I whispered, meaning every single word.

Chapter 29

Nina

"Good morning," Chase whispered.

"Hey."

"How'd you sleep?"

"After you put me out, amazing. Best sleep I've had in a long time actually."

The light of day was cruel on Chase's once perfect face. The dark circles under his eyes last night looked even worse. To say he was exhausted would've been a gross underestimation of the truth.

"Chase, are you not sleeping?"

"I'm sleeping," he answered emotionlessly.

"No offense, babe, but you look like shit."

"Thanks," he said sarcastically, getting off of the bed, standing, and stretching.

"You're still hot," I said, wrapping my arms around his neck from behind, and kissing the top of his shoulders.

"I'm fine, Nina. Really. We better get downstairs."

"You know you can talk to me about anything."

"I know." He smiled and left the room.

He might've been lying about his sleeping patterns and being okay, but he wasn't about having to get downstairs. Shoving aside the uneasiness which sat in the pit of my stomach, a quick shower was taken, but repressing the horrible feelings of openly doubting trust in Chase made it difficult to focus on such a simple task.

Last night the words just slipped out before they could be stopped. It wasn't exactly a falsehood, but it wasn't the complete truth either. Yes, a giant river emotionally separated us at the moment, but at the heart of both worlds, Chase could be trusted, and he'd do anything for me, but now wasn't the time to be analyzing any of this. Suggesting no faith existed between us had hurt his feelings. Apologizing for this was necessary, however, it would have to wait until later.

It was Christmas Eve and my mother would probably already be in the kitchen stressing out over having the entire family over tonight and tomorrow, cooking, and cleaning. No sooner did the last bite of bagel greet my stomach, my mother enlisted me to scrub the upstairs of the house, and when completed, help her finish tidying the downstairs. Whining and complaining wouldn't do a damn worth of good, so with an eye roll and a bucket of cleaning supplies in hand, the painfully tiring task commenced. Perhaps this mundane chore would keep my focus off of Chase and our relationship woes.

The first few hours were spent wondering about the necessity behind scouring the upstairs. No one ever journeyed up here, but over the years I learned never to question my mother's madness. Finally, Chase's room was the only space left to address. The area proved fairly neat with not much to do other than dust and vacuum. While dusting the dresser a small, full pill bottle with no label caught my eye.

"Dad," I yelled, charging down the stairs, clutching the bottle tightly.

"In here, princess," he called from his office.

The coast was clear because Chase had been sent to run ten thousand errands for my mother.

"What's this?"

"A pill bottle, Nina."

"This was on Chase's dresser. What is it?"

Don't play cute with me, Dad. I invented that little game.

My father reached for the bottle and quickly examined the contents. "Sleeping aids."

"Why didn't I know about this?"

"Some things are none of your business. Chase is under a lot of pressure and stress. You need to cut him some slack. Perhaps he didn't want to tell you about a self-perceived weakness. He's accomplished and has learned a lot in a very short period of time which is taxing on the body and mind."

"We're all under a lot of pressure. He's not the only one."

"You're right. We all are and we're all handling it the best and most comfortable way we can. Chase will be all right when all is said and done. We all will be," my father assured.

"He looks like walking death." My once harsh words were now filled with worry and sorrow.

"This transition is difficult. Keeping one's emotions in check is a full-time job. Chase is constantly focusing on feeling nothing. Sometimes when we're overwhelmed, we have a difficult time shutting our minds off at night. Sleeping pills often help remedy this."

"You keep saying he's going to be okay, but it really doesn't seem that way."

"Some things take time. Unfortunately, this is one of those times. Be patient and supportive, Nina. Chase truly loves you. Bluer skies await you both. We all have to endure this temporary confusion. While he's finding himself and how he fits into our other world, you should be doing the same. Focus on honing your own skills."

"Yeah. Thanks."

Looks like we're still keeping things from each other. Thanks a lot, Chase. Your little speech last night about how it's only you and me was bull and your way of getting me to tell you about my vision. For some reason my destiny is supposed to be a hard and long one, filled with misery at every turn.

I couldn't return to my cleaning chores. My anger was far too rooted. Grabbing a jacket and heading out of the front door, rage led me down the block to the schoolyard. I'd become a stranger in my own life; disillusioned and detached from reality. No one could be trusted, not even my own soul mate, to tell the truth about anything, but everyone expected me to be upfront and honest all day every day. What else was Chase hiding? I wanted to be someone, anyone, other than me.

The empty playground pleased me. Having to deal with anymore secrets and lies today would break me completely. A secluded area behind the school was the best place to escape to. Slumping to the cold, hard ground, my back braced itself against the crimson bricks. My fingers carelessly ran across the blades of almost dead grass.

Why does life have to be this trying?

My eyes stared into space while my brain attempted to recall the last time happiness, true joy, not for a moment, but rather for an extended period of time, had been experienced. It was useless because such a simple emotional response was void from my world, and that realization caused tears of loneliness to fall. Perhaps I was acting overdramatically. Maybe I was being selfish. I truly didn't give a damn because my entire being ached with sadness.

What if you never went to Tybee and saw Chase? What if your paths never crossed? Would you be happy?

A strong, overpowering depression settled inside of my core. Guilt joined the despondency for thinking about an existence without Chase, but on the other hand, we'd be in a better place if we were never aware the other was out there.

"Why is the prettiest girl in Savannah sitting all by herself seemingly upset?"

"Release me from this curse, this obligation. If anyone can do it, it's you. Figure out a way to remove me from all of this. I don't give a damn where you have to hide me or what I have to do. Talk to Michael or The Powers That Be. Please," I begged, not bothering to look up at Orifiel. His accent gave him away every time.

"I can't. I'm sorry. There's no way out."

"Can we try something?"

"Such as?" Orifiel questioned skeptically.

"A fantasy."

"What type of fantasy are we talking about?" He queried, sitting beside me.

"One where I'm not me and you're not you in our present states."

There wasn't a verbal response, but his golden eyes filled with longing while his face draped in anguish.

"Are you in?"

"That sounds dangerous, love," Orifiel warned.

"I really don't care. Neither should you."

While he searched for the right words, my brain shut

down creating a temporary imaginary world. A less complicated one where pain of any kind didn't exist and life was fun and exciting again. Straddling his lap, gradually inching closer, our faces met. Orifiel's lips were soft and warm filling every ounce of my existence with sheer pleasure and relief. His solid fingers dug into my hips as his mouth engulfed mine. Our bodies moved as one as passion I never experienced bubbled to the surface. His command was slow, deep, and rhythmical. Within a few simple moments his frame pivoted. Now on top of me, our legs tangled. His right hand took hold of my upper thigh while his left caressed the side of my face. The moment's thirst could've been ripped straight from the pages of a romance novel.

"We can't do this, Nina," he whispered breathlessly, rolling onto his back. His fingers tugged at his hair.

"Why?" I demanded, abruptly getting up and turning away from the situation.

"Because you're not mine. That's not to say I didn't wish you were, *especially* right now," he rationalized, rising off of the ground, and moving his frame around mine until we were facing one another again.

"Being me, living this life—it hurts too much. Give me a break where I can be normal for a change. I want to feel attractive, desired, wanted, craved. I don't want to be yelled at, ignored, or dismissed. Right now it doesn't matter what's right or wrong. Why can't you understand that? You said you were here to help with whatever. Well, help me. For shit sake, I'm even showing you how to."

"I do understand, love. I'd never overlook or take your presence for granted and I *really* do believe your physical form to be absolutely striking. I am here for you and I want to help, but snogging is a risky move for both of us. It's not that I didn't enjoy what happened, dare I say I enjoyed it a little too much, it's that it never should've happened in the first place," Orifiel said softly.

"Make this stop hurting. Please," I pleaded, holding back tears.

"Give me your pain," he urged, slowly moving nearer. His left hand found its way across my neck and up my jaw, finally wrapping around the back of my head. His fingers wove themselves through my hair with a gentle, but rather powerful tug. Our eyes closed in anticipation of what would happen next.

Delicately, patiently, and unhurriedly he brushed his lips and nose against mine allowing us to connect while breathing life back into my almost dead soul. His lips parted slightly as he deftly kissed me. It was almost as if his intimacy was absorbing my torture and grief. Orifiel's right arm firmly held me close. His other hand continued to stroke my hair. For the first time in a long time nothing was experienced except the moment we'd created. Life was occurring in the here and now with no emotional baggage. With one touch, my inner pain, pain no Angelic gift could ever seem to ease, vanished. Our souls silently spoke seeking comfort and rest from the other's. After some time he tenderly pulled away.

"Thank you," I murmured. His arms remained locked around my waist.

"I'm not sure what's going on or what's bothering you, but I hope that helped. I don't give a damn how much trouble I'm in for playing around with you. It was worth it, love. You're worth it," he replied, looking up at the sky.

"Why would you be in trouble? No one has to know

we spoke or even saw each other for that matter. In fact, I'm not even supposed to be here alone. I snuck out. Hopefully nobody will realize I'm gone," I said, still trying to hold onto the sweet escape he'd created.

"First of all, Michael knows all, sees all, and hears all. Secondly, you're the farthest thing for alone. Being here with me is the safest place you'll ever be. Lastly, true Angels are forbidden from carrying on relationships of any type, whether it be romantic or friendship, with Mortals—even Mortal Angels."

"Please don't up and leave. I need you." Worry returned when I processed what he'd said.

"What's going on, Nina? What's happening here? You need to snap back to reality. I joined you on your little holiday from sanity. We had some sinful fun, but now we're home. It's time to face the facts." His once kind, understanding tone had disappeared, as did his arms from my waist.

His curt action caught me off guard making me take the defense. "What's *not* wrong? That would be the easier question. Why is Chase pushing me away? Why is our love fading? What's wrong with him? Will he ever get better? Why does everything have to be so damn difficult? To top it off, you're going to bail on me too because there's some stupid rule about being friends with Mortals that all of a sudden you feel the need to live by. If we couldn't be friends, why did you show yourself to me? Why didn't you stay hidden in the shadows leaving me alone?" Hot tears of rage and sadness flowed freely from my eyes.

"You started this friendship or whatever the hell you want to consider it. *Not* me. You're the only one who can be trusted and I need you to help me make sense of this craziness—to right the wrongs, but forget all of that because you suddenly realize you made an epic mistake and want to bolt. Fine, Orifiel. Run away, but once you go, don't you dare ever look back."

He didn't answer, but rather roughly jerked my body back into his arms, resting his head on top of mine. Drawing away would've been a waste of time and energy. His hold was a firm declaration of unspoken words—words that couldn't be said, but needed to be felt.

"Please stop fighting with me, love. Seeing you like this is unbearable. Abandoning you isn't and wasn't even a thought. Last summer I promised to always be around, and I am a man of my word, especially when it comes to *you*. Michael sent me here to watch Chase, but honestly, Nina, I've spent more time focusing on you, because you mean more to me. You can always be free and open in my company; say or do anything you wish. We're friends. Always will be. As for your questions, the solutions are there, we just need to find them. Life's an epic journey filled with challenges. Embrace the adventure because you never know what wonderful places it may end up taking you. You're not alone. Everyone who walks this Earth has a certain amount of crap to deal with. You're enduring your allotment now so when it's over, you can sit back, relax, and enjoy your existence. Keep fighting, love. Eventually you'll find your definition of peace and true bliss. It's out there. I swear. Be patient because your future holds so much joy, love, and raw, uncontrollable passion like you've never experienced before."

"How do you know that? How can you be sure happiness will ever find me?"

A slight laugh escaped his throat. "I know a lot of things, and of all those things I'm one hundred and twenty percent certain an amazing future awaits both of us."

"I desperately want to believe you." My defeated confession caused me to bury my head in the crook of his neck. Orifiel's heady, masculine smell drew me in, but not in the sense of physical desire. Though Orifiel was devastatingly handsome and exceptionally gifted with matters of intimacy, the bolt of lustful electricity lacked.

"Escaping to a fantasyland isn't the answer."

"If you get into any trouble over what happened blame me."

"I'd sooner lose my soul then throw you under a bus allowing you to take the fall for anything we've said or done." A brief smile crossed Orifiel's lips before his eyes fell, filling with sadness. Tiny crease lines formed around his eyelids. "If you only knew what I know things would be a lot easier."

"We'll always be together, right?"

"Aye. In life *and* in death," Orifiel assured, sitting, and pulling me between his legs.

He held me close, not saying a word, allowing us to enjoy whatever time was left on our mental checkout. I doubted Chase would be aware of my absence, but my parents might. Chase had become beyond lost in his own damn drama and hung up on himself I probably could've dropped dead on the floor right in front of him and he'd never notice.

"I'd better go." Unravelling myself from Orifiel's tight, warm hold was difficult.

"Oi. Before you leave we need to agree to a few

things, okay?" His tone turned serious as he took hold of my left wrist.

"What's up?"

"What happened before stays between us—no one else. You have to promise me that you'll never tell Gabriel about it." Alarmingly strong traces of fear lived inside of Orifiel's words.

"Why would I tell your brother? I don't even know him, but yeah, sure. My lips are sealed."

That's an odd request.

"Chase. I meant never tell Chase, not Gabriel," he practically shouted.

The thought of Chase knowing about what happened shot me straight back to reality making my stomach churn.

What did I do? Seriously? You cheated on Chase.

"Oh my God." There didn't seem to be enough oxygen to breathe.

"Calm down, love. You're hyperventilating. You did nothing wrong. *We* did nothing wrong, but sometimes significant others, especially soul mates, feel threatened by the presence of opposite sex friends in their mate's life. This is coming out wrong." He paused, taking a hot second to run his hands through his hair. He appeared frustrated and edgy. "Nothing transpired. We're friends and that's all we will ever be—no that's a lie. I can't elaborate any further on that, but it's nothing bad. You were upset. I comforted you, but to Chase it might not seem that way. You two have to figure out your issues because based off of today's conversation, he's hurting you, and badly. Emotional pain and distress is far worse than physical. Talk to him. It might be difficult, but you have to. Be truthful about how you feel no matter how hard or uncomfortable it may be. If it were me, brutal honesty is what I'd want from anyone. This is a trying time for you and him. As for the roll around—it never occurred. Forgotten."

"You're right. Chase and I have a few things we need to discuss." Forcing a fake smile came easy, almost second nature these days.

Banging my head against a brick wall would prove more effective than talking to Chase, but maybe Orifiel was onto something. Sitting around, waiting for the situation to cure itself wasn't doing a damn thing. If one wishes to see a change, they need to be the change.

"I'll see you. Thanks for listening," I said, kissing his cheek, turning, and heading in the direction of home. He followed me, but I never looked back to check. My eyes focused only on the pavement straight ahead of me.

****

By five, Chase still hadn't returned from running various errands. Instead of opting to stand guard by the front window anxiously waiting, I headed upstairs to shower. Usually I loved this season, the decorations, shopping, time off from school, but not anymore and justly that didn't seem fair. This time last year Chase had dumped me. You'd think I'd be happy we were together, but the tension surrounding us had killed the mood. Something had to give for the situation to break free from its negative hold. The only solution was to do whatever it took to make the holiday and all of the days after it positive ones filled with hope.

Because that's such a realistic goal.

Before finding Chase in the kitchen, a decision to take Orifiel's advice and to forget about our brief intimate moment was made. It was wrong, *very* wrong and it would never happen again. An epic error in selfish, attention seeking judgement. I despised myself for giving into adulterous behaviors, but in order to move on, I had to forgive myself first.

Chase sat alone at the table flipping absentmindedly through a magazine.

Positive thinking.

"Hey. You look nice," I said, sitting down.

"Thanks. You look great, baby. Like always," he replied in a monotone voice, barely looking up.

He did appear good in spite of the deep, dark circles under his brilliant, emerald-colored irises which seemed to be swimming in a sea of despair.

"Listen, Chase, it's been tense around here lately, but it's Christmas. Could we try to have some fun?"

"Is that what you'd like?" he asked, lowering the periodical, and finally making eye contact.

"Yes. It really is."

"If that's what will make you happy, baby." A slight smile spread across his otherwise lifeless face.

"Thanks. I have something for you." Reaching into the bag on the floor, my fingers curled around the small, black box at the bottom. "Early present."

"What is it?"

"Open it and find out."

He flipped the lid viewing the contents. After several seconds he grinned while sliding the silvery black titanium band on his ring finger.

"Thank you," he whispered.

"Everyone in both our worlds needs to know you're taken. You're mine, forever."

"Nothing and no one could ever rip me away from you. I promise when this is all over, we'll be together, living our own life. We'll get through this, baby."

"Can't wait."

The evening with my entire extended family thankfully proved uneventful—a pleasant surprise. Wanting some alone time and to keep a distance between Chase and Steve, we followed my parents and Steve in Chase's car to Jenny's home for desert. Casually, I inquired if he intended on seeing George and Blanche. Apparently, he'd swung by while running errands in the morning to see Blanche. Nothing had changed. She still wanted him to come back and George remained angry. They both thought Chase would've returned by now needing money or support. Since he hadn't, the situation and tension had worsened. He admitted he'd been searching for an apartment, which didn't thrill me, until he suggested the apartment would be for us to start our future together in. Chase freely offering to engage in a dialogue with no pushing or prodding on my part had been a nice change of pace. There was no fighting or wild moods for once.

Everything seemed to be going smoothly well into the next day. Chase's temperament was calm and relaxed, and it appeared he'd gotten some sleep the night before. My aunts, uncles, and cousins were all on their best behaviors keeping conversations light, and Steve had finally backed off of Chase, even starting a few random discussions with him. It was okay to relax. Balance had been restored and nothing could ruin that.

Smile and take it all in because you know this isn't going to last long.

Chapter 30

Chase

Initially, when Nina asked if we could enjoy the holiday, I agreed because I'd been such a bastard lately. This was something she wanted. One simple action would get me back on the right path to regaining her trust and affections. After a few hours of faking happy, my body and mind adjusted to the sudden, unexpected shift. The task became increasingly easier by the moment. Smiling and levity were, for once, fairly genuine. Hell, even Steve fell for it and started a conversation. I indulged for Nina's sake, though stapling my head to the carpet would've been a hell of a lot less painful. However, if the jackass could pretend, so could I. After all, at some point we'd be brothers-in-law and would have to endure the others' presence from time to time. This was good practice.

"Nina, what field of medicine interests you most?" One of her aunts questioned.

"I really don't know," Nina answered.

For a fleeting second the thought of Nina in a white lab coat walking up and down the halls of a hospital caused a flicker of a grin to appear. She'd make a rather hot physician.

"You're sitting in a room full of them. You know you want to." My head twitched briefly while Vincent's voice hissed its return.

Keep cool, Chase. This will pass. Excuse yourself and go upstairs.

"I'm not feeling well..." My head ticked again, but this time more aggressively. A surge of great strength consumed me causing me to stand and grip the edge of the table. Free hands would equal destruction of catastrophic proportions.

"Do it. Do it now. Make me proud," Vincent ordered.

"Do you hear that?" I demanded, knowing no one heard anything, but secretly hoping someone had.

The idol table chatter stopped. All eyes were fixed on me. Jack swiftly rose, grabbing my shoulders.

"Ground yourself the way I showed you. Breathe through this," Jack whispered.

"They're the enemy. They're making a fool out of you. You're not one of them because you're one of us. Kill them all. Do it now. I command you."

"Did you hear that?" My eyelids opened wider. Sweat drenched my otherwise dry flesh.

"What are you hearing, Chase?" Jack questioned calmly.

"Break Jack's neck, then pick them off one by one. I'll protect and hide you. You're stronger than all of them put together. Do it. You're wasting valuable time."

"Get out," I heard myself shout.

"Let's get you upstairs. You need to lie down," Jack said, then turned to face the confused Luther clan. "He's been suffering from some pretty severe migraines lately. We've been having a difficult time getting them under control."

"No." For unknown reasons the look of pity on everyone's face set the Demon inside of me loose.

"Let's go," Jack urged, taking firm hold of my wrist.

His touch caused my eyes to roll back. The intense head throbbing broke free making the pain vanish as fast as it came. My hands rose. My fingertips pressed to my temples inviting Vincent's voice to creep deep within my soul. Several neck rolls allowed for something warm and soulless to seep into my extremities.

"Dad. Do something," Nina panicked.

Her raw fear finished the transformation. Feeding off of Nina's terror allowed me to grow stronger, more powerful than I ever imagined.

"Destroy."

Vincent's desire had to be sated. With great delight, I watched the Luther family scurry into the kitchen for safety as my hands took hold of the hundred plus pound solid oak dining table, flipping it effortlessly.

"Hurt them."

Anything in my way received brutal punishment. Her uncles and brother tried to subdue me, but couldn't. They were no match for this strength and they were simply flung to the side. Chase no longer held control. Only Vincent did, and he was too durable to fight.

"Dad," Nina shrieked.

Again, Nina's terror fed my Demonic state. Taking hold of her arms, my hands violently shook her as hard as possible. She had to scream. She had to fear me.

"Chase. Stop this now," Nina begged.

The sound of that beautiful, melodic voice pleading and the pained expression filling her captivating eyes tugged at my heart making all of my actions temporarily pause.

"What are you doing? Finish her."

"No, Vincent. Not her. Anyone else, but never her.

Not now. Not ever."

My head shook in an attempt to shake Vincent. The more it twitched, the softer Vincent's commanding voice became.

"Stop. Get out," I tried to shout through slurred words.

A sharp stab in my right thigh shocked the world still. In that one moment nothing made any sense, especially the falling darkness.

Chapter 31

Nina

What the hell?

I stood in a state of shock as my mother ran over to heal the areas Chase had bruised on my body. Normally, the warmth from this type of touch would've soothed me internally and externally, but it didn't. My entire being fell into a tragic state of numbness.

"It's all right. He's out," my father said, still calm as ever. "Jeff and Steve. A hand please."

The men hauled Chase's limp, lifeless body up the stairs and into his bedroom while I stared blankly at the wall, slumping onto the couch. Orifiel's warning about hearing voices began to play on a loop.

This is no good. Nothing positive can come from it.

Chase had become a ticking timebomb with no kill switch. I felt helpless and totally useless. Love alone wasn't going to save him this time or accomplish a damn thing. The dream from two nights ago coupled with Chase's outburst was terrifying—a terrifying warning to be exact.

Hold up a second. In the dream Chase was alive, beaten up, but still breathing and moving. Vincent, though angry with Chase, used me as bait to convince Chase to become a full-on Demon. If that's the case and the vision is a form of reality, Vincent's visits into Chase's head didn't work. If it did, Vincent wouldn't have come after me. Chase can effectively fight Vincent's hold, but who knows when the vision is destined to become a reality? How much time do we have?

My mind raced, desperately calculating various scenarios and forms of logic until my father reappeared in the living room. He took a seat beside me, ripping me back to the here and now.

"Dad." There were too many questions which required answers, but "Dad," was all I could manage.

"I gave Chase a sedative which should help him calm down and sleep. This transformation he's going through is rough. We were born into this with our gifts always present. Chase wasn't. Powers and abilities are growing and developing inside of his Mortal shell, but eventually everything will level off, and a new version of normal will be born from within him. He'll be all right. Once he wakes in the morning we'll discuss where we should go from here," my father informed.

"You're not kicking him out, are you?" Would my father do that? No. No way. He'd never do such a thing to someone in need, especially not to Chase. Or would he? Had all of this become too much for everyone?

"Not at all. We certainly can't force Chase to stay, but he's more than welcome to live here for as long as he'd like. That will never change."

"I need some air. I'll be outside. Don't follow me." With that firm declaration, I walked out of the front door.

"If we ever cross paths again, Vincent, I'll destroy you myself—bare hands and all. That's a threat and a promise, you bastard," I hissed angrily up at the sky.

"There are about a thousand Angels who already have dibs on killing Vincent, Gabriel being first on that list. I, right after," Orifiel said, pulling me behind a tree.

"Hey. Happy Christmas, love," he added, flashing a devilish smile, pushing me against the bark, and locking me in place with his hands.

"Orifiel." His presence provided instant relief. Wrapping my arms around his neck, my fingers dug into him, squeezing tightly. Orifiel's touch and soul melding with mine quieted my anxiety. It could make even the worst wrong appear right. It didn't matter how or why this occurred, as long as it always did.

He held me close in his powerfully strong arms for a few seconds before pulling away. "What are you doing out here alone mumbling like a crazy person?"

"Things are getting worse."

"Things often get worse before they get better," he offered. "Want to talk about it?"

"Yes, but not here." With my extended family still hanging around, probably being nosey over what happened, it wasn't safe or private enough to discuss anything.

"Okay, where?"

"Come on," I said, grabbing Orifiel's hand, and leading the way to the empty schoolyard.

"Here, put this on," Orifiel spoke, taking his red hooded sweatshirt off and handing it to me.

"Now you're going to be cold."

"You're welcome." He paused, raising an eyebrow, and pulling the zipper up once I'd put the jacket on, "The elements don't bother me. I'm already dead. Can't catch a chill."

"Good point and thank you." Plopping on a swing, I stuck my tongue out at him in a joking fashion.

"What's up, love?" he asked, sitting on the adjacent swing, deliberately swaying into mine. The action reminded me of something Steve would've done.

"I had another nightmare and Vincent's back in Chase's head. My father had to drug him to get him to stop raging."

"Whoa. You just said a mouthful there, sister," Orifiel said, trying to keep what should've been a tense moment light. "Start from the beginning and we'll figure it out from there. Take your time. Don't leave anything out."

This purge of new information needed to be delivered as quickly as possible because even though my family was currently distracted, it wouldn't stay like that for long. Eventually, someone would look for me.

It felt good not having to hold back, to speak freely with someone who listened without doubt or interruption.

"That's not too bad," Orifiel said.

"Seriously? Not too bad?"

Did he not hear what I just said?

"Okay, well, yeah, it is bloody horrible, but what do you want me to say? Everybody panic? We're all going to die? Not going to do that because there's an answer *and* a solution to every problem. Just because we might not know what that is right now, Michael will. We'll figure this out together."

"Together, huh?" An over exaggerated eye roll ensued.

Ha! Yeah, right.

"Yes, love, together. As in you and me, and obviously with some help from Michael, but primarily you and me. I'm here for you. Didn't I prove that yesterday? We're friends and our destinies are strongly intertwined."

"What's that supposed to mean?"

"It means you and me have a lot to do before our story is complete. Spoiler alert—it never is."

"Like what?" Orifiel's words caused a spike in curiosity.

"I can't tell you," he answered. His head hung low. His eyes stared at the ground. Whatever the secret, keeping it to himself caused visible frustration and torment which made wanting to know more intriguing.

"Why?"

Keep asking questions. In due course he'll slip a hint or provide a clue of sorts.

"There are rules which cannot be broken. Michael wasn't exactly thrilled over us snogging, but he let it slide. I can't disappoint him again."

"What did Michael say?"

"Aside from, '*don't do that again, Son,*' I can't share anything else."

"Orifiel," I started, getting up, pulling him off of the swing, and intertwining our fingers. "Can you see the future?"

"Can you read the stars?"

"Like constellations and stuff like that? A little."

"Reading stars is completely different than looking for pretty pictures in the night sky."

"Well then, what is it and why do you ask?"

"Star reading is fairly in-depth and very difficult to explain. Impossible to teach. Either you can or cannot. It's a secondary gift of sorts. I can, so yes, because of that, the future is clear to me. The stars will shift at times for various reasons therefore changing certain impending details, but what's read is never a lie."

"What do the stars say about me?" Breath caught in

the back of my throat.

"I'd love to share that information with you, but I can't. I'm sorry." Orifiel's voice was strained.

Emotions ranging from distress, to curiosity, to hope, coursed within me. What did Orifiel know?

"Please don't be scared. What's to come is glorious and filled with much love and joy. It's just going to be a slightly bumpy road getting there, but I'll be with you the entire time. You'll be fine."

"Are you part of my future? Like a key player in it?"

"I have a sizeable role in it actually. Before you ask, we'll always be close, best mates, though there'll be a brief period when you'll wish for me to piss off. It'll pass. Don't worry." He grinned at the thought.

"How's your brother?" If the subject wasn't changed, thoughts of what was to come, destiny and all that crap would drive me mad with inquisitiveness or dread over the unknown. Maybe knowing the future wasn't such a good idea, but if we continued this conversation, I'd either break him, trick him into telling me things he shouldn't, or I'd end up hearing my fate which Orifiel may deem as great, but in reality might not be. Some things should be left unsaid. This was one of them.

"He's good." A slight exhausted sigh was detected before Orifiel unconvincingly replied.

"Try that one again, but this time, make me believe you." I smirked.

"He's a complicated bloke."

"What's complicated about him?"

"Oh, lots of things. Another story for another time."

"Is Gabriel like you?"

"He's *nothing* like me."

"Would I like him?"

"As you American's like to say, *I plead the fifth*."

"What's that supposed to mean?"

"It means, my love, you better get back home. Keep strong. Should you have another vision, call for me. Things will get better. Have some faith in my sentiments."

"I trust *and* believe you, Orifiel. I don't know why, I just do. If you say things are going to get better, they will."

He hesitated, then took my face in his hands. "That's my good girl," he whispered before kissing my forehead.

"It was fuzzy," I blurted out remembering a key detail which had been left out while recounting the nightmare from earlier.

"Huh? What's fuzzy?"

"The dream. The edges of each scene were blurry. Usually, everything is crisp, rather sharp. Do you think that means something?"

"Yeah. It means you didn't see the entire future because Vincent's altering the plan. You saw part of the old plan and part of the new undecided one. It's not necessarily a bad thing. Our future is constantly changing through our actions and decisions, though we typically end up where we're destined to be. Your subconscious mind already knows what it wants and how it intends to obtain it. It's simply a matter of mapping. I'll tell Michael. Don't worry about it. When you see a sharp vision you need to tell me straight away."

"Of course."

Placing his arm around my shoulder we walked home, saying our goodbyes quickly. The house had finally cleared of all relatives. Quietly sneaking up the stairs to Chase's room I sat next to his sleeping body. Hot angry tears flowed freely as my fingers stroked his hair.

You have to have faith, Nina. Faith in the fact you and Chase will beat this. Faith that sunnier skies await you both. You can do this and you will not let Orifiel down. Lean on Orifiel right now and let Chase lean on you. Don't let Chase or anyone other than Orifiel see you sweat. Stay strong. The rest will fall into place. It's time for you to be the rock.

I took a deep breath, inhaling the positive and exhaling the negative.

"Nothing will break us," I swore before curling up beside him and seeking comfort from our silent closeness.

****

I must've fallen asleep on Chase's bed because when I woke, we were tangled together with me half on the floor. My neck and back ached. Chase remained perfectly still. The alarm clock read seven. Quietly and carefully, the untying and getting ready for the day process commenced. Returning to his room with my laptop after I showered, revealed whatever he'd been given last night knocked him straight into the land of nod. After a few minutes of checking e-mail and messing around on social media, a personal message bubble popped up on the screen from Tori. Part of me missed seeing her as often as we used to, but the other part, a much larger part, didn't. Tori could be a great person when she wanted to be, but often only a spiteful, arrogant version of her was visible. Tim had a lot to do with that. On the surface he appeared a somewhat decent guy, but underneath the charming exterior an abusive jerk who spent the better part of freshman year at college pickling his liver by consuming massive quantities of alcohol existed. According to Tori after Tim's last stint in rehab he'd been cured and was back to being the perfect boyfriend. I hoped and prayed this to be true. Heaven help that guy if he ever touched her in a harmful way again. This time I wouldn't let it go.

Once a loser, always a loser, but it's not your circus or monkeys to deal with. You have your own flying monkeys to tame.

"Hey, you. You're up early," Tori wrote.

"Yeah. How was your Christmas?" Tori being awake at this ungodly hour wasn't a surprise.

"Great. Tim got me these beautiful earrings. Rumor has it *you* got a *ring* from Chase."

"Jules must've told you. It's nothing really. Just a promise ring," I typed, not feeling up to elaborating on my personal life at the moment. It's not that the ring wasn't gush and brag worthy, the relationship rut we were in had stifled any possible enthusiasm.

"Still, a diamond is a diamond."

"True."

"What did Chase get you?" Tori fished, overly concerned with the value of material items.

"A necklace. I'll show you next time we see each other."

"How about tonight?"

"I don't know, Tori. Chase is a touch under the weather."

Not completely a fib.

"Aw, come on. We haven't seen each other in ages. Jules is probably free."

"Maybe. I'll call you later."

"I'm not taking no for an answer. *I'll* reach out to

Jules and set it up. Let's meet at the mall, back entrance, and let's say around seven. See you then."

Before I had a chance to respond, Tori had signed off.

Crap.

There was no way would Chase be up for hanging out with friends tonight and honestly, I wasn't either. Granted we hadn't seen them in a long time—running into Tori at the mall didn't count, and it would be great to see everyone before they went back to school, but the timing was off, way off. However, if we didn't meet Tori's demands, she'd show up at the house, tracking me down anyway. This defined a no-win situation.

"Baby?" Chase's groggy voice broke my deep thoughts.

"How do you feel?" I inquired, holding my breath.

"Fine, I think. What happened?" he asked, sitting up slowly.

"You kind of went bat crap crazy last night. My dad had to sedate you," I answered, trying not to make it seem like such a big deal, but being honest at the same time. There was no reason for Chase to feel bad or get set off. He'd only woken and was probably confused and probably feeling crummy enough. The condensed version of the truth worked best.

"Wow. So that wasn't a dream then. How bad?"

"Not as bad as you think. You flipped the dining room table and broke a few things."

"Did anyone get hurt?" Trepidation filled his eyes.

"No."

"Do you think this has anything to do with my abilities growing, or do you think I'm going crazy?"

"You're not going crazy, Chase."

"In your mind you believe it's completely normal that Vincent's voice lives inside of my head?" he questioned sarcastically.

"Well no, but it doesn't have to. You have to fight the evil inside. Once you defeat it, you'll be all right."

"Easier said than done."

"You have to try."

"What do you think I was doing last night? It worked, but obviously not well enough because if it had, nothing would've been destroyed."

"It's a work in progress. You have to keep doing it every time Vincent pops in for a visit. Eventually, he'll leave, never to return. You'll get better at it."

"I feel like an ass."

"Don't, Chase. Everyone understands what you're going through. No one is faulting you for it."

"If you say so."

"Hey, listen. We kind of have plans tonight. The timing is awful and I really don't feel like going either, but you know Tori and how demanding she can be. We can cancel if you want," I said rapidly, attempting to change the subject to break the tension.

"No, it's okay. What time and where?"

"Seven. We're meeting her, Tim, Jules, and Mark at the mall."

"All right. My errands shouldn't take too long," Chase replied, getting up off of the bed, and digging through a dresser drawer.

"Where are you going?"

"A few places. Nowhere special."

"Want me to join you?"

"I'd rather you didn't. Family stuff. It's personal."

"You don't have to hide, Chase," I comforted,

fearing there were no errands, but rather only a strong desire to not be around anyone who witnessed evil Chase's rampage.

"I'm not hiding, baby," he defended, kissing my forehead, and taking off down the hallway to the bathroom.

He's up to something and damn it, I'm going to figure it out. We share a connection and it's definitely telling me to be suspicious.

Chapter 32

Chase

Everyone lies and besides, I did have a few errands to run, but said errands certainly wouldn't last all day. Truth be told, I missed personal space and privacy. Back home, no one really bothered me aside from my mother. That luxury simply did not exist in the Luther household. Nina, Jack, or Ellen always wanted something. Nina wanted attention. Jack wanted time to work on my gifts, and Ellen always needed a chore boy. I obliged because they'd welcomed me into their home, but most days, being left alone would've been nice.

Today, I'd scope out apartments and fingers tightly crossed, rent one. Nina could've tagged along. After all, at some point we'd be living together, not anytime soon, but soon enough. However, there was nothing left to say, and she'd harp on last night which held no interest for me. It happened. It would be processed, addressed, and corrected. No one would hold it against me. How could they? Well, maybe Steve would, but who *really* cared? After a few quick pleasantries with Jack and Ellen, neither of whom brought up anything negative other than asking me how I felt, I took off.

Armed with a newspaper and a strong desire to find a place to live, the local coffeehouse was the perfect place to go—though my peace and quiet were interrupted by the buzzing of my damn cell phone. It was Bristol.

Damn it. Go away.

Hitting the ignore button got old, fast. This girl wasn't taking the hint. Shutting the phone off would be a stupid move. What if Nina needed me? Bristol had to be blocked. No contact needed to be enforced. Feeling bullied into taking this drastic action wasn't sitting well with me because she meant no harm, but life, especially mine, didn't have any more room for another complication. Twelve missed calls and one text message in less than an hour was insane. Before the final cutoff, I clicked on the message. My heart sank.

'I know you're avoiding me and that's fine because I'm used to it, but I need help.'

Immediately my thumb touched the dial button.

"Hey."

"Finally," Bristol snapped.

"What's up?" Ignoring her nasty tone was best because arguing with anyone wasn't going to happen today.

"I can't really talk long. My parents are close by. Chase, things have gotten really bad here." She sobbed heavily.

"Don't cry, beautiful. What's doing? Talk to me." Within a split second the old Chase, the one who adored this girl, crept back inside of me.

"Everything."

"If you don't tell me what everything is I can't help."

"Mom and Dad dumped a ton money into private investigators to find Sean, and now we're broke. We have to leave Savannah because we can't afford to live here. A realtor is coming over later to talk with them about selling the house. If we move to Montana to live with my grandparents Sean won't know where to find us when he comes back."

"What can I do to help?"

"Do you have ten thousand dollars you don't need lying around that we can use to pay our bills and catch up on the mortgage?" she scoffed.

"Actually, yes. Call me in two hours."

"What? No, Chase. I was kidding. Blowing off some steam."

"Bristol, call me in two hours. You always want to go head to head with me, but this isn't up for debate or discussion. Do what I say for once. Don't challenge me. I'm not in the mood."

"Chase," she started.

"Case closed, beautiful."

Last summer I'd made a promise to be there if a need should arise. Even though Bristol wasn't my problem anymore, I'd honor the commitment. She, nor her family, deserved to suffer. They'd been through enough losing Sean, and were now dumping money into finding him. Perhaps my motives were guilt induced because I knew the truth. Sean wasn't coming home, but that didn't matter. Bristol's family recouping their financial loss did.

Folding the newspaper and downing the last of my coffee, I headed to the bank. After withdrawing the cash, which took considerably shorter than expected, I went to the library and buried myself in a random, empty section of the stacks, unfolded the classified section and continued to search for an apartment waiting for Bristol to call. About an hour later, she finally did. There was never any doubt she wouldn't, but a small part of me suggested otherwise. Perhaps wishful thinking this nightmare wasn't real.

"Chase?"

"Who else would it be, Bristol?"

"I don't know. Maybe you're with your girlfriend."

"No. I'm alone."

"Now what?"

"Meet me."

"Where?"

"South University by the administration building in a half hour. Do you know where that is?"

"Yes, but Chase," she began.

"Hey, I want to help. Stop worrying." Hopefully, she pick up on the soothing tone I'd used and would take her high energy level down a few notches.

"You're a good man, Chase James." Her smile could be heard through the receiver.

"We both know that's a bold face lie. Half hour. South University. Administration building. See you there."

For the second time today apartment hunting had to be placed on hold. Thirty minutes later, my emotionally drained body leaned against the administration building, clutching the envelope containing the money.

"Hey," Bristol said, throwing herself into my arms. The moment her body touched mine, the fragrant smell of her strawberry shampoo took me back to easier days. My eyes closed as I inhaled deeply several times.

"Hey, yourself," I said, pulling away. Immediately, my attention drew to the coat she wore—my old varsity jacket. She'd kept it and still wore it which caused an internal debate to occur over whether to feel flattered or worried. "Nice jacket."

"Yeah it is, isn't it?" She laughed.

"Where'd you get it?" I joked, playing into the game.

"Oh, some guy gave it to me."

"Some guy, huh?"

"How are you feeling?"

"All right, but we're not here to discuss me. What's going on with you?"

Chapter 33

Nina

I knew something had been off with Chase, and now the proof was right in front of me. Following him and hiding alongside a nearby building wasn't right, but necessary. Consumed with shame and guilt over spying on him, I decided to head home. I would've made it to the parking lot if his phone hadn't rung, stopping me dead in my tracks. Curiosity as to who called got the better of me. Chase's eyes appeared sincere, like he really cared about the girl he'd met up with. The two sat on a nearby bench, chatting in low, inaudible tones.

She was attractive. Loose, almond curls cascaded over her shoulders. Sunglasses hid her facial features, but the girl's body appeared slender, toned in all of the right places, and short. Pulling a man's high school varsity jacket tighter around her torso for warmth gave off an air of innocence.

Chase slid next to the girl, placing an arm around her shoulders, voiding any space between them. She rested her head on his chest and laughed softly. There were no words in the English language to describe how I felt. Part of me wanted to jump out and attack them both, while the other part wanted to lie down and die.

What is he doing and why?

Who knew how much time had passed? It didn't matter. I continued to watch in horror. It was like seeing a car wreck. You didn't want to look, but your mind made you. Their body language showed an intimate relationship existed, which really tested my gag reflexes and personal restraint. Chase handed the girl the envelope he left the bank with and stood. Both moved closer to where I'd concealed myself. Their conversation could now be clearly heard.

"Thank you. You have no idea how much this helps. I owe you," the girl said.

"No, you don't. Call me if you need anything, anything at all, even if it's just to talk," Chase said, tracing her jaw with his thumb—the same way he did with me.

"I promise. Same here. Does your girlfriend know about any of this?"

"No. Let's keep it that way. This is between you and me. Tell your parents whatever you'd like, but leave my name out of it. Okay?"

"That's fine. I'll make something up. They're so deep in the ozone layer they won't ask many questions anyway. Totally not worried about it. Nice ring."

Chase glanced down at his left hand. "Thanks." He smirked.

"Is that *her* way of telling the world she owns you?"

"Maybe." Chase shrugged, nervously playing with the piece of jewelry.

"It's serious then?"

"It's complicated. I better get going."

"Do you have to go, or do you maybe want to grab some coffee?"

"Sorry. Got plans. Can't break them. Trust me, I wish I could."

"Oh yeah? What are you doing?"

"Some triple date thing with Jules Warner, Tori Wylie, and their boyfriends," Chase answered. His eyes rolled.

The girl's facial expression instantly soured. "*Tori Wylie*."

"Let's not go there, darling," Chase warned, shaking his head. His once slight southern drawl had evolved into a full-blown accent. He truly sounded like a person born and raised in the Deep South and I didn't like it.

"Don't go. Tell them you made other plans, and spend time with me."

"Hanging out with you would be considerably more fun, but my hands are tied, beautiful."

"Coffee. Saturday. I'm not taking no for an answer. I'll call you," she said in a cute playful manner.

"Deal," Chase agreed, and winked.

He pulled the girl into a tight embrace, kissed the top of her head, and inhaled deeply. Placing his hand on the small of her back, he escorted them to the parking lot. Chase watched the girl's green, shit box, hatchback pull out of the lot and onto the street, leaving moments later himself.

What the hell just happened?

Once enveloped inside the comfort of my car, I reached for my phone.

"Hello?" a familiar voice answered.

"Jules, it's me. You need to listen *very* carefully and think *really* hard about this." My voice and hands shook.

"Are you all right?"

"Do you know a girl who's about our age with almond colored, wavy hair, cute, short, and knows Chase?"

"I don't know, Nina. Why?"

"Think, Jules. Think."

"What's going on?" she demanded.

"He was with her."

"Huh?"

"Chase."

"Chase was with the girl you just described? Nina, it's obvious you're upset, but you need to develop this a bit more because you're not making much sense."

"Yes. I overheard part of their conversation."

"And?"

"Chase met this girl on the South campus by the administration building after she called him earlier, and he handed her an envelope. They knew each other and seemed close. A little too close. When Chase told this person about our plans tonight, she got bent after hearing Tori's name. What's worse is he suggested hanging out with her would be more fun than with me. Oh, and whoever the bitch is, she mocked the ring I gave Chase, and you know what? He allowed it. He welcomed it. He told her our relationship was *complicated.* What does that even mean? Please don't repeat any of this." Jules wouldn't, but at that moment sadness and shame overrode my anger. Chase was more than likely cheating on me, which in turn, aside from being the most hurtful thing one could ever do to someone, was embarrassing and belittling.

"Your secret is safe. You should know by now that I'd never betray your trust, or anyone else's for that matter. A lot of girls fit that description around here. Half of the girls in Savannah are blonde, short, cute, and if they went to our high school, dislike Tori for one reason or another. Can you tell me anything else?"

"No."

"All right, we'll have to find out more about this mystery chick then. We'll figure it out." She paused. "Chase never struck me as the type of guy who'd cheat. There has to be more to this. I'm sure of it."

"The two of them are meeting up for coffee tomorrow. Any chance you'd come along and stalk the situation with me?"

"Normally, no, but for you, yes. Guess this means you're not coming out tonight?"

"I don't know. Probably not. I wouldn't want to torture Chase by having him pretend to want to be out in public with me."

"You should come, Nina. If you're going to play this off until tomorrow, you need to act like you didn't see anything. That means keeping your plans, unless you want to tell Chase what you witnessed and see what happens from there. Be warned, if you choose the latter, don't start spraying him with verbal bullets and accusations. That's how wars begin. You have to speak calmly, which I don't believe you're capable of currently. There's a reason behind his actions and though it looks bad right now, it may be something harmless and innocent. You have to try to keep that in mind."

"You're right. There's no way we could have a conversation without me blowing up. The thought of looking at Chase and having to pretend everything is fine is making me feel physically ill."

"It could be something benign. You quite possibly are getting yourself worked up for nothing."

"Maybe."

"Are you going to be okay?"

"Once this is all cleared up, sure. Until then, no. I'm almost home. Thanks for listening."

"No problem. See you later?"

"Yeah."

My eyes glanced at the speedometer. The car was traveling well over the legal speed limit. My attention was definitely not on the task of driving. This inner rage coursed in angry waves. The more I tried to focus, the more images of Chase and that girl kept popping into my head feeding the beast within me. Without any real proof I'd already decided he lied, cheated, and deserved to be dumped immediately. A small, sensible, rational part of me struggled to convince me that appearances needed to be kept up until definite answers were had. What pissed me off the most was I got the shitty Chase—the moody, sulking, grumpy, fuming guy, and she got the happy, sweet, romantic good version.

Maybe he was looking for an out, but if we were destined to be together, how could that even be possible?

"Where have you been? You know you're not allowed to leave the house alone. Chase got home a few minutes ago and he had no clue where you were either," my father scolded the moment I stepped foot in the door.

Damn it, but at least the cheater is around.

Being on lockdown sucked. The freedom to come and go as I pleased was sorely missed.

"I had a few things to do today and you and Mom were busy. I hate bothering you guys." An obvious lie which hopefully came across as believable.

"It must've been really important because you didn't say goodbye or leave a note, plus your cell phone is off. Your mother must've left a dozen messages. We were really worried about you."

"I'm sorry, Dad. The battery must be dead. It won't happen again."

"It better not."

"It won't. I promise."

After apologizing profusely to my mother, it was time to get ready to head out for the evening, though cancelling would've been a better option, especially for Chase who obviously held no interest in being with me. He'd made that crystal clear to his *girlfriend* earlier. The thought of them made my eyes close tightly and my head shake as if the silly gesture would cause the image to vanish for good. Deciding to utilize a passive aggressive approach, I styled my hair with loose curls like the bitch Chase had been screwing around with wore hers. Maybe that would make him want me. It all made sense now why he had no interest in me physically. If you're getting it from someone else you certainly don't need what's waiting for you at home. Do you?

"Hey, baby. Ready? It's almost seven. We probably should've already left. Your hair looks great by the way," Chase said, standing in the bathroom doorframe.

For what seemed like the hundredth time in less than two hours, that girl and Chase danced around my brain, but this time my imagination had them kissing.

"Ugh. Gross," came out, coupled with an icy shiver.

"Huh?"

"Nothing. Let's get this over with," I snapped, walking past him, and down the stairs.

"Mom. Dad. We're leaving. We'll be back later and yes, I have my cell phone. It's on and fully charged."

"Be careful, kids. Have fun," my mother called from the laundry room.

I slammed the car door shut. Sitting ramrod straight I crossed my arms tightly against my chest, making sure to keep any expression other than neutral at bay. Initially,

Chase didn't speak a word. He kept his eyes on the road, but the silence finally wore him down.

"Why so quiet, baby?"

"Got nothing to say."

"Why don't you tell me what's wrong now this way we can deal with it, I can apologize, and not have whatever it is screw up the entire night," he replied calmly.

"Does it really matter? It's not like you want to be doing this anyway."

"Yes, it does matter, and yes, I do want to be doing this with you."

Liar. That's not what you told little Miss Goldilocks earlier.

"Fine. Then everything is great."

"Is it your time of the month or something?"

"Excuse me?" I hissed.

"You're acting all moody, I just figured—"

I cut him off mid stupid thought. "Just so you know for future reference, you should never ask a girl that. It's rude. And, no. It's not. You're not the only one around here who's allowed to be sullen."

"Sorry."

"Yeah, right. Sure you are. And don't even think about using your divine gift on me," I warned, making sure to stop any future manipulation of the situation. Recently, on several occasions, he used his mind control gift to sway conversations in his favor.

We sat in silence for the rest of the ride. Normally I would've grabbed his hand the second we got out of the car, but not today. It didn't matter if he walked behind or beside me.

"Ni. Over here," Tori called.

"Hey." A fake squeal forced its way out.

Holy over compensation for not wanting people to know you and Chase are in the middle of an argument and possibly breaking up. Take it down a notch so you're not as transparent as tissue paper.

"You look great," she said, throwing her arms around my neck.

"As do you. Hey, Tim. What's going on?"

"Same old, same old. Where's Chase?" Tim questioned.

"Back there, somewhere," I said, pointing vaguely behind us. "Where are Jules and Mark?"

"At the restaurant, grabbing a table. We stayed behind waiting for y'all because we knew you'd be late." Tori Wylie, a girl who always came equipped with a jab.

"Well, let's go find them then," I said, trying to come across as genuinely excited, which proved difficult.

Chase caught up and was now awkwardly speaking with Tim. It couldn't be more obvious the two harbored deep distain for the other.

Before we arrived a Mexican restaurant had been decided on. It wouldn't have been my first choice, but it would do. Tori insisted that she and I take the ten-minute ride to the restaurant together and Tim go with Chase allowing us time to catch up. Happily I agreed because this would annoy Chase. Being stuck alone with Tim would drive him nuts. The trip was short and filled with happy, light conversation almost making me forget the hurt and upset that had settled in hours earlier. Finding Mark and Jules already seated at a table when we arrived provided relief. The sooner this night ended, the better.

"These are the earrings Tim gave me for Christmas.

You have permission to be jealous," Tori cooed.

"They are gorgeous," I exclaimed, but I wasn't really impressed by the gold love knots. They were ordinary. Chances were Tim grabbed the first thing he saw or had his mother pick them out. Tim never struck me as the giving type. A taker, yes. Giver, no. How could someone as selfish as him, someone who often showed others Tori was his lowest priority, have any form of a loving emotion within his heart?

"Really nice, Tori," Jules added.

"I know," Tori said casually. "Ni, show me this ring Jules told me about and the necklace Chase got for you."

"You know? I took the ring off before showering and I forgot to put it back on, and the necklace didn't go with this outfit. Next time."

Chase shot me a dangerous look from across the table. For the rest of dinner Tori dominated the conversation. Chase, Mark, and Tim carried on their own socialness leaving us girls alone. Tori decided after we left the restaurant we should hit up this new club which recently opened downtown. It really didn't matter that no one else had any desire to go, Tori ruled, and complaining wouldn't do any good. It would make the spoiled southern belle have an all-out tantrum and who really wanted to deal with it and hear that?

Tori was beautiful and genetically lucky, unlike me. Tall with long, flowing, chocolate brown hair framing a perfectly flawless face, coupled with rich, sparkling honey-colored eyes and legs that went on for days, made her lethal to the opposite sex. All of the guys at our high school used to drool over her classic beauty. All but Chase for some reason.

This time Jules insisted the two of us ride to the club

together. Neither Mark nor Chase objected which infuriated me. I wanted Chase to be as uncomfortable and miserable as humanly possible.

"You need to calm your attitude," Jules warned the second we got into her car.

"No idea what you're talking about. I've done nothing wrong. Hell, I haven't even said a word to the cheater."

"That's the problem. You're not acting like you. Everyone sees it. We'll get to the bottom of this tomorrow, but for tonight, chill."

"I am being *chill*."

"No, you're not. Stop it, okay?" she said.

"Wow, Jules. I've never heard you get pissed off before."

"Yeah, well, sorry. It happens from time to time."

"This sucks. It hurts like a bitch. Every time my mind lets it go, some random image of them pops up. Then my stomach turns and all of the pain comes rushing back."

"For all you know you could be jumping to conclusions, making something out of nothing. Let's wait and see what happens, *then* deal with it once we know for sure."

Easy for you to say. Mark isn't the one in question.

"You're right." She wasn't, but this was one of those no-win conversations.

"We're here. You're going to relax, right?" Jules asked nervously.

"Yes. I promise."

"Fake it till you make it. I can't imagine what you must be feeling, but you have to at least try."

"Okay. Got it." A forced smile grew. Hopefully this

gesture would be enough to convince her I'd be good for the rest of the evening.

"Thank you," she replied with a hint of uneasiness.

The club was packed. Making our way to the dance floor was harder than expected. Once there, Jules's advice of feigning normalcy came to mind causing me to grab hold of Chase and dance with him. He responded by pulling me close. It felt bittersweet being held that tightly. I wanted to forgive and forget everything, but I couldn't. Chances were all he saw was a pissed off girlfriend who was acting crazy, *not* the life missing from my eyes. How could he? He'd become the most self-centered person lately. I felt wounded, alone, and horribly self-conscious even though Chase stood smiling inches away.

Around two in the morning, we said our goodbyes in the parking lot, promising to make time to see each other again before we had to return to school for spring semester.

Fat chance of that happening. Tomorrow by this time I'll probably be single again.

"Call or text me in the morning to let me know what's going on," Jules whispered.

"Of course."

"One way or another we'll get to the bottom of this."

Not knowing how much longer this charade could be kept up, closing my eyes and feigning exhaustion to avoid a conversation while Chase drove us back home was the safest option.

"Did you have a good time?" Chase asked.

"Yeah," I said, forcing a yawn.

"Baby, you've been awfully quiet tonight. What's going on? If I did or said something to upset you, please tell me. Causing you to feel bad is never my intention. If that's the case, allow me the opportunity to apologize and make it up to you." His words appeared sincere.

Though my heart wanted to purge its secrets, it was too late to embark upon a weighty discussion. "It's nothing really. I'm tired and under stress too."

"Do you want to talk about it?"

"No."

"If you change your mind, let me know. You know where to find me."

I wanted to say something clever and witty letting him know I knew about his girl on the side, but silence fell because tomorrow was another day. I'd have to be patient and wait until then to discover exactly how ugly the truth would be.

Chapter 34

Nina

Making sure to wake before Chase was the hard part. Even though he'd be asleep, I still set the alarm for five in the morning. There was no chance in Hell I'd risk missing the opportunity to bust him. By six, I sat in the living room, dressed and ready to go at a moment's notice. Anyone entering or exiting the house had to pass through this area. Around ten, Jules showed up pretending to have some sort of random problem she needed to discuss privately. We sat in my room looking out of the window and watching for Chase to make a move. At noon, his car started up. We took off down the stairs waiting a few seconds before heading out. My father was at the hospital and mother was out shopping. The coast was clear.

I slid down in the passenger seat to avoid being seen. Thankfully, it wasn't for long. Chase pulled into a local coffeehouse parking lot and reached for his phone. For the next few minutes he sat waiting. Finally, the girl arrived. My heart skipped a beat as she hopped out of her hatchback and knocked on Chase's window. The two shared a long, intimate embrace the moment he stepped out of his car. Hand in hand, they walked into the café.

"We have to go in there," I hissed.

"How do we do that without being seen?" Jules questioned.

“Think.”

After a pregnant pause she spoke. “Come on.”

I followed Jules inside allowing her to push me into a corner booth.

“Stay here and don’t move an inch, Nina.”

Jules walked to the counter and ordered drinks. Her head darted from side to side sizing up the place. Calmly, she made her way back to the table, handed me a large green tea lemonade, and grabbed my arm, guiding me to a booth not too far from where Chase and the girl sat, but out of their line of sight. The white noise coming from the patrons proved a major hindrance while trying to overhear their conversation.

“Can you hear anything?” I whispered.

“Yeah. Be quiet and hold this,” Jules said, shoving a newspaper at me.

“Do you know her?”

“She went to our high school. Now hush.”

After a few minutes Jules spoke again. “They’re catching up. Nothing serious. She asked how last night went. Chase complained a bit about Tori and Tim, but who doesn’t?”

“Is there any flirting?”

“It’s hard to say. Everyone flirts differently.”

My head pounded as I sat there pretending to read the paper. Beads of sweat formed on my forehead as surges of adrenaline coursed inside of my every cell. I wanted to get up and go postal, but I couldn’t. All that could be done was to stay seated, ask questions, fidget, and pray for the best.

“What’s going on now?” I asked nervously.

“Not much. They’re chatting like friends. Son of a bitch,” Jules spat.

"What?"

"He's holding her hand and it looks like they might kiss," she said. Her tone revealed tremendous disappointment.

"That's it," I hissed allowing the fury roaring inside of me to take over.

"No. Sit your butt back down. Move an inch and I'll smack you."

Her sudden confidence was comforting. Jules's voice never rose over a certain pitch. Her attitude never hardened. Usually when calm people grew upset their target, in this case Chase and the girl, should fear them. It's the quiet ones one must always worry about, right?

It appeared time was moving backwards while I waited for an update. I was going out of my mind expecting the absolute worst.

"It looks like she went outside to get something. You need to go to the counter and order something, anything, and wait there until I come get you. I'm going over there to surprise Mr. James," Jules instructed.

"But the line is almost out the door."

"That's the point. Don't look at me at all. Look away or you'll ruin this. Got it?"

"Yeah."

"Go."

Taking a place at the end of the insanely long line and making sure my focus remained off of Chase was considerably harder than expected. I wanted him to see me and know his epic joke of a soul mate knew the truth.

One way or another I'll have the last laugh, Chase, and the joke will be on you.

Chapter 35

Chase

Sitting at a café having coffee with Bristol was wrong, but why did it feel so right? The relaxed mood and light conversation made the experience nice and rather enjoyable. Bristol seemed happy, an emotion she hardly ever showed when we were together. Well maybe not always. We met when we were kids, but I noticed her when I was a sophomore in high school. While hanging out at Sean's house one afternoon, Bristol came home from cheerleading practice. Her blonde hair had been pinned up in a high ponytail. We exchanged a brief smile before she disappeared into the kitchen. The moment Sean got up to go to the bathroom, I found her leaning against the fridge. Her right foot was bent, tapping on the stainless steel behind her. She was drinking a bottle of water and reading some chick magazine. I shouldn't have touched her, she was Sean's half-sister and he'd always been fiercely protective of the bond they shared, but I couldn't help myself. She was beautiful and I had to have her. A few weeks later we were sneaking around seeing each other, trying to hide our budding romance from Sean. We were successful until he caught us making out in their basement. Initially, he'd been annoyed, but then Jules Warner moved to town. From that point forward, Sean spent most of his time obsessing over Jules, and leaving us alone. We were the perfect couple. Captain of the baseball and lacrosse teams dating a varsity cheerleader. You couldn't find a more all-American, apple-pie couple. Things were great at first, but then Bristol started getting possessive and controlling. Originally, her insecurities were endearing. She was gorgeous and I'd fallen in love. Because of that, I actively ignored all of the red flags. As time passed, her actions and behaviors became progressively worse. Way too often she'd accuse me of cheating, lying, or of hiding something when no such act had been committed. Enough was enough and one night I let her go. On my way home from our last argument as a couple, the accident happened.

"Chase? Are you okay?" Bristol questioned.

"Huh? Oh yeah. Just thinking."

"About?" She raised an eyebrow, smiling coyly.

"Remember the game against that high school from Atlanta?"

"Oh God, yes. Remember how we celebrated your bottom of the ninth, game winning, grand slam?"

"Yes," I whispered, and winked.

"Damn it," she cursed, looking down at her phone. "It's Mom. I'll be right back."

"Hey there, Chase. How's it going?" a familiar voice spoke sharply moments after Bristol left the café.

Slowly, I looked up to find Jules standing over the table.

Holy crap. Why the hell is she here? Play it smooth.

"Jules. What's up?"

If things couldn't get any worse, Bristol re-entered the building.

Damn it.

"Who's your little friend, Chase?" Jules questioned,

not breaking eye contact once. Her curt behavior caught me off guard. Jules had always been as quiet as a church mouse, but here she stood bold as brass.

"This is Bristol. Bristol, this is Jules."

Why is there never a hole deep enough to crawl inside of and die in when you really need one?

"Nice to meet you," Bristol said cheerfully.

Oh, sweetheart. If you only knew this girl is Nina's best friend you wouldn't be acting so chipper.

"Could you excuse us for a minute, please?" Jules snapped.

"Uh, okay. I'm going to go freshen up," Bristol said leery, leaving the table.

"Look to your left," Jules instructed.

"You've got to be kidding me," I hissed out of frustration and horror. Nina, girlfriend and soul mate, whom I'd been less than perfect with lately, was standing in line maybe fifty feet away from where we sat. A hot surge assaulted my neck causing noticeable small beads of sweat to form everywhere.

"I'll get Nina out of here *if* you tell me what the hell is going on," Jules demanded.

"Nothing is going on."

"Are you cheating?" she asked flat out, obviously not trusting me. Hell, I didn't even believe myself. Why should Jules or anyone else?

"No. Bristol is a friend. I'd never."

"Then why are you worried about Nina being here?"

"Jules, quite frankly I don't have time for this. If Nina sees me with a female friend, she'll freak out. It won't matter what's said. She'll jump to conclusions and a scene will follow shortly thereafter insuring the fact that none of us will ever be able to show our faces here again. We hit a rough patch and have been having some issues, which we're working on. It's complicated and honestly none of your business, but no matter how bad things might get between Nina and me, cheating on her would never be an option. Regardless of what's happening, we are in this together, for life."

Jules's facial expression softened. "Chase, it's great that you love Nina and see a future with her because she loves you too, but you can't be sneaking around with other girls, friends or not. Nina won't understand, even if it is innocent like you say."

"I miss normal," I whispered not knowing why I'd say that to Jules, someone oblivious to all things Angelic and Demonic. It unintentionally slipped out.

"All couples have their ups and downs."

"Please get Nina out of here. I promise I'll tell her about Bristol today."

"If you don't tell Nina, she'll find out eventually. Lies and deceit always rear their ugly heads at some point."

"I owe you."

"Make this right, be happy, and you won't owe me anything. Nina is like a sister. She loves you, all of you, even though you've been acting like a real jerk lately. She's been putting up with your crazy mood swings and standing by your side. I'm aware you're enduring some drama with your parents and it's been hard on you, but Nina deserves better. You know that. It's not okay that she walks around doubting herself—all of herself from intelligence to physical appearance. She's been stretched to the max these past few months. Step up. Tell and show her, her value in your life. I'll see you later," Jules said.

"You're right. She does and I will. But Jules, I love

Nina too. I'll make this right," I replied, meaning every word.

As promised, Jules quickly ushered Nina out of the café. My heart sank the second Bristol returned.

"I have to go," I said, standing.

"What's wrong? What happened? I thought we were having a good time. What did *Jules* want?" Bristol questioned in a snotty tone.

"Nina was here."

"So?"

"She's my girlfriend, Bristol. If Nina were to have seen me with you, it would've broken her heart. She doesn't deserve that, especially after the way I've been dumping on her."

"But I did?"

"I'm sorry for that. I've apologized numerous times, but I'm not paying for that mistake for the rest of my damn life."

"Mistake? Mistake! I loved you. I must be the biggest idiot ever because I still do. No. You know what? You're the idiot. You let me go and baby, there isn't another woman alive or dead who's better than me. Go to Hell, Chase James," Bristol spat, storming away.

Oh, I'm already there, beautiful.

"Had that coming. Definitely deserved it too," I mumbled to myself, picking up the two empty coffee cups, tossing them in the trash, and heading back to Nina's house to face an uncertain punishment.

Chapter 36

Nina

Still waiting in the long line, resisting the urge to steal a glance at Jules and Chase, my fingers clutched my cell phone so tightly it should've broken. Finally, Jules pulled me close and whispered, "Don't turn around. Just walk out the door. Got it?"

"Uh, huh."

She practically pushed me to the car, taking off before the doors were even fully closed.

"What the hell, Jules?"

"He's not cheating, and he's going to talk to you about whatever it is that's going on later," Jules informed.

"I'm sorry for dragging you into this." Some relief he hadn't been with the blonde chick was experienced.

"Why? You're my best friend, Nina. I don't want to see you get hurt. Besides, you'd do the same for me."

"You're mine too. I'll always have your back no matter what," I said, really wishing right then and there I could tell her everything about being a Mortal Angel, Chase being a Lost Soul, and how all of this was completely and totally stressing me out.

"Did you know the girl?"

"He introduced her as Bristol, but the name doesn't ring a bell. I vaguely remember seeing her around school. She wasn't in our grade."

"Tori." If Bristol went to our school, Tori would definitely know the scoop. For the first time ever, Tori's gift of gossip would come in handy.

"What about Tori?"

"How much do you want to bet Tori will know who she is?"

"True, but Nina, tread lightly. Don't make Tori think something's going on or else you'll end up being her next piece of juicy gossip."

Ignoring Jules's advice, I dialed Tori's number praying she'd pick up.

Damn. Voicemail.

"Hey, it's Nina. Give me a call when you get a chance, okay? Talk soon."

"It's probably for the best she didn't answer. Let Chase come clean independently of Tori. You know I'm not the kind of person to pry, but exactly what is going on?"

"I wish I knew."

"Rumor around town, or rather the gospel according to Tori, is Chase is living with your family and suffered a nervous breakdown."

"He is living with us, but there wasn't any nervous breakdown. Chase was ill and had to be temporarily hospitalized."

"How is Chase adjusting to such a big change?"

"I'm so sick and tired of everyone always worrying about him. What about me?"

"Your family and friends do worry about you, but Chase is currently dealing with a heck of a lot more than you. Again, what's going on? I have a right to know being you shoved me in the middle of your spy mission."

"Chase had some family issues. It became too much,

so he thought it best to move out. My parents invited him to live with us, probably because they were afraid we might do something stupid like elope. Chase was admitted to the hospital because he passed out. It ending up being the result of exhaustion, prolonged stress, and dehydration—nothing too terribly serious. As for his recent behaviors, maybe you're right and he's feeling displaced and depressed. I'm sorry for getting snippy, but it's been a big adjustment for me too."

"It sounds like it's been rough for everyone involved. You can always vent to me."

"Thank you."

After Jules dropped me off at home, an anxious energy set in while I waited for Chase. To pass the time, I lounged on my bed, online shopping. The sun set with no sign of Chase.

Maybe I should call him? No, don't do that. Eventually he'll return and find you. Where else would he go? Maybe he decided to be with Bristol? Stop. Be patient and remain calm.

Waiting for him felt more painful than watching the interaction from earlier. Ugh. Bristol. Now the bitch had a name which made matters worse. Around seven, headlights shined brightly through the window, flooding the dimly lit room with pools of yellow light. Quickly, I got off of the bed and peered outside. Chase. My heart raced disregarding the desire and need to remain cool. My hands and feet tingled as the sound of his footsteps grew louder.

"Nina?" Chase said, knocking.

"Yeah," I said trying to remain as emotionally void as possible.

"Hey. How was your day?" he asked, sitting on the

desk chair.

"Fine. Spent most of it with Jules."

"What did you do?"

He was curious to see if Jules had said anything. "Oh, nothing really. We hung out here, then went to get some coffee, but Mrs. Warner called, and Jules had to go home to babysit her brother. What about you?" I'd never sell Jules out. Chase needed to come clean without coaxing or threats.

"Had coffee with a friend."

Chase's internal freak out wasn't shown through a projection of his emotions, but rather with jittery mannerisms and tone of voice. If the situation had been anything else, I would've been proud of him for controlling his gift.

"Do I know them?"

"Maybe. Not sure."

"Do you want to give me a name? Or are we playing who does Chase James socialize with?"

"Bristol Scott."

"Okay."

"She's a friend."

"Okay."

"She's an ex-girlfriend. Something came up. She needed help. I didn't touch her or anything like that."

"How come you couldn't tell me, and why are you telling me this now?"

"Because we have enough going on at the moment. I'm telling you now because honestly, Jules spotted me and Bristol having coffee this afternoon."

"If you weren't caught would you have told me?"

"No. Probably not. If Jules never saw me I would've let it go because again, there's nothing going on. We need to focus on other things, not this petty bullshit. You can either be pissed off and I can walk on eggshells for the next few days kissing your ass or you can believe me, accept my apology, and get over it. It's your call, Nina."

"You'd be pissed off like no one's business if the tables were turned. What if I went to grab coffee with Tommy Ashley because he called out of the blue needing help with something? You'd hit the roof. Please," I yelled.

"You're right. I'd be annoyed, but if you told me nothing happened, I'd believe you and know that since we were made for each other, in the end, it's you and me, not you, me, Bristol, and Tommy. Even if I wanted to cheat on you, Nina, I couldn't. Neither could you. The bond between us is too strong, too unbreakable. You should realize that by now."

"I don't, Chase. It actually makes sense that you'd cheat. These past few months have been nothing but horrible. You freaking out over learning and mastering new divine gifts makes your mood swings out of control. *I* feel them. We *all* freaking feel them. You don't talk to me. You hear voices. I never know what I'm going to get with you—it's frustrating the crap out of me. Can't we have one damn day where you're not brooding over something? I'm tired of being the calm, rational one. I'm scared too." I paused. "See me. Look at me. I'm drowning, Chase. There's too much weight on my frigging back."

"I'm sorry. You deserve to be treated better. Much better actually, and I plan to make every effort to fix that. The mood and sense gift is in check. As you can see, I'm keeping my emotions to myself right now, and I'm not using the gift on you to lessen your anger. I'm fighting fair, *not* cheating because I *don't* cheat. Strength and the channeling of it is something I need to be constantly aware of, and slowing down time is a gift that's still up in the air. Why Vincent pops in and out of my brain is an unknown, but I'll find a way to evict and beat him. Better days are ahead of us. You have to trust me. I'd never, *ever*, do anything to hurt you, Nina."

"You seemed happy with her."

"You already knew," he said, running his hands through his thick, messy hair, turning slightly, and producing an evil laugh.

"I saw you two the other day on campus," I admitted.

"You should've said something yesterday. At least the mystery of your attitude from last night has been solved."

"Does she make you happy, Chase?"

"Honestly? Yes and no. Yes, because when we talk life seems normal again. Yes, because she's blissfully unaware of this double life. To her I'm just Chase James, *not* Chase James, Lost Soul. Yes, because moments of levity between you and me actually hurt when I experience them and I don't know why. Happiness shouldn't be painful when shared with the person you love, but let's not lie to each other. When was the last time we were content together? *But*, there only needs to be one no to cancel out all of the yes responses. No, because she's not you. I love you and only you, and I never want to experience life without you by my side. I don't want to lose you, baby, but we can't keep going on this way. We're both miserable."

His words stung. His honesty wasn't lost on me, and there was no denying some of it had been true, but it didn't lessen the ache and sadness.

"Did you sleep with her?" I inquired, not really wanting to know the answer, but feeling compelled to ask.

"When we were dating, yes." Chase's eyes dropped upon admission.

"How awesome for Miss Bristol. Maybe one day I'll be good enough for you."

"Nina, you know that's not true. We already talked about this. We're not talking about it again. *I'm* not ready. Why do you keep forcing the issue? When the time is right, we will. Until then, case closed. Where's the cross necklace by the way?"

"Over on the dresser. Why?"

"Because I told you to never take it off of your neck and what did you do? You got pissed at me and took it off. You need to promise me right now that you'll put it back on immediately and never remove it, even if you're as mad as hell over something I said or did." Chase's tone was dead serious.

"Why?"

"It will protect you, Nina. Please put it back on," he begged.

"How will it protect me?"

"Put it on and stop challenging me. Damn it," he shouted.

"All right, fine. I'm putting it on," I said, walking to the dresser and securing the necklace around my neck. "Happy?"

"Yes." His attitude turned considerably softer.

He got up and stood in front of me. Slowly and gently his arms slid around my waist. He was testing the waters by keeping a safe distance between our bodies.

My initial rage turned to desolation. Moments of shared joy apparently caused Chase pain. Knowing this information hurt most. We were being torn apart by something we couldn't control, but yet still in control of our decisions and actions. How could I fault him for talking to Bristol when I'd done the same thing with Orifiel? I needed someone to lean on and ran to someone other than Chase. We might not ever be able to find normal in the conventional sense, but we had to at least try to find some livable version of it.

"Baby, do you want this? Do you still want us?"

How could my soul deny him? I loved Chase. Even his worst fault could be forgiven. Our shared bond was powerful, consuming, and blinding. A lot of girls in this situation wouldn't be able to get past this moment and truthfully, the memory would always remain locked inside of my head, as would my dejection and doubt. Fork in the road time. Keep going forward or walk away.

"Yes, of course, and I always will. However, if you sneak around again, we're done. Soul mates or not."

Maybe kicking Chase to the curb would've been the better option, but I'd already lost him once. Reliving that dark period of time wasn't something I wished to repeat.

"I'm sorry, baby," he said, tugging me closer.

"Let's leave this life behind us for a while."

"Okay. I like where this is going. How do you propose we do that?"

"We start by being Chase and Nina. Not Mortal Angels or Lost Souls. Let's not talk about or stress over our other world. Let's worry about this one and try to have some fun."

"We can do that."

"What was her problem?"

"What are you talking about?"

"What did Bristol want from you?"

"Family financial problems, but you know something? She means nothing and isn't worth wasting any more time on. Besides, I'd much rather do this," he whispered.

He leaned forward pressing his lips to mine. Chase's kiss and touch felt beyond satisfying. We stood kissing slowly and passionately. I yearned for the day when we could be together without life getting in the way. For the moment, we appeared stable again. Perhaps things might start looking up for once. It was doubtful, but one must always have faith, right?

Chapter 37

Nina

Days turned into weeks, then months. Before I knew it, spring had arrived and my nineteenth birthday was rapidly approaching. Chase and I had been spending our time reconnecting, trying to find the paradise we'd lost. Free moments were used for engaging in activities other couples our age did. Often, we'd talk until dawn's first light about everything and anything—a new favorite of mine. However, the awareness that our happiness hurt Chase mentally and physically still wounded my soul. Who really knew what was lurking behind a laugh or a smile? Were his expressions true and genuine, or were they inflicting some form of turmoil inside of his core? His words about how moments of levity pained him remained a constant thought disrupting any form of peace. It became a goal of mine to chase that feeling away, far away, praying it never returned. We hardly ever spoke about Angels, Demons, or Lost Souls. The few conversations which involved that portion of our lives were brief, solely mentioned as a means for us to make sure the other was okay—him with the emergence of gifts, and me with the nightmares. Honestly? I lied suggesting things were okay and no more vision were had. Chase did the same. We desperately needed the time off and we both knew it. Telling white lies was our only option. I hated it, but loved the denial and falsely believing we could be ordinary people.

Our relationship had grown stronger and closer. Nothing would be allowed to destroy that. Many times I wanted to call to Orifiel to purge a vision—they hadn't stopped, if anything they'd grown worse, but I didn't. Inviting him in could harm the progress I'd made with Chase. We needed to lean on and seek comfort from each other, not others. For the first time in a long time Chase seemed relaxed and at ease, making the bi-polar mood swings ancient history. Ignoring the desire to keep my birthday as low key as possible, Jules, along with Chase's help, was up to something. Being part seer wasn't necessary to pick up on Jules's bad lying and their not so subtle sneaking around.

"Happy birthday, honey," my mother exclaimed as I entered the kitchen.

"Thanks, Mom."

"What does the birthday girl want for breakfast?"

"I hope you're not going to do that all day."

"I remember the day you were born." She sat and sighed.

Great. Here we go.

Every single year the story of Nina Olivia Luther's birth had to be told. I could probably tell it better than her at this point.

"You were supposed to be born May thirtieth, but you had other ideas. We were living in Chicago and your father had to go to a convention in New York. He swore up and down that Dr. Carter miscalculated the delivery date and you'd be an early June baby. The last thing your father said before he left was, '*Are you going to believe Dr. Carter who's been an OBGYN for five years, or me who's been one for over fifteen?*' Good thing Jenny and

Bridget stopped by to drop off some toys your brother left at Jenny's house because no sooner did the front door open, my water broke. By the time your father got to the hospital you were already born. We were expecting to have another boy, but when Dr. Carter said you were a girl," she paused, holding back tears over this memory, "you were so small and had the sweetest eyes and face."

"Thanks for the traditional birthday kick off, Mom."

"What's the birthday girl up to today?" she asked, ignoring my sarcasm.

"The mall with Jules and then lunch." Around March, freedom to leave the house alone had been restored. Since there'd been no more talk of nightmares or visions everyone eased off. Personally, I believe they were trying to reestablish a certain sense of lost normalcy in the house as well. It didn't matter. Coming and going freely again felt fabulous.

"No big plans for tonight?"

She knew Chase and Jules had organized something and wanted to check to make sure I remained blissfully unaware.

"Nope."

Jules arrived thirty minutes later, and we hit the mall with a vengeance. My passion for shopping had trickled over onto her. Finally, Jules allowed herself to try on more daring looks which showed off her hidden beauty. Casually, Jules tried to encourage me to buy this deep purple, silk halter top that tied together mid chest creating some major cleavage, and a pair of tight, black flair bottom pants, suggesting I looked stunning in it. She continued to urge the outfit should be worn tonight, no matter what I did.

Smooth. Real smooth, Jules.

After the mall we hit up a fast-food place opting to sit in the car instead of going inside. More than anything I wanted to tell Jules the truth about everything, but I couldn't. It would've been nice to talk to someone other than my family, Chase, or Orifiel about Angels and Demons, Heaven and Hell. Maybe one day I'd be able to, but now wasn't the right time. She'd understand and would have something insightful and helpful to offer, but jeopardizing my family's secret was out of the question. The rules of this game which had been forced upon me were clear. Besides, who knew if my reality would freak Jules out? If it did, we'd have to pack up and move again—something none of us wanted to do.

"What are you up to later, Jules?"

"Babysitting," she replied, attempting to conceal a smirk. "Is Chase taking you somewhere special tonight to celebrate?"

"Not sure."

"He probably will," she said, looking down at her watch for what seemed like the hundredth time in less than two hours.

"Hot date?" I joked.

"Oh no. I've got to be home before three is all—to babysit."

"Then we should probably get going."

"You know what? I forgot your present at home. I'll stop by tomorrow and give it to you. I'm sorry, Nina."

"It's not a big deal. You didn't have to get me anything at all."

On the ride back to my house we sang horribly to the songs on the radio, laughing, and having a great time. If life could always be like that then I'd be the happiest person in the world. This was normal and what regular teenagers did. Mundane moments were what kept me going. The realization and acceptance of my double life was something I'd come to terms with, but the ordinary part would always be a work in progress. However, the simple things people often took for granted provided me with the greatest joy.

"Happy birthday." Chase wrapped his big, strong arms around my waist, kissing me as soon as Jules pulled away. "How was the mall?"

"Fabulous as always. Your day?"

"Much better now that you're here with me. I missed you, baby."

"I missed you too."

"How about we get dinner and see where the night goes from there?"

"Sounds good."

"Pick you up at five?" Chase joked.

"Will you need directions?"

"Maybe. Keep your cell phone close by."

"In that case, I better get ready."

Rushing upstairs excitement set in. This was going to be a memorable, amazing birthday. I could feel it.

****

"Knock, knock," Chase said, entering my room at exactly five o'clock. "Ready?"

"Yeah, almost. What's the rush?"

"No rush."

"How do I look?" I asked, exiting the bathroom. A self-conciseness weighed heavily inside of me. Though we'd moved past the Bristol incident, the blow to my ego was still healing, and at times, required validation.

"Wow. Really sexy, baby. Well worth the two plus hour wait."

Chase helped secure the clasp of the cross necklace around my neck.

"Mission accomplished." An inner sigh of relief surged forward.

Hand in hand, we walked down the stairs and into the foyer. I opened the hall closet to grab a lightweight sweater. Hanging beside it was Orifiel's red hoodie. My heart instantly filled with desolation.

When you have a free second, call to him. No one has to know. It's not like you're doing anything wrong. He's a friend, an Angel, and someone you care about. You don't throw good people like him away.

"Happy birthday, princess" my father called.

"Hey, Dad. Thanks."

"Could you come into the living room for a second?"

"Sure."

"You look pretty. Where are you kids off to?" he asked.

"Dinner," Chase replied.

"Before you leave, give Mom and me a minute to give you your gift."

My mother disappeared into the dining room. Seconds later, she reappeared with a gigantic box and a card.

"Happy birthday, honey," she said, with a huge smile.

Inside of the box were two very expensive designer travel bags, a makeup bag, and a valet bag.

"Thanks, but are you planning on sending me off somewhere or looking for me to move out anytime soon?" I asked nervously. "These past few months have been hard on all of us, but don't you think kicking me out is a bit drastic?"

"No. Don't be silly. Your mom and I thought you might be able to use this someday. Open your card."

As my eyes scanned the sappy sayings and heartfelt sentiments, a check fell to the floor.

"This is a lot of money," I said shocked, processing the amount of zeros.

"Oh, we think you'll be able to put it to good use," my mother said.

"My turn," Chase said, handing me a long envelope.

Carefully opening the flap, two first class plane tickets to New York revealed.

"I love it," I exclaimed, throwing myself into his arms.

"You're always telling me how much you miss living in New York—how badly you want to go back to visit. Now we can this summer. We leave next month," he said, smiling widely.

"Where are we staying?"

Chase took the envelope containing the airplane tickets off of the coffee table and handed me a business card.

The Waldorf Astoria. I'd passed that hotel a hundred times when I was in the city and always wanted to stay there.

"How did you know?"

"Your mom told me."

"This is too amazing. Thank you."

"We thought this would make you smile. You both could use a break from Savannah. Plus, we trust you two to be alone so far away from home," my father said.

"Thank you so much, Mom and Dad."

"We better get going," Chase urged.

“We’ll see you later,” I said, hugging them one last time.

Dinner at Gino’s was great, like always. The conversation was light and fun, the way it used to be. We chatted and laughed while planning our trip. Chase had never been to New York. I wanted to make sure when we were there he got to see everything. The night couldn’t have been more perfect. Not once did we mention Vincent, Chase’s powers, or anything pertaining to things that only happened in our alternate life. Definitely one of the best birthdays ever.

“Shit. I forgot my phone. Here are the keys. Start the car. I’ll be right back,” Chase said, heading into the restaurant.

“You got it.”

Within a few minutes he returned. “Sorry,” Chase said, sliding into the driver’s seat.

“No worries. We all forget things from time to time. Nobody’s perfect, but you’re pretty damn close to it,” I said, reaching over and grabbing his thigh, hoping the action would elicit some imitate emotion and not a dismissal.

“What do you…” he started, but the sound of my cell phone ringing interrupted the moment. “Damn it. Hold on a second. Hello?”

“Mark and I had this huge fight. He dumped me,” Jules said sobbing.

“What happened?”

“He just came over and we started fighting. Something about how he’s sick and tired of me always having to help take care of my brother and grandmother.”

“What a jerk. Are you still at home?” I’d never heard Jules cry like this before. It was rather concerning. It truly bothered me that one of the sweetest people in the Universe was in emotional distress.

Mark will pay for this.

"Yeah. I know it's your birthday, but could you please come over?" she begged through heavy bawling.

"Without a doubt. Stay where you are. I'll be right there."

"What's the matter?" Chase inquired.

"Mark dumped Jules. We need to get over to her house. Hey listen, could you call Mark? See what's going on?"

"I could, but I'm not sure what good that would do. Guys really don't do that, Nina. We don't talk about our emotions with each other. We hang out and act like nothing's wrong. Girls talk about everything until there is nothing left to talk about, then you talk about that." He laughed.

"Maybe you could find him."

"And do what with him? Say it's okay to cry? Hold him? Help him pen an entry in his Burn Book? Nina, I'll say this again—guys don't do that. If it were me, I'd want to be left alone."

"Mark really sucks. Jules is such a great person."

"Maybe they'll work it out. We're here," he said, throwing the car in park.

Dashing for the front door, I pushed the doorbell button at least a dozen times before Jules's mother opened it. "She's upstairs in the game room. By the way, happy birthday," Mrs. Warner said.

"Thanks," I replied, hauling ass up the steps.

"SURPRISE!" Was all that could be heard while a blinding light smacked me in the face.

"Holy crap, Jules. I'm going to kill you," I said

stunned, aggressively rubbing my nearly blinded eyeballs.

"Oh get over it, Nina. We didn't get to celebrate last year. You deserve this." She embraced me tightly.

Tori, Tim, Mark, a bunch of friends from college, and several from high school were all there.

"Did Chase and I really surprise you?" Jules questioned nervously.

"You did." Hazy black dots still floated about freely in the air.

After several minutes of being bombarded by friends, Jules approached me.

"Hey. I've got to show you something," she said, grabbing and dragging me across the hallway to her room.

"What is it?" I asked, sitting on the bed.

"I did a little digging into Bristol Scott. Here, take a look at this," Jules said, shoving a yearbook at me.

"What the hell happened to this?" The cover looked like it barely survived nuclear war.

"My brother happened. Just look," she demanded.

My eyes glanced down on the page. Bristol's flawless, ready for the cover of a fashion magazine face stared back.

"You're showing me this because you're trying to destroy my self-esteem completely and totally tonight? This chick is the only person in the world who can take a badass school picture. Everyone else looks like death—even Tori who's drop dead gorgeous. Not fair especially since the thought of her and Chase together doesn't haunt my nightmares anymore. I'd rather let this go and forget about it."

"Oh my God, Nina. You can't see the forest for the

trees. Look." She pointed at the picture again.

"I am looking, and what does that figure of speech even mean?"

"For time and frustration's sake, here goes. Bristol *Logan* Scott—she's Sean *Logan's* half-sister. Sean's biological father bailed on Mrs. Scott and Sean after Sean was born. Mrs. Scott remarried almost immediately. A year later Bristol happened," Jules informed.

"How do you know this?"

"I asked Tori who seemed to totally dislike Bristol. My guess is because Bristol is pretty and Chase picked her over Tori. I knew the girl looked familiar, but I couldn't place the name. According to Tori, Chase and Bristol dated for a while before he dumped her. That was right around the time of his accident. If you notice the date of this particular yearbook, it's not recent, but rather from a couple of years ago—before you arrived in Savannah. After they split, Bristol went all bat crap crazy. The Scotts put her in some sort of private school for girls only, telling people she'd been accepted to a school for the gifted. Tori didn't elaborate much after that, *but* this is where it gets strange. No one, not even Sean's parents, have seen Sean since last summer. It's as if he vanished into thin air."

"Huh."

"Tori said the Scotts dumped all of their money into hiring a private investigator to hunt Sean down leaving them flat broke. Mrs. Wylie seems to think Sean was on drugs or something like that," Jules added.

"Good work, Perry Mason."

Holy overload of information right there. It made sense why Chase omitted the part about Bristol being

Sean's half-sister, but why put himself in harm's way for an ex? What was Chase up to? Could this entire situation be a trap of sorts?

All kinds of random thoughts popped in and out of my head.

"You okay?" Jules asked.

"Yeah. We better get back to the party. Thanks for the info. It was rather enlightening."

"Don't start a fight with Chase over it please," she begged.

"No way. Things have been going pretty good lately. Nothing is going to ruin that. Besides, I'm over the Bristol crap. She's not worth it." My words were mostly true. Chances were, part of me would always remember Bristol. The mind is a powerful organ, but seemingly something as simple as erasing a memory baffled it.

"Ni," Tori said, knocking and entering Jules's room. "You might want to see what your boyfriend is up to," she suggested, sounding a bit too devious for my liking.

"Excuse me?"

"Bristol Scott showed up and dragged *your* boyfriend downstairs away from the party. If I were you, I'd go see what that piece of trailer trash is doing, then sanitize him from toe to snout." Tori smirked.

"They're friends. I trust Chase. He's not doing anything wrong. You make mountains out of ant hills. Stop thriving on drama." The tone I used may have sounded bitchy and strong, but my inner confidence was anything but.

"Oh yeah? *Just friends*, huh?" Tori snapped, turning me around so Chase and Bristol were in full line of sight through the window. To clarify, Chase and Bristol in an intense lip lock. Rage coursed through my bones. My hands balled into tight fists.

How could Chase do this? Weren't we trying to make us right again? How long was this going on for?

Wait, maybe Chase never cut ties with Bristol?

Liar. Horrible, deceitful, nasty liar. Soul mate or not, Chase James, we're done.

This felt worse than being kicked in the stomach and having the wind knocked out of you.

"I'm sorry, Nina," Jules said, placing a slender arm around my shoulders.

Without uttering a word, I stormed down the stairs and past Chase and Bristol, who were on the porch still giving each other mouth to mouth. Jules's lived close. Walking home, especially fueled by anger, would take five minutes maximum.

After a few moments, my cell phone started ringing nonstop. First, Jules, then Chase. This wasn't going to be dealt with right now and maybe not ever. I'd played the role of the stupid girlfriend for far too long.

Blinded by every negative emotion known to man, I'd hardly realized how far I'd walked until the elementary school down the block from home came into focus. Pausing to find my house keys buried deep within my purse, the sound of rustling bushes eerily broke the night's quiet calmness. An instant chill shot up my spine. It was one of those moments where you know you're in danger and want to run, but your feet freeze up.

"Orifiel?" I questioned hesitantly, hoping the sound had come from him.

"Well, well, well. What do we have here?" a snake-like voice hissed.

There were no words as my eyes locked on the blood

red irises staring straight at me. My nightmares were about to become reality.

Truth & Consequences—IV

My Dearest Love,

The stars and flashes of prophecies I've recently seen have shifted tremendously, and for the worse. I don't know what to do to stop this. Without being able to tell Michael, Raphael, or Gabriel what's known is horrible. A helplessness has set in. I'm Heaven's greatest asset, most powerful weapon, but currently the weakest link. Holding onto this secret—the one being kept from Gabriel, is destroying me.

Foresights keep presenting themselves at an alarming rate. Though you won't be brought into creation for several years, know I'm doing everything to make sure that moment occurs. Perhaps I should say something to Michael, but fright over my soul being released into nothingness because of purging this knowledge due to distress isn't worth it. We'd never meet. I'd be gone for eternity, never knowing if your lips taste as good in reality as they do in my dreams. I'll figure something out.

In fifteen minutes, all Hell will break loose. Fate and life paths will be altered drastically, enough to send everything which had been preordained to happen into a chaotic state of disarray. I can't even think of that right now. Fixing this mess, ending it before it's too late has to happen, and my love, *it will*. If this doesn't bode well, know my heart will always belong to you even if I'm not around when you read these letters. The second the stars and prophecies revealed your presence you were loved, deeply. You became eternally mine. As long as I'm part of the Universe, I'll always fight like hell for you, for us.

I love you.

Always,
Your Betrothed

Chapter 38

Chase

There were zero complaints to be had concerning the past few months. Initially, I felt bad for telling Nina moments of happiness hurt, but it was the truth and often the truth is painful to hear. When all was said and done, opening up had been the best thing for both of us. Together we worked to rebuild our relationship. We took the time to get to know each other anew, while enjoying the others' company, never speaking much about our other lives aside from the occasional, "*how's it going*" question. Our answers were brief providing comfort and assurances that no threats had presented. The more we connected, the closer I felt to her. Nina was smart, witty, funny, bold, passionate, blunt, and loving. The sound of her voice started working its magic again soothing my soul, reviving lost joy. Listening to Nina speak for hours allowed for an escape to a personal paradise. Her laugh was the kill shot every time. Nothing could ever describe or do justice for how that particular sound inspired me. Apartment hunting became a low priority. Mending our relationship was the most important area of my focus. Once we did, I'd start looking again. The Luther's continued to welcome and accept me as a son, ultimately placing no real pressure to leave anytime soon. Steve would be coming home for the summer, a happening I wasn't looking forward to, but we'd find a way to get by.

I'd re-enrolled at South University, starting classes again in the fall. Life was good. Dare I say, peaceful for once.

Since this was the first time I'd be celebrating Nina's birthday, last year we were broken up, something special and memorable needed to be created. After several hours of trying to figure out the perfect present, a trip to New York popped into my head. She'd love that. Often she speak mournfully about how much she missed New York. Going back for a visit would be good for her soul and would allow for some more insight into her past. Jack and Ellen had no objections. If anything, Ellen provided information on a particular hotel Nina liked. Nina appeared elated with the gift which made me genuinely happy, and the happiness we shared this time didn't hurt. I felt whole and cleansed.

Going to Jules's house for the surprise party she'd planned was the last thing on my mind. Being alone with Nina, seeing where the night would take us would've been much more enjoyable and exciting, but Jules invested a lot of time, effort, and energy into this gathering. How could anyone say no? After dinner and the party, I'd take Nina somewhere finally allowing our relationship to progress to the next level. The time had come. There were risks, but none of that mattered. My frame of mind was strong and able to quickly push the lurking evil aside. The headaches occurred from time to time and Vincent's voice could still be heard, but shoving him away became easier. His voice and hold had weakened making it manageable to void his negative energy. No new abilities had presented, while daily work with Jack enhanced the existing ones. Normal sleep patterns resumed. When a headache struck, Jack's herbal mixture, along with positive thoughts, and some relaxation techniques chased them away. Within minutes, balance was rapidly restored. This was the best I'd felt in a long time.

After Jules called, the plan of getting in and out of the party in two hours or less was set into motion.

Play it by ear. See how it goes. Remember, you can alter others' moods and senses, something you've gotten pretty damn good at it. You can control and manipulate people without them even realizing it. Granted, you shouldn't use your gift on others because it's morally wrong, but you can. It's a great weapon to have in your arsenal. Do what you have to without regret because showing Nina, physically showing her, you love her is the most important thing at the moment. By this, you'll strengthen your already strong bond.

Once we arrived at Jules's, I checked the clock mentally marking off two hours. A bunch of people we went to high school with as well as several people I didn't know, but assumed went to college with Nina and Jules were there. Nina made the social rounds disappearing into the crowd. Finding a seat on the sofa while screwing around on my cell phone would entertain me until she returned.

"How's life in the fab lane?" a sweet southern accent drawled.

"Fab lane, Tori?" I asked, smiling and looking up. Deep down there was a good girl dying to come out, but her social status prohibited this from ever occurring.

"Oh, whatever with you." She grinned, plopping on the cushion beside me, and placing her left hand on my right knee. "Let's visit. How are things?"

"Not bad. Living the dream. You?"

"Chase, I heard about your parents kicking you out

and about the breakdown. Seriously, *how are you*?" Tori appeared sincerely concerned.

"I'm fine. Glad to know Chase James is the toast of Savannah." Sarcasm hung from my every word.

"*Talk* of Savannah. *Not* toast. Don't flatter yourself, and never refer to yourself in the third person, please. It's not cool or attractive. Anyway, I'm glad to hear you're doing better. I understand though, you know, what you're going through and all."

"Okay, thanks?" How does one really respond to that?

"I'm fully aware of what it's like to live a lie. How hard it can be to pretend everything is okay when it's not."

Unsure of where this was going, my next few words would have to be guarded and calculated. After a couple of seconds of silence, Tori broke the ice.

"Your dad is cheating on your mom, and you and your dad don't get along well. Your relationship with Nina has been strained, but you're living with her. You dropped out of college, and had a nervous breakdown. All of that has got to be hard on you." She paused and moved closer. "My dad hasn't been very good to my mom either, and things with Tim have more downs then ups, but smile through the pain. Don't think about it. Never let people see inside of you because if they do, that's when you find trouble. I'm rather familiar with you, Chase James. You're not a weak soul. Oh, and the first moment you can, get the hell out of this town because it's only going to bring you down more. Move as far away from everyone as possible. It helps."

In Tori's own distorted way, she was trying to help, though her views on life and how to deal with it saddened me greatly.

"Thanks, but let me tell *you* something. You're a good girl even though you don't show it often. You shouldn't have to laugh through your tears. If you're not happy, do something about it. We can't control what our fathers, mothers, or significant others do and honestly, Tim doesn't deserve you. You're a beautiful, smart, talented woman who has a lot to offer someone. Find someone who will worship you, someone who won't make vulnerability a bad experience," I said, meaning every word.

"Can I ask you something?"

"You can ask me anything."

"Why didn't we ever *hang out*?"

I couldn't control the slight laugh which involuntarily came out. "I had a girlfriend. You had a boyfriend. *And* you had a very bad attitude which was a major turn off."

"I always liked you. You were the hottest guy in our school."

"Truth be told, before Nina moved to Savannah, I thought about it. Hell, you were a prime topic of arguments between Bristol and me."

"Bristol?" Tori's head shot up.

"Looks like some things never change," Bristol hissed, grabbing a fist full of Tori's hair.

Immediately, my hand grabbed hold of Bristol's wrist, forcing her to let go of Tori. "What are you doing? What's wrong with you?" I demanded, trying not to make a scene. "Are you okay, Tori?"

"Yeah," Tori replied, visibly and audibly shaken.

My fingers ran over Tori's soft curls as my eyes examined her face. She appeared all right. My attention returned to Bristol, who seethed with rage. She didn't speak, but rather cracked me as hard as she could across the face before storming off. I had to go after her.

"Mark?"

"What the hell, Chase?"

"Don't ask. Where's Nina?"

"She didn't see a thing. She's with Jules doing something in Jules's bedroom."

"Do me a favor. Keep Nina up here until I return. I'll be right back."

"Sure. You got it. Good luck with whatever that was." Mark smirked.

Aggressively exiting the house, Bristol was found sitting on the porch swing.

"You have exactly one minute to tell me what that was all about," I shouted.

When she turned to face me her beet red, swollen eyes reveled that she'd been crying for possibly hours.

"Bristol, what's going on?"

"Sean's dead," she wailed.

"What?"

What the hell?

"Some cop called this morning. He said they found Sean's body. We went to the morgue to make sure. My brother is gone, Chase."

"I'm sorry," I whispered, trying to piece the story together.

How could Sean be dead?

"I didn't mean to bother you or attack Tori, but I knew you wouldn't answer the phone for me. A friend mentioned your girlfriend's birthday party tonight. That's how I knew you'd be here. Help me, Chase. Make this better. Please," Bristol begged.

Not knowing what to say or do, mainly because processing this new information proved almost impossible, pulling Bristol close felt right. “It’s going to be okay,” I murmured, as my fingers stroked her hair in a feeble attempt to ease the pain of our shared anguish. Emotions, especially absolute horror, make you do crazy things.

“My world is crashing down, Chase. Nothing makes any sense.”

“I’m here. We’ll get through this.” Bristol’s grief stricken expressions and sentiments were pure torture.

Slowly, she moved closer until our lips touched. Every ounce of hurt and love this girl possessed flooded back to me in the form of a kiss. Though committing this act was wrong, it happened anyway. Broken up or not, feeling confusion and anxiety over the latest development with Sean didn’t matter. A connection to Bristol still existed. The moment resembled temporary insanity in its purest form.

“How dare you,” Jules screamed, startling us. “I thought you were better than this. I believed you when you said nothing was going on.”

“Where’s Nina?” My heart dropped as my stomach tightened. Nina had to have seen us.

Pushing Bristol away, my feet sprang to desperate action.

“Chase,” Bristol said loudly.

“Where is she?” I shouted, grabbing Jules’s shoulders.

“You don’t deserve Nina, therefore you don’t deserve to know where she is. You’re a pig and you,” Jules turned, fixing a hard stare on Bristol, “are an evil whore. He’s got a girlfriend. Who the hell do you think you are? I know all about you, how the two of you used to date and Chase dumped you, and now you go to some all-girls school because you couldn't handle some loser letting you go. You're Sean Logan's sister. Though I'm sorry about the hardships your family must be dealing with, and I pray Sean is okay and comes home soon, you have no right to take what's no longer yours. I don't know who invited you, but I sure didn't. Get off of my porch and don't ever come back here," Jules hissed.

"Jules," I began, reaching for her arm. With one swift movement she slammed a fist square into my abdomen knocking the wind straight out of me.

"Touch me again without my permission and you'll find out how hard I can knee you in the groin."

Collecting myself and attempting to stand after Jules's freakishly strong punch, something inside of me snapped, but remaining calm was key.

Jules is not the person you want to push over the edge. This seemingly sweet girl turns into a vicious Pit Bull when provoked. You can appeal to Jules's softer side without using your gift while still maintaining balance.

"Jules, Sean is dead. His body was found this morning."

"Oh God." Color fell from her face as tears formed. Slowly, Jules sat, staring into space.

"Where's Nina?"

"She took off toward Oak Street. Probably heading home."

Without thanking her or worrying about Bristol, I hopped in the car. Jules didn't live far from Nina's house. When she wasn't spotted on the road, I assumed she'd made it home already. Entering the pitch-black house, my thoughts went wild when Nina didn't respond. Scaling the stairs, then slamming through each room, coming up empty caused a panic like nothing I ever experienced. A note from Jack and Ellen saying they went out to dinner and would be back shortly had been the only thing I found. I raced down the porch steps and back to my car.

"Hello, Chase," a deep voice hissed.

Stopping, paralyzed with fright, my body slowly turned to find Vincent standing before me. I tried to speak, but all words ceased to exist.

"When someone greets you it's polite to greet them back," he informed.

"What do you want? Where's Nina?" I spat, boldly showing fear didn't exist. This bastard wouldn't see me sweat.

"Not the salutation I'd been looking for, but I'll let it slide. I want what I've always wanted from you. Your precious Nina is safe and sound. Well, for the moment, that is."

"Touch one hair on her head and I'll destroy you myself."

Vincent threw his head back laughing hysterically. "You wish."

Brewing rage granted me the strength to grab hold of his throat, squeezing as hard as possible.

"You can't kill me," Vincent said, taking my wrist, and effortlessly withdrawing himself from my grip.

"Then I'll die trying," I screamed, seething with hatred.

"Your gifts won't work on me. Don't waste your time or energy," he said in a very matter-of-fact tone.

Defeat. Absolute defeat. Vincent had me by the

balls. Nothing could be done physically or mentally to beat him or rescue Nina.

"Fine. You win. I'll come quietly *as long as* I see Nina."

A wicked smile spread across Vincent's otherwise horrifying face. "Oh you're coming, quietly or not, but I'll dictate *if* and *when* you ever see Ms. Luther again."

Out of nowhere, someone took hold of me from behind and roughly placed a cloth over my mouth and nose. My mind spun. My body fell numb. It didn't matter how much fight existed inside of me. The urge to shut down ultimately triumphed. With each inhale Vincent's voice grew more and more distorted until I gave up, passing out, silently praying Nina was still alive and would remain that way.

You must always protect her…

****

Painfully slow my eyes opened to a sea of blurriness. Wrestling the desire to submit to the peaceful nothingness I'd experienced earlier was tough, but I was keenly aware something was horribly wrong, something that would require complete and total focus. Forcefully rubbing exhaustion away, my wobbly legs stood. The room was painted stark white with no windows. Bright florescent lights buzzed casting blueish shadows on empty walls. The sound of a lock turning jarred my awareness.

"Where am I, Vincent?" I demanded, still unsteady on my feet.

"Exactly where you're supposed to be," he stated calmly.

"And where might that be?"

"Doesn't really matter." He grinned, taking a seat on

the lone folding chair in the corner of the space.

"Where's Nina?" I yelled, staring him down.

"She's here and safe, but that can change at a moment's notice."

"What do you want?" The overwhelming sensation of going crazy because there was no way out, combined with not knowing how to get to Nina became all too real.

"You already know the answer to that question."

"Let Nina go and I'll do whatever you want."

"No. You had your chance. There will be no more deals. I tell you what happens next. Not the other way around."

"You're going to have to kill me because I'll never obey or do your bidding," I stated, fully prepared to die right then and there.

"Have it your way." He smiled as though he were claiming victory. "Abaddon and Apollyon," Vincent called.

The twin Demons entered the room.

"Please show Mr. James what happens to people who do not follow orders," Vincent instructed before exiting.

One of the twins locked my arms from behind, while the other started beating the crap out of me. The first few blows to my abdomen hurt beyond belief, as did the punches to my face, but after a while the involuntary moaning stopped when they made contact mainly because everything went numb. All I could feel was the warm blood that was trickling down my cheeks.

Use your gift or at least try to.

Focusing enough to check into a better place mentally wasn't difficult to achieve. Once this happened, total control over both Demons occurred. First, I shut off their hearing, then sense of touch, finishing off with vision elimination. Maintaining the hold was effortless. Once released, I grabbed the chair Vincent had sat on earlier, slamming it across their windpipes until both remained motionless on the floor.

"I should end you both," I hissed, taking one of the twins by his neck and shoving him forcefully against the wall. The Demon didn't move, but a slight cracking noise indicated I'd broken at least part of his spine.

"Enough," Vincent ordered. "Let go."

"Why? No fucking way," I said remarkably calm, still strangling my victim, fully intending to kill both twins.

"Neither will touch you again. You have my word, which unlike yours, I never break."

I paused, but maintained hold over the twins momentarily while contemplating Vincent's words.

In the past when Vincent said he'd do or not do something he stuck to it. Why would now be any different? Besides, maybe he'll let you see Nina since he knows what you're capable of.

With one final swift slam of the twin's head against the concrete, I let go, watching the body slide to the ground. A few seconds later, the mental hold over them broke. Slowly, they came back to life.

"Come," Vincent ordered.

I followed him down a long, narrow hallway and through a door.

"See? She's fine," Vincent said, waving a hand at a table-like bed to which Nina had been tied to.

Vincent's firm hold on my shoulder stopped me from moving. His touch felt like fire. Instinctively I wanted to drop to the ground, but showing pain or fear wasn't going to happen. No. Never. Remaining stoic was necessary. Vincent's eyes locked with mine causing the burning sensation to heighten. I'm unsure of how long we stood there while I fought to remain conscious through his intentionally inflicted agony. Finally, a wail escaped as my body gave in, desperately struggling to be free from Vincent's hands. It had to stop.

"Impressive," Vincent said.

I dropped to the floor, broken, gasping for breath while an icy chill extinguished the internal blaze.

"Most men would've crumbled and begged for mercy the moment I touched them, but not you. Curious. Let's see what else you can endure without the use of your gifts."

Immediately, Vincent's left index finger stroked my forehead. He did this over and over. The pain increased, while tolerance for it remained steady until the palm of his hand replaced his finger. A brain explosion would've been less torturous, but focus remained on Nina, who was still out cold.

Stay strong. Don't break. Eventually, Vincent will stop.

A sharp stabbing pain, coupled with a harsh pulling sensation occurred the second Vincent's hands moved to my heart. My vision diminished as my heart rate lowered. With little energy left, I turned to see Nina. She had to be the last thing I saw before dying.

I'm sorry, baby.

With my final Mortal thought, Nina's eyes opened, and Vincent's hold released. His attention was now on her. My frame slammed to the ground. Breathing seemed impossible. Getting up and protecting Nina had to happen. There was no way in Hell Vincent or one of the other Demons would make her suffer. Nina's life and existence were far more important than mine. If it meant sacrificing myself, so be it.

Chapter 39

Nina

My eyes shot wide open. I was desperately trying to gain a sense of awareness for this unfamiliar space, but the crippling pain made it impossible. Instinctively, my hands wanted to move to where the debilitating sensation radiated from to heal it, but I couldn't. Panic and dread quickly set in once the realization I'd been bound and tied up struck me. Thrashing wouldn't help. Whoever put me here did not want me to leave.

There had to be a hint, a clue around somewhere, but nothing was revealed, only darkness in a cold room. A stale smell lingered in the air assaulting my nostrils with every breath making me believe this place hadn't been occupied for a long time. Desperately trying to recall the events leading up to my present predicament caused frustration. I'd been at Jules's house and was upset with Chase. There were keys and the school yard, then nothing. Everything faded to black.

"Vincent, it's time," a hard female's voice hissed.

"Patience, Lahash. I want to make sure Chase completely understands the pain she'll be in," the voice laughed.

Vincent.

Fight, Nina. Destroy this bastard once and for all.

"You will not hurt her," an all too familiar voice wailed in agony.

"Are you ready?" Vincent's voice sang.

"No," I screamed, struggling to free myself.

This was it. Vincent and his Demons were moments away from destroying us and nothing could be done this time to save us or stop them.

"It's nice to see you again, Nina Luther. You look well." Vincent paused. His blazing crimson eyes took me in with a solitary casual glance. "The great amount of patience and time spent waiting for just the right moment to find you alone has paid off. Your Angelic boyfriend became a touch of a problem because he never left your side. He was always following you even when you didn't know it. Curious though. It was to my understanding Chase was under Angelic surveillance, not you, but yet his eyes only followed the life and times of Nina Luther. So very odd, wouldn't you say? Perhaps not though. You did share a fairly intense, intimate moment with the Guardian. I bet an ungodly amount of restraint had to be exercised on his part being how attractive you are, and how he's conscious of whom you *truly* belong to. After that the damn Angel hawked you morning, noon, and night, completely forgetting about his initial mission. He became obsessed with you, which is why I suppose Michael pulled him from Earth, forcing him back to The Heavens. Regardless, plotting and planning to make sure this would all turn out in my favor wasn't a waste. Nothing is ever done in vain when valuable information is obtained along the way. Who would've guessed in the end preying on the grief of a family was the way to go? Not me, but it's a moot point."

"What do you want from us?" I seethed.

"So much anger for someone who is supposed to be an Angel. Chase. That's all I seek. We can do this one of two ways, Nina. The first, the recommended choice, is for Chase to come join me. If he does, I'll let you leave, unharmed. The second is you take turns being tortured until Chase sees things clearly." Vincent grinned.

"Why do you want him?" I asked knowing the answer, but trying to buy time.

"For such a bright girl you ask such silly questions. Why *wouldn't* I want him? Remarkable abilities are still developing within his core. When the transformation is complete, he'll be an anomaly. There will be no other being or form that could compare, not even the beautiful Lilith. I can teach him, mold him in my image. With Chase in Hell's Army, we will rule Heaven, Hell, *and* Earth. His tolerance for pain is uncanny. That will make us an unstoppable force." Vincent's greedy eyes widened at the thought of eternal glory.

"How do you know what Chase can do?"

"I know everything, Nina Luther. Much like your Angel friends, I've been watching Chase too. Speaking of your Angel friends, where are they? Aren't they supposed to help their own kind? Or maybe the Guardian is too consumed with addressing his own personal desires and regrets."

"Untie me. Let me speak to Chase. I might be able to help."

"How? Better question—why should you be trusted?" Vincent mused, toying with his goatee.

"You have your ways, I have mine. As for believing me? You shouldn't, but you should realize you have everything to gain and nothing to lose. If we try anything stupid, you alone are stronger than both of us combined. Kill us. You have my permission."

"Reasoning and logic. Impressive. I'll untie you, but

be warned. One false move will cost you your lives. There'll be no foolish journey to Heaven and there'll certainly be no reward in Hell. You'll be eliminated, erased from the Universe's knowledge. Do you understand my terms and conditions?"

"Yes."

"Lahash, please release Ms. Luther," Vincent ordered.

A short, stout woman with greasy, black, matted, spiked hair and a hard, vacant expression, lumbered over to where I lay and freed me. Trying to keep a neutral facial appearance was nearly impossible. This woman's touch repulsed me. Lahash grabbed hold of my arms, forced me off of the table, and practically threw me into Vincent's arms.

"Thank you," I said to Vincent.

"There might be hope for you after all, Nina Luther. You have manners, a trait that's rare to come across these days. Maybe in time you'll wish to join Chase on our side. I could offer you much, but first you must prove yourself to me," Vincent said, running a long, yellow, dirty fingernail down my cheek. Reaching up and intertwining our fingers caused great internal disgust. Vincent's soft, cool hand welcomed mine. "Be smart," he urged.

"If you're serious about accepting me into your family, I'm interested. Tell me you will and I'll give you everything you desire."

"You seem true, Nina Luther. You show no fear for your own life at this moment. Yes. You'll be welcomed into my family with open arms should you wish, but why the sudden change of heart?"

"Like you said earlier. If the Angels really cared

about me and Chase they'd be here. They're not. Plus, to be honest, being with Chase is all that really matters. Our loyalty rests with whomever can keep us together and will provide the best protection. Allow me to heal Chase. Please."

"Go ahead," Vincent said, pointing to Chase's body which was lying limp on the floor.

Chase's face was covered with deep gashes and bruises. Lord only knew what the rest of his body looked like. Whatever the Demons did, it weakened Chase to the point of agony spiked with exhaustion. Remaining emotionless to the situation while assessing the brutality of the damage caused anger beyond simple human nature. However, since I wasn't aware of what abilities these Demons possessed, appearing and thinking only cold callous thoughts was crucial.

"Rumor has it next to Raphael you're the most powerful healer in existence. I also hear you're part seer—an ability we'll strengthen once you've fully committed to serving me. For now I have one request," Vincent mused.

"Yes. Anything."

"I'd like to see your ability to heal in action."

"Of course."

Rolling Chase onto his back, my hands went to work locating and hovering over his numerous injuries. The warmth pulsating from my palms grew from a dim light to a bright one in an instant, successfully healing Chase's form with remarkable speed and accuracy. Quickly and quietly, I worked from the bottom up. By the time of completion insane fatigue had settled into my brain, but no one could see that.

"Marvelous. So the rumors are true." Vincent spoke.

"Thank you. I suppose they are."

"You probably require a few moments to recover. We'll leave you to rest and discuss matters with Chase."

"Thank you."

"Take all the time you need. We have eternity." Vincent laughed. "Whenever you're ready, come find me."

He helped me rise and ushered the others from the room. The faces hidden under the long, dark cloaks were finally visible. Images from last year flooded my mind while the twins, Abaddon and Apollyon—who appeared to be hunched over and limping, Lahash, Enepsigos, Xaphan, Vassago, and lastly a figure that vaguely resembled Sean, glided past me. I waited to hear the door click closed before rushing back to Chase's side.

"Chase?"

"Are you okay, Nina?"

"Yes. A little spent from healing you, but other than that fine. You?"

"Now that you've healed me, one hundred percent."

"What happened? Where are we? And how did we get here?"

"Does that really matter right now? The point is we're here and have to find a way out."

"My parents," I panicked.

"They're safe—out having dinner."

A part of me flooded with relief. At least someone would make it out of this alive. "Did you hear what I told Vincent?"

"Yeah. What the hell, Nina? You can't be serious."

"I had to, Chase. It was the only way he'd untie me. Listen, there's no help this time. It's you and me, but we can get out of this by playing along with Vincent's crazy ass scheme. He knows you're strong and possibly fears you're going to be, if not already, stronger than him. The problem is, there are eight of them that we know of and only two of us. You're going to have to try to alter senses and emotions."

"I can't alter Vincent. Divine gifts don't seem to work on him, but the others can be manipulated. I'm not strong enough to screw with at least eight Demon's moods for very long while engaging in combat *and* fleeing at the same time."

"Let me think. This is the place that I've been dreaming about, but I can't seem to recall a clear picture of the layout of the building. There's a hallway which leads to another room, I know that for sure, but I cannot remember if there's a door anywhere inside of that space though. Shit," I cursed, getting frustrated with my memory, or rather lack thereof. What good was being a seer if the gift couldn't help me when I needed it the most?

"We'll figure it out as we go. The more you force yourself to remember, the less you'll be able to," Chase replied.

"What if there's no way out and we have to join Vincent? Then what?"

"We join or die, but whatever the outcome, we do it together. Call him back in."

Silently I prayed Chase had something up his sleeve—something he wasn't telling me.

You can't depend on a hope. Think, Nina. Think.

Suddenly, and rather quickly, a flash entered and exited my brain.

Orifiel. I'm in trouble. Please help me. Please find me. I don't know where I am, but I need you. Please.

Vincent has me and Chase. Hurry.

As promised, Vincent and several of his followers were patiently waiting on the other side of the door.

"We're ready," I said, faking a smile.

"Good girl." Vincent grinned and stroked my face with his fingernail again. Strangely enough his touch didn't seem to inflict pain on me like it had for Chase. His gesture actually felt soft and warm, almost fatherly. Perhaps torture by burning was one of his gifts? Why not? The Demonic twins possessed it. I clearly remembered that from last summer's living nightmare. It only made sense Vincent, the most powerful Demon of all, would encompass every gift imaginable.

"You have no Demonic healers and your recovery time is slow and painful. I can fix that as long as Chase always belongs to me. Chase will strengthen his skills under your guidance for the same terms."

"I have already promised you this and I will not go back on that, Nina. Come now. Your transformation must begin. Then, we will celebrate."

"Thank you." Chase spoke strongly.

"Ah, Chase. The Son I thought I'd lost for good. I'm thrilled you've finally seen the light. Your mate is certainly a force not to be reckoned with." Vincent paused and laughed. "Sean is anxiously awaiting your arrival into the circle."

"Let's not keep him waiting then," Chase said, grinning eerily.

Hand in hand, we followed Vincent down a hall, the same hall which appeared in the dreams, to a door which led outside. The air smelled cleaner and felt warmer. A circle of Vincent's followers formed. They were now standing around a large ring of fire. It appeared we were in an open field. There were no trees, bushes, or brush, only dirt and dead dry grass that crunched underfoot as we walked closer to the flames. He motioned for Chase and me to stay where we were as he literally walked through the blaze, taking his place in the center of the space. I finally knew what true evil was as I watched his figure glide through the flames. It was him. Devil, thy real name is Vincent.

"This is a celebration, children. You will welcome Chase and Nina into our lives with open arms. Anyone who disobeys this order will suffer consequences. You'll treat them like your brother and sister as you show them the way, our way, the *only* way. All of you who stand before me today have proven yourselves as loyal servants. Xaphan, for I have known you the longest. We rose to power together. Remember the good old days?" Vincent said and hooted while Xaphan, the only normal looking one in the bunch, nodded in agreement.

"Abaddon and Apollyon you've watched my back for years, destroying anyone and anything on a single command, proving to be my most loyal servants," Vincent continued. This time he glanced at the identical twins, whose onyx, pin straight hair made their lean figures and sharp noses stand out. The twins merely grunted in response.

"Enepsigos, my beautiful dark Angel with your Angelic face, but Devil-like heart and soul. You've never betrayed me, nor have you ever left my side. Through thick and thin you've always remained loyal and mine," he said to the woman who resembled a porcelain doll with her long, jet-black hair, tall frame, slender figure, and perfect complexion. Enepsigos's cold, hard eyes met Vincent's red ones. However, an expression of adoration shined brightly. Her Demonic love for Vincent was blatantly obvious. I felt an odd connection to Enepsigos in that moment. Much like me, she too knew what true love and a spiritual connection felt like. She'd die for her mate, no questions asked—something I was currently preparing for.

"Vassago and Lahash. You've both walked through the depths of Hell and Earth to seek valuable information for me all while messing with Micha's divine plans. The two of you have entertained me with the art of supreme destruction over the years," Vincent praised loudly as two of the ugliest creatures ever seen moved towards him. Both resembled weasels with rotting, yellow teeth and protruding jaws.

"And Sean, my newest child," Vincent started, gliding from Enepsigos's side to Sean's, who looked vastly different from the last time I'd seen him. I'd hardly recognized the once blond haired, blue eyed man. Classic features had been replaced with long, jet-black hair making his face appear harder and meaner than usual. The dirty looks he'd cast last year were nothing compared to the hatred and evil that filled his soulless, black eyes tonight. Sean Logan had evolved into a new being. A being so scary I'd never consider mouthing off to him the way I had in the past.

"You'll be rewarded the most tonight by getting your old friend back. I'm proud of the way you were able to manipulate that dullard sister and family of yours. Look at the result. Chase finally found his way home, *but* you're not only gaining Chase as a brother. You'll be acquiring Chase's bride as a sister. How lucky for you." Vincent beamed at Sean the same way a father would look at his son after he won the big homecoming game.

"Yes, children, I said bride. As a sign of good faith, Chase and Nina will be wed prior to their transformation and in front of you tonight, thusly providing assurances they'll always be one. Come, Chase and Nina. Stand before me." He gestured for us to join them in the fiery blaze.

Chase grabbed hold of my hand. We walked over the now low ring of tremendous heat to Vincent, whose palms rose and lowered prompting us to kneel before him. Chase pulled my rigid body down next to his. The others formed a tight loop around us chanting in a strange, yet familiar language. The louder they chanted, the higher the scorching, reddish orange flames grew. The end was near, even a fool would've realized that, but somehow I remained calm, holding onto hope that we'd survive this and live to die another day. Surely there had to be a way out of being a Demon for all eternity. Yes. We'd accept our fate here tonight, then figure out a path back to the side we truly belonged on.

Chase's fingers squeezed mine tightly. Was he wondering the same? Suddenly the chanting stopped and the flames subsided to almost nothing. A searing pain radiated from my left ring finger. It felt as if one hundred tiny needles were stabbing the skin under Chase's promise ring. I looked at Chase's face which also was holding back pangs of discomfort.

"Your request has been granted. You are wed. With this you must, *and will*, provide me with more children in the years to come. We shall raise them together. Now, it is your turn to honor me. The time has come for you to join Hell. Stand," Vincent spoke in an unnaturally happy tone. A chill shot straight up my spine.

As we rose a powerful vision almost knocked me

back down. Flashes of bright blue light colliding with brilliant red rays were seen through my mind's eye. Anguish and pain were heard, while urgency and strength were sensed. The vision, though short and vague, filled my core with hope.

"Are you all right?" Vincent queried.

"Yes. Of course. Better than all right actually, but before we begin, may I kiss my husband?"

"How rude of me. I apologize for not allowing you to share in that Mortal ritual. Please." Vincent smiled exposing perfect, pure white, even teeth.

Leaning over, wrapping myself around Chase, and pulling him close, my lips softly pressed against his for a brief moment.

"It's going to be okay. They're coming," I whispered.

Chapter 40

Chase

Out of nowhere, bright blue lights stormed the night sky accompanied by the sound of sharp objects cutting through the air. Something reached down forcing my and Nina's bodies backwards.

"These children belong to me. You will not harm them," a voice heavily laced with a thick Australian accent warned.

"Nina and Chase have made up their minds. They no longer wish to serve you, Michael," Vincent spoke.

"You've threatened them with death, Vincent. What else were they to do?" Michael's tone was rather matter-of-fact.

"You're too late, Angel. Give up. Leave immediately or suffer my wrath," Vincent threatened.

"We're prepared to fight, but we would prefer if it didn't come to such drastic measures. You haven't transformed them yet, *and* you will not threaten me either. Let us take what's ours and leave in peace." He paused. "No one has to lose their soul tonight if we all walk away."

"Answer me this. How did you find us?" Vincent questioned. It appeared that he was buying time. Why? I had no idea, but I was almost certain he was.

"We watch and protect our kind. Again, these children are property of The Heavens. The girl, Angelic by birth. The boy, Angelic by choice."

"Oh dear, Michael, we both know there's more to it than that," Vincent said, approaching Michael, stopping a few inches away.

"No, there really isn't," Michael answered, seemingly unaffected by Vincent's invasion of his personal space.

"Where's Gabriel? I haven't seen the Arc in a while, though he's been a busy little boy killing off key members of Hell's Army. You made the same mistake the idiotic Thirteen did. You turned that man into a cold blooded, heartless, soulless murderer. But, you righted the wrong in your mind by creating your other son to be Gabriel's voice of reason and conscience. How's that working out? I know Gabriel well. He's a killer with a dead heart and a soul filled with pure hatred and evil. He laughed the entire time he was destroying Leviathan. How does that make you feel, old friend?"

"Leave *my* children out of this. If anyone is to blame for Gabriel's actions it's you," Michael growled. Vincent's attempt to get under Michael's skin had worked.

"How about a little trade? Gabriel for these two?"

"You've truly gone mad."

"Tell him Lilith sends her undying love," Vincent said, smirking.

"Times up, Vincent. Do we fight or part?" Michael said flatly.

I held my breath waiting for Vincent to respond. I prayed both sides would walk away allowing for all of us to survive this nightmare unharmed, but deep down I think we all knew better. A war was going to ensue and I would have to fight in it. Thankfully, Nina wouldn't.

She'd be off on the sidelines safe, healing the injured. That's all that mattered. My life for hers. Seemed like a no brainer.

Chapter 41

Nina

Michael's auburn hair was pulled back into a severe ponytail, making his already commanding appearance bolder. Unlike Vincent's followers, the Angels were dressed in normal, everyday street clothing. The only thing besides their unreal beauty causing them to stand out was their skin. It glistened in the pale light the fire cast.

"The Demons want to fight," Ezekiel said to everyone but Michael, who still stood face to face with Vincent.

"Muriel and Chase, begin controlling emotions and senses. Chase, you possess the ability to alter everyone's perception aside from Vincent. Don't waste your time on him. You must project away from us or you'll inhibit our God given gifts to assist you while finishing them off. The rest of you, prepare to fight. Nina, you'll stay with me and heal the wounded," Raphael spoke. His Irish accent was heavy and thick.

Raphael's round face appeared peaceful. His vocal tone was relaxed, but his delivery of words was firm and direct. This crisis didn't seem to affect him.

"Orifiel, where's Gabriel?" Raphael asked.

"He's coming," Orifiel replied.

"When?"

"I haven't the foggiest. He's dealing with something

Michael deemed top priority."

"Damn," Raphael hissed as his expression fell. Taking Orifiel by the arm, he spoke privately to him in a quick, hushed manner.

Micah moved next to me placing an arm around my waist.

"Fear is what makes you Mortal, but your gifts are what make you divine. You're more than human tonight. You're one of us, *cousin*," she whispered.

"I'll do everything possible to keep Chase safe," Hadreniel added.

Seconds later, all hell broke loose. Streaks of blue light were shot down by beams of red. Raphael's arms braced me because he knew I'd want to run into battle to assist Chase.

"You cannot fight, Nina. You know this. You do not possess the ability or knowledge. Save your energy because you're going to need it," Raphael said firmly.

Both sides fought like starving animals in the wild. Screams and howls of pain and agony cut through the night sky. Feverishly my eyes looked and my ears listened for Chase, but I couldn't seem to find or hear him. The Angels and Demons were moving too quickly making it impossible to know anything for sure.

"Finish them, Chase," Muriel yelled. "Take away their sound and sight. Project away from us. Keep focus."

"Destroy them," Vincent hollered.

"I can't see," Lahash shrieked.

Bodies stumbled and faltered. Chase and Muriel were taking them down one by one while the others attacked. The only time I stopped watching was when Michael appeared in front of me dragging Ezekiel's lifeless body.

"Ezekiel needs to be healed immediately. He's been struck close to his core," Michael spoke speedily, placing the body in front of me, and vanishing.

Instinctively, I dropped to my knees allowing my hands to hover over the Angel's beautiful body. There were no visible cuts or damage aside from a quarter sized burn mark hidden beneath his torn, filthy clothing. An intense sense of warmth pulsated from my palms creating a bright light on the central most part of his form. Within seconds, Ezekiel's eyes snapped open. He examined himself before reaching into his left pocket producing a necklace of sorts. After he roped the chain around his neck he took off back into the thick of the fight.

"Angels, true Angels, not Mortal ones such as yourself, do not bleed or bruise. This is why your hands searched for the center of 'the being,' in other words 'the core,' which is where one's mortal heart once lived. It's the only way we can heal the dying and the only way we can be destroyed. We wear charms or amulets much like the one you're wearing to protect ourselves. If we're struck by evil we'll be injured, but not demolished. However, if our uncovered cores are directly struck, we'll cease to exist. Our soul will vanish forever. In this case, Ezekiel was hit close to his core causing his amulet to shatter, creating a small burn over the point of impact," Raphael informed.

My hands grabbed the cross Chase had gifted me for Christmas. It now made sense as to why he'd gotten so bent when I didn't have it on.

"You're to never take that off. Though you're not a true Angel, the amulet will provide a certain amount of protection against evil. Do you understand me, Nina?"

"Yes, but what about the Demons. How do you destroy them?"

"Fire is the only way we know of. They have to be burned alive and the ashes must be doused in holy water."

As we spoke Muriel and Urim were brought to us for healing. Once I had rehabilitated Muriel she softly assured me that Chase was fine and fighting well. A huge rush of relief swept over me. Healing the injured Angels was physically and mentally taxing. My movements became slower while my reaction time doubled.

"You need to do something," I said in a dream-like voice to Raphael as I grabbed the sides of my head. An extremely cloudy, vague vision formed.

"What's wrong?" Raphael responded quickly in a tone spiked with concern. "Nina, talk to me."

I didn't answer. The vision had to come into sharper focus first. Blurs of light flashed and Chase fell. He'd been struck down by one of the twins. His body hit the ground, then nothing. He'd been killed.

"Chase, he's going to die. You have to do something *now*," I shouted.

"We cannot interfere with fate, Nina. The battle must play out the way it's intended to." His tenor was cool, almost as if he didn't care.

"Maybe that's the way situations go down in your world, but not in mine," I said, defying orders and taking off after Chase.

Chapter 42

Chase

There was no time for thinking, only for focusing on the here and now and acting accordingly. Muriel stayed close by, frequently yelling orders. Once the war broke out all horror, surface and from deep within, vanished because good always prevailed over evil, right? Fighting through exhaustion, pushing myself to the limit seemed impossible. The more my gifts stretched, the weaker I'd become. Out of nowhere Nina came into my line of sight. She should've been safe, healing the injured on the sidelines, *not* in the middle of this war zone. Her mouth moved quickly, but I couldn't hear her words.

What the hell?

Nina's body dove in an attempt to push me to the ground as one of the twins fired a bolt at us. If she made contact with me before the bolt struck, she'd take the full impact. Instinctively, my arms stretched as far as possible to push the energy away so Nina's body could collide safely with mine.

If the situation hadn't been as life threatening I would've taken a moment to soak in the beauty of my gift. The flame and the space around it slowed down. Nina's body hung in the air. Movements were viewed second by second, almost like watching a video in slow motion. Once our bodies met, we leisurely rolled out of harm's way. The hold broke once our frames tangled and my focus waivered. At that point the world caught up to real time. A bright blue flash struck the twin who attempted to strike me. The twin fell to the ground, mortally wounded. Wanting to create more time for Nina to escape the crossfire we were smack in the middle of, I raised an arm again, but this time at no one or nothing in particular. Everything slowed down at my command, even Vincent, but using this gift drained me by the second leaving only a small window to make a move. The problem? Where do we run to?

Chapter 43

Nina

"Release your hold, Chase," Michael commanded.

For a brief moment, Chase's soul was viewed through my eyes. The strong, fierce façade Chase gave off when told to fight covered his intense anxiety and doubt which now hung heavy. I wanted to grab him and run far, far away from here, from all of this never to return. Time sped back up as Chase practically threw me away from the battlefield with incredible strength. Amazingly, I landed squarely on both feet.

"Seize the injured and retreat," Vincent ordered. With a sharp crack, the battle ended.

Immediately, Michael called the names of the Angels waiting for them to answer. I could breathe again once Chase responded in a strong voice claiming he'd sustained no bodily harm. Raphael took hold of my arm guiding me to where the others congregated. Even covered in dirt, dressed in torn clothing which hung limply off of their bodies, the Angels still represented peace and beauty. Michael had everyone lay down, insisting a once over from Raphael be performed even if they appeared okay.

"I realize you coexist in two completely different worlds filled with rules, but when you're in this one you listen to and take orders from me. Are we clear?" Raphael spoke firmly.

"Yes, but—" I started.

"Yes, period. No buts. Your reasons, valid as you may believe, do not matter."

"In time she'll learn our ways, laws, and rules. Nina acted on impulse and she will be taught to control that. From time to time we're guilty of the same, Raphael," Michael said, placing a hand on Raphael's shoulder. "She's still a Mortal. Don't forget that."

Raphael nodded in agreement. "Your gift is strong, almost as strong as mine. Healing is an art and you possess tremendous skill. You're an incredible asset for both sides," Raphael said, taking my hands in his.

"Ouch," I cringed at the touch.

In the midst of everything the soreness and aching radiating from my beet red left ring finger had been pushed aside. A black barbed wire band was seared onto the skin. Without thinking I lifted the injury and prepared to heal myself.

"That won't work," Michael said.

"Why not?"

"Because that's the mark of the Devil. We cannot heal or erase a mark that evil," he said.

"What does that mean? I'm not one of you anymore? I'm not a Mortal Angel?"

"You're still one of us. You always will be. That mark doesn't affect anything regarding your abilities or powers, nor does it dictate whom you side with. In our world you were taken as a wife by the Lost One Chase, who bears the mark as well."

"Excuse me?"

"In the eyes of The Thirteen, you're married which means the Lost One Chase has sided with you," Michael said.

"Nina, as far as the Angels and Demons are concerned, Chase is your husband. You both bear the mark and it doesn't matter who gave it to you. Once you leave us and return to your other life, you go back to being friends for now, but don't worry. The future holds more for you both. What you did wasn't a bad thing. You should be proud of yourself. We are. Chase is now one of us because of you. He's no longer a Lost Soul, but rather a Mortal Angel. By committing himself to you, his fate was sealed," Micah clarified.

"You fought well, Chase. Your powers and abilities are strong and will develop more over time. You've suffered, but everyone endures some Hell in order to find a piece of Heaven," Michael said.

"Nina will always be kept safe as long as she's with me," Chase said.

"Remember that sentiment always. You may need to draw upon it one day should your soul ever wander," Michael advised. "One more thing, Nina. Your connection with Chase, your love and devotion for one another sparked the new ability which rests inside of you. Sometimes we're granted additional gifts. Why this happens, I could not tell you, only time can, but use it to your advantage. Seeing the future, no matter how limited, is a rare trait. Lastly, do not worry about Vincent's whereabouts. His Army will require much time to heal, as will he, and we'll be watching the process every step of the way. Go in peace." Michael leaned toward me gently kissing my forehead. His warmth and love radiated deep within me. "Orifiel, please guide them home. When you're finished, return to The Heavens. Gabriel is anxiously awaiting your arrival."

"I know. He called to me earlier," Orifiel replied,

locking eyes with Michael. Some sort of unspoken communication transpired between the two. After a brief pause, both men looked away.

"Your car is parked not too far from here. When the battle ended, I retrieved it," Orifiel said to Chase, then he turned, and started down a dark path. His body illuminated creating ample light allowing for us to see where we were walking. He didn't say a word, which made me feel ill at ease. We'd spoken candidly in the past and had been so open with our emotions and thoughts. This uncomfortable, awkward silence was unbearable. Initially, I wanted to question the distance, but thought better. Instead, I kept quiet and my head down focusing on getting away from all of the madness. Chase gripped my hand tightly making sure we were pressed together at all times.

"We're here," Orifiel informed us.

"Thanks," Chase said.

Orifiel nodded and started to walk away.

"Wait," I shouted.

He stopped and turned to face me. "What?" His tone was icy.

"Give me a second," I said to Chase who nodded in response.

Once the car engine kicked over it was safe to talk because Chase was out of ear shot.

"What's with the attitude, Orifiel?"

"No attitude here. Got to go."

"Try again, but this time with the truth."

"Why did you cut me off?"

"Cut you off? I'm sorry, but what are you talking about?"

"You disappeared, severing ties, when all I wanted

to do was help. You still believe that you're in this alone and anything I say or do will not change that."

"That's not factual."

"Obviously it is."

"What are you getting at, Orifiel?"

"I've been watching your life spiral out of control. Not once did you think to call for me. Not one bloody time. The nightmares didn't go away and Chase broke your heart. I saw you at the school hiding behind a building spying on him. Your face and the pain on it haunted me for days. Why didn't you look for me? Nina, I want to catch you. Let me," he said harshly, but his golden eyes told a different, softer, kinder story. Orifiel inched nearer. His voice lowered drastically. "You're not uncomfortable around me or embarrassed because of what happened between us?"

"No. Not at all, but Vincent knows about it. He mentioned it several times tonight."

"Did you tell Chase?"

"No, and I don't plan to even if he asks. That secret dies with us, okay?"

"Aye."

"It was wrong to cut you out. There's no excuse. I won't even attempt one because it would cheapen what we share."

Our hands met and joined. He looked down at our

intertwined fingers before locking his eyes with mine.

"I'm glad you called when trouble started tonight, love."

"I knew you wouldn't let anything bad happen to me."

"Never, but promise me you won't close the lines of

communication between us again."

"I promise."

"I shouldn't be sharing this, but this war isn't over. It's only beginning."

"How so?"

He breathed deeply before pulling me closer. "Gabriel is third in command in our Army and the best Demonic Assassin in our world. He's been sent on a lot of missions lately. Michael must think or know something big is coming down the pipeline or else he wouldn't be relying on Gabriel as heavily. The mission he was on when you called was intense, like nothing I'd experienced before."

"You were with him?"

"Partially. Without getting into too much detail, Michael pulled me from watching you. He sent me to assist Gabriel in gaining access to a heavily guarded area of Hell. We were inside of Hell's gates when I heard your call, alerted the others, and came to get you."

"What kind of mission are we talking about?"

"I can't tell you."

"Have you asked Gabriel about what's going on?"

"No. Even if Gabriel knew, he wouldn't say. You don't know him. He's unlike any Angel in The Heavens in both a good and bad way. He's powerful and very angry which is a bad combination."

"Sounds like a real catch," I mumbled sarcastically, happy he wasn't my problem to deal with.

"Gabriel is and your paths will cross. When that happens, well let's just say, you'll know." Orifiel smiled.

"What's that supposed to mean?"

"Fire and ice, love." He smirked. "I've already said too much. If Michael, or any of the Angels for that matter knew what I just shared I'd be in serious trouble. Got to go. Watch your back. Be safe. When in doubt call to me immediately," he said, leaning over and kissing the top of my head before walking a few feet away.

His back arched as two wings slowly erupted. It was a breathtaking experience to witness. The moment rendered me speechless. Naked exposure to Orifiel's true form caused an unexplainable emotion.

"Orifiel?" a deep, unfamiliar voice summoned.

Orifiel didn't speak, but rather stood stone still. After a few seconds, he responded. "Thirty paces to your left, twelve forward, then fifteen to your right."

The hurried rustling of footsteps grew louder. Unsure of what this person wanted or whom they were, panic set in.

"Don't worry, love. You're not in any danger." Orifiel took hold of my wrist.

"Mother said you were injured and when I called, you didn't respond," the voice spoke, grasping Orifiel's free arm and roughly turning him, thusly freeing me. It was too dark to get a good look at the mystery person. Desperately, I wished he'd move out of the shadows.

"I'm fine, Brother. Raphael healed me. A very minor burn nowhere near my core, but you know mother." Orifiel laughed flippantly.

"Why didn't you respond?" the voice demanded.

"Father had me guide the targets back to safety."

"They survived?"

"See for yourself." Orifiel rotated slightly. His glow created ample light for everyone to be able to see. "Gabriel, this is the Mortal Angel Nina Luther. Nina, this is my brother the Archangel Gabriel."

"It's nice to meet…" He'd finally come into full

view. Everything around us seemed to vanish into thin air—like the world stopped spinning and we were frozen in time. Our eyes locked. Neither of us dared to move a muscle, only stare because exactly what does one say or do when they're unsure if what's being felt is good or bad? A powerfully odd emotion coursed through my soul, tugging at my gut and heart. I held no clue as to what expression Gabriel wore, his hair color, height, weight, or appearance in general because his big, brown, expressive eyes were my prime focus. Gabriel's tragedies were seen and felt though them. He was a tortured soul filled with agony and suffering that had to be healed. He needed me and I needed him. A mere foot away, Orifiel's voice and soft touch stopped me from reaching out and taking hold of Gabriel.

"You can't use your divine gift to heal him, but in time you'll help each other in more ways than one," Orifiel whispered.

"I can feel his torment. Please let me stop it," I mumbled, trying to break free and get to Gabriel.

"I know you can and he can feel yours. *For now* Gabriel and I must return to The Heavens and you to your mate, but remember, the brightest light always comes from the darkest of places. Happy birthday, love."

"Brother," Orifiel spoke. "Father is calling. We must go."

Guided by Orifiel's tugging, Gabriel mechanically walked backwards into the wooded area.

Run after him.

Some unknown force from deep within me kept urging me to chase them down, but I didn't, mainly because my mind couldn't handle anymore drama tonight. It was better to let them go. He'd be back. This I was sure of.

Chapter 44

Chase

"Are you okay?" I asked Nina as soon as she returned to the car.

"Yeah."

"What was that about?"

"He wanted to make sure we were good," Nina replied, brushing the question off. Obviously she didn't want to share any more details and honestly, now wasn't the time to press for answers. Nina and Orifiel had spoken several times in the past, but I doubted Orifiel posed a threat. Besides, Angels and Mortals were forbidden to embark upon romantic relationships, *but* Vincent's comment about how Orifiel had been sent to watch me, but was focusing on her, and how Vincent referred to Orifiel as Nina's "*Angelic boyfriend,*" gnawed at my gut.

Enough. Let it go. Vincent was trying to needle you and get under your skin. He probably would've said anything to instigate jealousy. Nina and you are destined to be together. You know Nina well enough to be sure she'd never go behind your back or cheat. She's a good girl, but above all, she's your girl and only loves you.

Surprisingly enough, we weren't too far from Nina's house. We drove in silence mainly because we were both still processing what had happened and we knew once we walked into the house we'd have to verbally relive the night. Nina stared blankly out of the window hardly moving.

"Ready?" I asked, after parking.

"Yes. No. Yes. I don't know," Nina answered. Her brain, much like mine, was fried.

Taking the lead and getting out of the car, my arm slid around her waist, holding on tightly, while guiding us to the house.

"It's over and life will return to normal. We're both alive because of how brilliantly you acted," I whispered.

"It shouldn't have gone that far."

"He would've found us at some point. At least it's done with."

"I guess."

"Come on. Let's get this over with."

Nina was now my wife and no one or nothing would take her from me.

No. One.

She was mine.

All mine.

Till death do us part and then some.

Period.

Chapter 45

Nina

"Chase?" My hand paused on the doorknob. The moment we enter the house there'd be questions, lots of them. We needed this time before everything became real.

"Yeah, baby?"

The only thing to do was smile and breathe because there were no words to describe anything. Who knew a half-baked plan would actually work? What if Chase didn't survive? A life without him would be a life not worth living.

Chase was aware of what I was thinking. He always seemed to know. A shiver shot up my spine as we stood there staring at each other. Looking down, the beautiful, deep purple, silk halter top was now dirty, torn, and practically falling off of my body. Chase removed his shirt and wrapped it around my shoulders. Great pain entered my soul once a gash on his tank top undershirt came into view. The tear was inches away from Chase's heart. Had the blow been a little higher, Chase would've been killed and I'd be standing here alone.

Not today. Not any day. Put it out of your head.

Together we walked into the house without saying a word.

"How was the party?" my father asked as we entered the living room.

"What in the name of good and evil happened to you two?" my mother shrieked in terror.

My father rose swiftly, racing to where we stood.

"Are you harmed?"

"No, Dr. Luther. We're both fine," Chase replied.

For two hours we sat, explaining everything that had transpired. Chase did most of the talking. It was better that way because his composure had returned much faster than mine. My mother's face reflected horror, but my father's remained calm. There'd been a moment when Chase showed them our branded fingers where tension rose, but it broke shortly thereafter.

"What happens next?" Chase asked.

"I'm not sure. We need to work on strengthening your powers and abilities now more than ever and Nina, you must work on honing your healing abilities. You said Raphael believes you're one of the more powerful, but power develops after mastering a skill which takes time. We'll find a way to figure out how to address the seer talent. As for being married, if anyone should ask about your rings, you're to tell them you suffered a moment of insanity and got matching tattoos. In this house you're still boyfriend and girlfriend."

"When do you think Vincent will return?" I asked.

"I don't know, but—" A knock coming from the foyer interrupted our conversation.

My father headed to the door and opened it.

"Dr. Luther. My name is Michael and this is Raphael. We were with your children tonight. We feel it prudent to discuss certain matters in private, if possible."

"Of course. Please, come in," my father said, ushering the two men inside to his office.

"Shouldn't we be a part of that conversation?" I

questioned Chase.

"No. Let your father handle whatever," Chase said, taking my hand and guiding us up the stairs.

"The fire in your soul was the only thing that saved us from Hell tonight. If and when a war breaks out, we will fight together and die together. I can't live without you," Chase whispered, kissing me slowly before going to his room and closing the door behind him.

Maybe I should've disclosed what Orifiel had said, but now wasn't the time. Vincent would surface at some point, but as long as it wasn't for a while, I could handle that. It was always darkest before dawn, and if that darkness meant fighting together in the dead of night to see that dawn, so be it.

Exhausted, I fell to the bed. Moments later sleep entered in the form of two big, soulful, tortured, brown eyes. Pleasure spiked with copious amounts of pain existed within his gaze. The eyes belonged to Gabriel, but oddly enough it felt as if I'd been staring into my own. Part of me was terrified by this, the other part embraced it falling victim to the power Gabriel held over me which could prove dangerous.

Fear can only grow and thrive in darkness, Nina. Move out of the shadows and into the light. The pain won't stand a chance.

Chapter 46

Chase

"*It's not over, Chase. This will never be over until I've won. Sleep in peace because you're going to need the strength and energy for when I destroy you. You've been warned.*" Vincent's words hissed inside of my head.

"Not if I find and kill you first, Vincent."

A word about the author...

A lifelong storyteller, JP Barry specializes in crafting heart stopping, compelling, unique, emotional page turners for a variety of genres. A New York native, Barry is always on the hunt for ideas for her next novel. When not writing, Barry enjoys spending time with her family.

Thank you for purchasing
this publication of The Wild Rose Press, Inc.

For questions or more information
contact us at
info@thewildrosepress.com.

The Wild Rose Press, Inc.
www.thewildrosepress.com

Milton Keynes UK
Ingram Content Group UK Ltd.
UKHW010233111224
452348UK00011B/742